Dream On, Tom

LONG TOWER

A Long Tower book from
GUILDHALL PRESS

Shane White

First published in June 2004

Guildhall Press, Unit 15, Ráth Mór Centre,
Bligh's Lane, Derry BT48 0LZ
T: (028) 7136 4413 F: (028) 7137 2949
info@ghpress.com www.ghpress.com

ISBN 0 946451 78 8

Cover image courtesy of Belfast Visitor and Convention Bureau
Typesetting and cover design by Kevin Hippsley

Supported by the Arts Council of Northern Ireland

This Project is supported by the European Union, administered by the Local Strategy
Partnership for the Derry City Council Area.

**EU Programme
for Peace and Reconciliation**
in Northern Ireland and the Border Regions of Ireland

**ARTS
COUNCIL**
of Northern Ireland

LOCAL STRATEGY PARTNERSHIP
DERRY CITY COUNCIL AREA

Acknowledgements

First and always, to Una for her support. My thanks to
Paul, Kevin, Declan, Michael, Seána, Pepper and all at
Guildhall Press for their professionalism and courtesy.
Their input is much appreciated. Also to the Arts Council
of Northern Ireland for supporting this publication and
Guildhall Press.

The Author

Shane White was born in Newry in 1955. Which makes
him almost a neighbour of, and ten years younger than,
his boyhood hero, George Best. Pelé once called George
the best player he had ever seen. His comments on
Shane's football prowess strangely go unrecorded.
Crestfallen, Shane took to writing. His previous work
includes *Before The Bandits* (Guildhall Press) and
Frontier Folk (Lagan Press).

In memory of my brother, Leo, who taught me two worthwhile things: how to build a go-cart and, more importantly, that life is always worth staying up late for.

Chapter One

'You're a useless bastard, Tom Dooley, a drunk, a lazy get. A loser. I wish I had never married you.'

She slammed the front door in my face, the door of the house she and Roger shared. Aye, and with my wee daughter, Siobhan. My wife had a hell of a voice for someone so small and frequently offered me this tirade of insults. Mairead had stood there, all guns ablazin', in her blue matronly nightdress, an angry bundle of five foot nothing, her rumpled long red hair framing her face like a raging bush fire.

I steadied myself on the gravel path, as usual a number of pints waylaying my ability to focus properly. But I still notice things. Like, despite her love of literature, her insults were limited and, worse still, predictable.

'Arse, Mairead Dooley, you forgot arse,' I shouted with the misplaced satisfied grin of the drunk who thought he had got his opponent back to deuce.

Pulling up the collar of my leather jacket, I stared at the shut door. Seems the conversation is over. *Finito*. Ah, well, she was losing. Jesus! That frigging woman does my head in. She is so bleeding unreasonable. *I'm* not the one who moved in with Roger. *I'm* not the one who kicked me out of the marital home. Oh no. Well, I wouldn't, would I, kick myself out, eh, now that would be daft? If I did try, I can assure you, as God's my judge, I would refuse to go. I can be an obstinate bastard when the mood takes me.

So, I like a pint or two; what man doesn't? So, okay, I was unfaithful on occasion; what man isn't? True, I find most jobs arse numbing. There appears to be this standard requirement to be surrounded by prats. Oh God, that job in the DSS. Prats in suits; me in jeans, cowboy belt. No gun. They carried their lunches in briefcases; I brought my peanut butter and tomato sandwiches in a Spar bag. One that was replaced on a regular basis, I might add. Counted for nothing come promotion. They said I continually under-achieved; I said they continually over-expected. As Confucius said, 'Choose a job you love, and you will never have to work a day in your life.'

She wished she had never married me. Oh yeah? Should have made that clear all those years ago in Belfast. She didn't realise what a catch she was getting. Jesus! All those years ago. At times, just like yesterday.

'Here, Thomas Dooley,' the young girl shouted across the road, a Brit personnel carrier whining its way down the brick-laden Corsta Street. Another girl, wild red

hair flicking at her freckled face, grabbed her mate and tried to shut her up. 'Thomas Dooley, Mairead Canavan fancies you, so she does.'

'I do not,' Mairead squealed, her face aflame.

Thomas Dooley turned round, hands in pockets, flicked his head back, slightly disturbing his jet black hair, curly at the front, like his mother's, and strutted across the street. His blue eyes, as mischievous as his father's, who died when he was three, winking at his mates. They, in turn, started laughing and shouting after him.

'And why wouldn't she?' he asked, rubbing his bum-fluff-going-on-bristle face.

Mairead pulled her friend away. 'I do not, ye cheeky get, ye.'

Thomas stopped and laughed, watching them walk away. St Dominic's maroon uniforms. Mairead turned and smiled. Thomas winked.

I had little alternative but to walk away. Did I leave their house gracefully? Define graceful! I fell backwards over an overgrown prickly hedge. 'Get that frigging thing pruned, Roger,' I shouted. 'It'll grow better next year.' I thought that stylish at the time.

There was no further point in my standing there in the rain watching the neighbours' bedroom lights popping like a firework display. I could hear Siobhan crying. Shite, shite and double shite.

I soon stood alone on Ealing tube station. I needed a drink.

My mobile phone rang. It was my mother ringing from Belfast. I couldn't answer it, not in that state. Jesus! If there was one thing I hated, it was my mother knowing I was drunk. And she always did. I do have a form of respect. If not self-respect, as my mate Cathal always reminded me. Bollocks! I let the phone go to Voicemail and quickly put it back in my pocket.

I made the Royal Oak, Camden Town, for the last hour. The once-cream walls, now cheaply tanned with nicotine, and the beer-smeared furniture providing a haven for the usual crowd who rested their laurels there. The place was like them; it made little effort. Amid the rubble of human decay, there occasionally appeared the odd one or two optimistic sods. Not tonight, though. Misfits, miscreants and lost souls. If they had been dressed in black, you could well have mistaken them for a reunion of the Sisters of Mercy and the Christian Brothers.

Cheap aftershave chasing cheap perfume, all wrapped up in a tidy little package of despair. Saturday night, fun filled, fun packed. Get pissed, fish and chips, puke, and not necessarily in that order. Ageing lovers holding hands as they arrive, holding throats and avoiding punches as they left. Holding on to what was left of their marriage. Love's sweet dream turned sour. Fuck, don't they all? I'm not embittered, just still slightly sober.

The Royal Oak is a good old English boozer, full of Irish and Scots with an Australian barman. It had been a while since the decorators were in. On an outer wall, you could just make out the once-pleading graffiti – FREE GEORGE DAVIS. Why do I come here? It's my local.

Cathal was there as usual, the big bastard. His large frame tucked into his recent dress mode: green corduroy trousers and green check shirt. One day he'll get that thinning greyish hair cut and he'll no longer resemble a fat John Lennon. He filled the ripped bar stool and then some. He claimed he was only a few pounds heavier than the national average for someone living at his address. Yeah, he had a fine line in bullshit. A Scouser, and him a Tranmere Rovers fan. Tells you something about him, that. God, the rows we had over football. I used to be a Man United fan; *used to be*. Well, if you're brought up with vintage United, you're not going to settle for this third-rate mob. Aye, despite their trophies. They've gone and sacrificed the Busby soul for astonishing success.

Ferguson may well be a Scot, I kept telling Cathal, but he's no Busby. Regardless of the trophies. He didn't have 6 February 1958 to contend with.

I slapped him on the shoulder. 'You'll have a drink, Cathal?'

He raised his eyes in mock shock. 'Is the Pope a Catholic?'

'Don't know, don't get the *Vatican News* anymore,' I said, holding up two fingers to the barman.

'Had a few already, then?' he asked. I nodded. 'I take it your meeting with Mairead didn't go too well?'

'How can you tell?' I asked, always thirsty for knowledge.

'You're well on and you're frowning,' was his response.

Oh aye, and another thing about the Scouser, he has tapes of *Dallas* which he frequently watches. He has got to be the only person in the whole wide world who thinks JR shot himself. Said he reckoned it was a cry for help.

I really must stop frowning. My mother always pulled me up on it. When I saw her. She was the only one who didn't criticise me for not going home. Actively discouraged me, so she did. Twenty years is a long time to be away from your homeland. But I'm not going to bore you with the details. To be honest, I try not to dwell on it. I don't always succeed. Mairead never blamed me though. She's good like that. Tell a lie, she did once, not long after she came over to join me in London. I can still hear her crying out in pain. It used to really get to me.

'I just wanted to see Siobhan, Cathal, that's all. But of course when I got there, who did I find? Aye, Roger the Codger was there. Tell me, Cathal, what on God's earth does she see in him, eh?'

'Eh, now that's a difficult one,' said Cathal, looking deep in thought. 'Let me see, how can I put it? Oh yes. He's educated, sophisticated, got a good job, money…'

I didn't let him finish. 'Do women still go for that sort of thing?'

'They do, young Dooley, when the alternative is a bit of a drunk, a bit of a lazy sod and a bit of a cheater. They do, Tom, when the alternative is you.'

I had to laugh. Cathal never bullshits me. Yeah, sure, he listens to me and throws a few philosophical comments in my general direction, but he doesn't allow me self-pity.

'That's what your ma's for, Dooley boy,' he would often say. Not long after we first met, he said I had a season ticket to self-pity. I had known Cathal for about three years. He once tried to be a priest, not in the accepted way, you understand. Technically speaking, he dressed up as one to escape the attention of a member of the local Constabulary in and around Lime Street one beer-sodden evening. Rag week or not, they were going to do him.

Cathal slowly slid off his stool. I hoped he was off to the bog, for if he wasn't, then he was getting ready to give me a lecture. He steadied himself. Bollocks! It's a lecture.

'I take it your Siobhan saw the row you and her mother had, eh?'

What am I supposed to say?

'You told me when you left to go and see Siobhan that whatever happened, you were not going to row with her mother.'

Ah, but you weren't there.

'And don't be giving me any old shite about me not being there, not knowing what went on.'

Okay, I won't.

'Whatever mess you and Mairead make of your lives, Siobhan comes first. You said that the other night. And there you go upsetting her again. I suppose she was crying when you left?'

I felt hammered to the ground. 'But nobody will ever…'

He butted in, wearily shaking his head, 'Yeah, yeah, nobody will ever love Mairead the way you do.'

Remind me not to discuss anything ever again with this excuse for Marjorie Proops. I signalled to the barman for another round, to shut Cathal up. I didn't really need to be reminded that I could be an arse. If I did, I would be first in the queue. Now, come on, how's that for self-examination, appliance of guilt, holding my hands up, eh? I'm not all bad, all self-pity. Mairead's a bitch, though. That's why I am the way I am.

Cathal and I liked the Royal Oak. So what if you wouldn't eat off their plates, bring a woman here or spend more than a couple of hours within its walls. Well, you could if blindfolded. In its defence, it was one of the very few London pubs that have managed to escape the corral mentality of the big breweries.

A couple of hours later and the old eyes were becoming blurry. A rush of alcohol was in the fast lane, rapidly loosening my senses. I was getting tired, wanted my bed. However, the thought of getting out of the bar, trudging home, mounting the stairs to the flat above the Indian always made me feel more tired. So, I ordered another round.

Aha, what is that I spy in the corner? Visions of sweet slumber nudged aside as I noticed a young ginger-haired girl smiling at me. I elbowed Cathal; he just looked at me and shook his head.

'Leave it, Tom,' he said. Forceful advice. 'You're not fit for it. Give it a rest. You're not up for it tonight.' I half-expected Cathal to take out his stethoscope – he'd done a couple of years at medical college – to check my vitals. I told Cathal not to worry, I felt A-One.

Okay, so a succession of women had caught my eye over the years. With some, I even struck up a relationship. More than one lasted over three weeks. I get bored easily. Am I supposed to apologise for being the way I am, for being me? Sod Mairead, bollocks if I was going to hang about forever waiting for her to come to her senses. One day, Mairead Dooley, one day I am going to make it big and where will you be, eh? With Roger the dentist in some big flash house off Ealing Broadway.

I took a deep breath and steadied myself on the bar. I quite elegantly dealt with a surge of wind as I swatted a burp with the back of my hand. I was more up for this than I thought. Cathal just stared, non-committal-like, with that smug grin on his face. I was flexing my diminishing brain cells, checking to see if I could muster enough to pull. I didn't think I was going to have much trouble with this one. I looked again at the girl. She looked sort of attractive. In a darkened-room, full-of-smoke, what-the-fuck sort of way.

'You're lowering your sights again, Dooley,' Cathal's voice jumping into the haze.

I grinned; she grinned. Two grins – first prize – a firm basis for a meaningless, sordid liaison.

The door opened; my eyes spun round. In walked Dotty. My glance swung round to take in her walk to the bar. Even Dotty looked attractive, and she looked ninety. In any light. She was ninety if she was a day. With her dyed jet-black hair always in a bun. You could count her ribs through her see-through black blouse. Dotty was one of the local good-time girls, believe it or not. A lady of the night, although recently more of the late afternoon. Understandably, her stamina had waned over the years. Apparently she had a phobia of baldheaded men. On the streets, she sips gin from a coke bottle (to keep the heat in, she explained) so as not to put her clients off. Not the done thing to be seen drinking on the streets, she says. Dotty claims only ever to talk to her clients, nothing else. So many just want to talk, she says.

My glance – okay, leer – returned to Ginger. I heard a resigned sigh from Cathal.

I walked over to her, a burp from her direction catching both of us unaware. She wasn't as quick as I was in nullifying wind. We chatted. Don't let anyone ever tell you that working in a jam factory is not without its fascinating stories!

Next morning, I awoke with the usual taste of stale lager capturing my first thought. There's a few more brain cells who've taken a hop, skip and a jump, never to return.

Jesus!

My mouth was bone dry. After a couple of attempts, I managed to wedge my tongue from my palate. A thumping head was in time with a bedside clock. I could make millions if I could turn that into a rap song.

There was a slight gap in the curtains admitting some niggling sunshine. I peered at my watch. Nearly half-seven. Late for work again. Stocktaking that morning.

Sod it!

Where's my jacket? I reached down and tapped the floor in search of my trousers. Cold lino. I'm sure I had carpet in the bedroom. Threadbare it may well be, but there was a wool content hidden in there somewhere. No luck. I raised my head slightly and leaned over the side.

Man overboard!

Pulling myself up, I tried once more to locate items of clothing. Ah, underwear. Not my size, but my colour, I think. Locating my mobile phone, I switched it on. Ah, a message.

I'll call now; that will really piss them off.

'Morning, Roger,' my voice was quite bright and definitely sneering. The bollocks knows that Mairead loves me. Why doesn't he just piss off? Oh aye, she may well be living with him and about to divorce me. I know, disgraceful, isn't it? And her a good Catholic too. But she still loves me, and even if she didn't, which she does, she sure as hell doesn't love him.

'Yes, Roger, I do know what time it is. I have a watch and am conversant in the big-hand-wee-hand conundrum. Is my wife there?'

My wife. That always pisses him off.

'Keep your voice down; I have a hangover.'

What! I turned round. It was Ginger.

'Have you no home to go to?' I asked, a bit pissed off.

'Apart from this one, no,' she groaned.

'Oh sorry, I thought… Oh hello, Mairead. Never mind the bloody time. You left a message on my mobile at two minutes to twelve last night. What, why can't you tell me now? Okay, okay, I'll see you tonight. Give Siobhan a big kiss for me and give Roger a big…' She hung up. With hardly a sideways glance, I tried to swing my legs out of the single bed. The duvet came with me. Ginger swore and quickly grabbed it back.

Location, location, location. I really must be more aware of where I end up at night.

It wasn't a good day for swing. My foot caught in the duvet and I fell face forward onto the cold floor, exposing my naked ass. I noticed I still had my shirt on, and indeed my socks. Took off my shoes, at least. I've always maintained it's this thoughtful, romantic side of my nature that will inevitably be my downfall. Surprisingly, what with all that was going on, Ginger was now snoring. Not loudly, but enough to ensure that I wouldn't be seeing her again. I truly have this thing for women who snore: it's called a pillow over the face.

Mairead used to snore when she had a couple of drinks too many, which wasn't often. Her nose used to twitch a little and her mouth moved like she was blowing bubbles. I used to cod her on about it, used to really annoy her.

Dragging on my trousers, I hoped I could leave the flat without further, unnecessary, embarrassing small talk. I couldn't even remember Ginger's name, but I felt somewhat amazed that I should be surprised by that. Ginger stirred and turned on the bedside lamp. Even crumpled, she looked okay; she looked good, in fact. I still choose well, under the influence. Cathal said I was lowering my sights; he must have been well on.

'Got to go; late for work,' I said as pleasantly as I could. I still had pangs of guilt doing this, even though I've had enough practice. My face goes red, would you believe it? I had come to terms with my interpretation of my good Catholic upbringing. A feeling of guilt, but not intense enough to spoil the fun. Morality and pleasure: what a brilliant combination! Sure they'll have a special place for me in heaven.

'We must do this again sometime,' I added, immediately regretting the offer as I stood at the door. I promised I would stop saying that. Chandler once had the same trouble in *Friends*. I didn't mean it. I didn't want to see her again. Just go, don't look back. Game's over; no action replay. Indeed, no peek at the highlights even.

Chandler always got a laugh. That morning, there was a distinct lack of joviality in that room. Ginger yawned and brushed back her hair with her hand.

'Bog off,' she said as she turned over in the bed. 'Let my cat in on the way out, will you?' She had freckles on her back. That's a "no-no" with me. Phew! That was close. There was me thinking I was falling for her. I slammed the door shut before the cat could get back in.

Bog off! Callous bitch. Jesus! Women of today! No guilt, no regrets.

I often wondered if Mairead had any regrets about taking up with Roger. I'd asked her often enough. She asked if I had any regrets brawling with Roger on their front lawn in front of Siobhan.

At one time it was just me and her against the world. Some would say that coming to London from parochial Belfast at the age of seventeen could well be a rather daunting task, but not for me and Mairead. We were in love. Oh boy, that old crap again. Trust me: it *does* work when you're that age or when you think Daniel O'Donnell brewed the tea especially for you and you alone. Aaah.

I came over first on my own. Mairead had spent four weeks in hospital before she was anyway fit to travel.

What an adventure. When I first arrived, easing into Euston on the boat train from Holyhead, I just stood in wonderment as a mass of people scurried around, no time to stop, less time to stare. But I tell you, that's what I did: stare. The diversity of people was, for me, both breathtaking and stimulating.

Black people, Chinese, Japanese, all colours, not only our small-town, unimaginative, restricting orange and green. A small, stout West Indian man struggled breathlessly with suitcases, the sweat glistening on his forehead, his British Rail uniform too big. Football fans shouting and waving their tribal scarves (I searched for the red and white of United) being eyed up by real-life British peelers. Loved the helmet. A Brit soldier sat on a rucksack looking relaxed; never saw that before. It was all such a contrast to the mediocrity that was Belfast. Our colourless, bog-standard, two-dimensional society. Soon, though, I felt the sudden chill of loneliness.

I had been given a couple of addresses of cousins who lived in West Hampstead and a friend of a friend who lived in Willesden; no chance, I *so* wanted to avoid Irish areas. Someone told me to buy the *Evening Standard*; it advertised flats and bedsits.

Eventually, after wasting a fortune on phone calls, and travelling halfway round London to look at overpriced slums, I managed to nail a bedsit in Kentish Town, not far from the tube station. The many Irish voices I heard nearly put me off staying there, but it was cheap and clean. I really wanted to go and have a few pints, but I decided to get a carry-out and, in solitude, attempted to bring some much-needed oblivion to my new surroundings.

I was overjoyed when I picked Mairead up from Stranraer; she looked ill though, the boat journey from Larne not agreeing with her. It was so good to know that at last she was with me. I had been long enough on my own. I'd got a job in an Estate Agent's: crap pay and boring as hell, but no way was I digging roads. On more than one occasion, I had to plead with Mairead to join me in London; her family, see, they were trying to stop her, turn her against me. I was a bad lot, according to them. I have to admit, Mairead's incessant crying over the first few weeks did my head in. I mean, *really* did my head in. I took evasive action – went down the pub.

What did she want me to do? What's done is done. Did she really think I wanted it to turn out that way?

They made us leave, remember?

Ah, that was the past; the present had me spruced up and at the Royal Oak for a few jars with Cathal before my meeting with Mairead. I felt credit was due for the effort I had made to make a suitable impression this time. Now, I'm not one for putting any great store in appearances, but I felt the need to feel good that night. Cathal even got off his stool to have a closer look at the scrubbed, clean-shaven individual who stood before him. The white shirt wasn't new, but it was ironed. Leather jacket looked good. New jeans, most definitely. Always kept on top of my jeans. Beige heavy boots. I looked the part.

'You're putting in a hell of an effort for your missus, Tom. Not like you,' Cathal said, getting back on his stool.

'It's funny, Cathal, I feel nervous,' I said, accepting his offer of a pint. 'The thing is, I don't know what she wants, but I have a sinking feeling that I won't like it. So, I thought, get yourself ready, Thomas Dooley. Look good, feel good, feel confident.'

Cathal sniffed and drank deeply from his pint. 'And look like one of the Village People.'

I grabbed him by the lapels, failing to dislodge his big grin. I had some advice for him delivered in a deep voice. 'Better than looking like Fred Flintstone.'

'Yabbadabbado! Or Fred Dineage?' Cathal offered. 'Or Fred Gee; remember the barman from *Coronation Street?*'

'He's dead.'

'So? Fred Flintstone never existed.'

Before I had time to consider that remark, the barman put another couple of pints and two whiskeys on the bar. I don't know how people cope in modern bars when you have to continually order your beverages. Better not get too pissed, I thought, might say something I shouldn't. I downed the whiskey in one go. Better not be too sober, might not say something I should.

'As we speak, Mr Dooley, Mairead could be getting rid of Roger the Lodger,' suggested Cathal, now immersed in *The Times* crossword.

I sucked air though my teeth. 'I prefer Roger the Codger; doesn't remind me of the fact that I took him into our house. If I had stuck at that job, we wouldn't have needed the money and we wouldn't, therefore, have needed a lodger.'

Didn't mean she had to take up with the get. Oh, that was all her own doing. He was in our house for about two months only, for Christ's sake! Me and Mairead had known each other since we were kids.

It wasn't done unkindly, but Cathal reminded me I hadn't exactly done myself any favours by being found in bed with our next-door neighbour. Although I was more than aware of it, I hated being reminded that my marriage break-up was my fault. Mostly. Of course, I could have put more into my marriage. Would, if I got the chance. That's all I needed: another chance with Mairead. Get shot of Roger, then I would get my family back. Then, then the sky's the limit. Watch me go.

Yeah?

I looked at my watch. I was due in the Indian in twenty minutes. There was a match on the telly; Man U against some team from the Ukraine, whose name even the commentator had trouble pronouncing. "Man U, Man U" began to reverberate throughout the bar. Bollocks to Man U! I had lost my heart to them when Bestie had taken to the field at the age of seventeen. I loved George; he was one of us. Me and Bestie share the same birthday; I'm twenty years younger than him. Bestie was God. Imagine God needing a liver transplant at fifty-seven. Another double whiskey made me wince a little. Man U; no style now.

Law, Bestie, Charlton, Paddy Crerand, Tony Dunne, Shay Brennan God rest his soul – and the one and only Norbert Stiles.

Some rave about Beckham. He paints his nails, for Christ's sake!

Mairead used to get so annoyed at my having so many photos of United on the walls of our grotty flat; we moved from Kentish Town about a month after she came over. Couldn't go to a pub without some frigging Irish sod being there. We found a place just off the Edgeware Road. One night, though, the man who lived above us was knifed. We heard a terrible commotion. Turned out he had a row with a prostitute and she knifed him in the knees and legs. Bit of advice there for anyone using the services of those ladies: never take up with a small whore. Funnily enough, I bumped into him a few months ago. He's doing fine. He's permanently disabled, but he gets by with some DSS disability allowance. Has a wee car and all.

Whether it was my nerves or what, but I was suddenly stabbed by the sword of despondency, and it dug deep. 'Here, Cathal, I've been thinking: about life, you know. Our lives in particular. There's me, working in a frigging off-licence and there's you, working, eh, … occasionally, I think that's the term to describe your employment pattern. I've been thinking, Cathal: are we a couple of losers, mate, eh? Maybe now's the time to be honest with ourselves. We've had a good run for our money.'

Cathal bared his teeth, tutted a little in thought. This one would warrant deep consideration. Maybe he would get off his stool. Cathal was not one for jumping in with mindless comments; he left that in my capable hands. He liked to think a while. He supped a little, swirling the liquid round his mouth like it was a fine wine rather than the watered-down crap we habitually drank. Soon, however, it seemed he had the measure of my quandary.

He explained that in order to be an actual loser one had to enter things, be there at the kick-off, when the bell goes type of thing. 'As you know, Tom, out there, there is controversy, circumstance. All manner of things, just waiting for active participation. So, you see, by evading them all, you neither win nor lose. Of course, at times it can be difficult, for one's natural instinct periodically eggs you on. There is, however, a definite satisfaction, achievement even, in saying NO to it all.'

With that, Cathal's lips stopped moving and, sighing slightly, he conjured up a satisfied, if somewhat bemused, smile. A Stan Laurel look. You can always rely on Cathal for reassurance. I stared at him, then at the barman who, with undue haste, threw in his two pennyworth.

'I think you're a couple of losers,' he said.

Cathal seemed untroubled by the comment and shrugged his shoulders. 'Merely one man's opinion, and he's an Aussie.'

I decided it was time to be off. 'I'll see you later, Cathal.'

'So long, partner.'

I hated drinking with Cathal on a Tuesday. On a Tuesday he always rented a John Wayne film and stayed for the regular Royal Oak Country and Western evening. Cathal wanted me to stay, wanted to prove that Willie Nelson's rendition of *Always On My Mind* was better than Elvis Presley's. Yeah, right. Not interested.

Indeed, a Willie Nelson lookalike was standing in the corner chatting up a few girls from the nearby nurses' home who came into the pub on nights like this for a laugh. They'll get a laugh tonight, for Wee Hughie, a Govan reject of indeterminate age, was also chatting to them. Wee Hughie always wore a black woolly hat and squinted through bottle-thick glasses. You could guarantee the wee man was telling them how he had appeared on local radio and TV, for he, too, was a lookalike. The nurses looked mystified, as well they might. They gave up guessing.

I felt like shouting over to him, *Not tonight, Hughie. Just this once, don't do it. Don't do it, Hughie, man.*

Too late. You could tell by the sudden explosion of laughter that he had. Yep, Wee Hughie had once again proudly revealed he was a Ronnie Corbett lookalike.

How could you miss Belfast with these lunatics on tap?

Chapter Two

'Here, son, take these. You'll be hungry by the time you get to England,' Tom's mother said, her voice now weakened by sorrow, as she filled a carrier bag full of soda farls, potato bread and crisp baps bought that very morning from Kennedy's bakery. She apologised for not being able to get any Paris buns. She tried so, so very hard not to show her fear but her shaking hands betrayed her. He was angry with her. For accepting he had to go.

I sat munching on a couple of poppadoms. The Indian Restaurant had a smattering of seated customers, mainly couples. Four lads, custom built, beer guts to the fore, stood waiting for a takeaway. The background sitar music was a bit loud for me. As I lived above the restaurant, I was a good customer and was treated as such. Only once did I have a few too many in there and fell over, breaking a couple of glasses. I sat at a window seat so I could spot Mairead arriving. Give my face the opportunity to convince itself that my heart was wrong and that I didn't really give a damn about her.

The waiter took her coat. She was dressed casually, a red blouse hanging over a pair of faded blue jeans. She had her hair cut since I last saw her: short at the sides, long at the back; it suited her. Her green eyes still sparkled. Couldn't miss that. She looked ill at ease, though, as she approached my table, her eyes flitting between a warm smile and shyness. Understandable, eh, when you're meeting the love of your life. I stood up and pulled out a chair for her. That was definitely not a familiar perfume she was wearing.

'You're looking well. Hope you didn't get dressed up for me?' I smiled as warmly as I could. I, too, felt tense.

She deflected the warmth. 'Now, why would I do that?' Her voice was laced with tiredness. I felt a little hurt, a little awkward in her presence. Catch yourself on, Dooley boy, for Christ's sake! This is your wife, as a dyslexic Michael Aspel might say. You may be estranged, but you are no strangers.

The waiter brought her half a lager and me another pint. Mairead asked about my mother and then told me she had been speaking to her the other night and she didn't seem herself. Thick as thieves, Mairead and my mother. I sheepishly admitted I hadn't spoken to her in over a week.

Mairead picked at her curry; I devoured mine, compelling it to soak up the alcohol. We chatted about Siobhan. Mairead still seemed tense; her responses were limited to a word or two only.

'Tom, I want to…'

I jumped in. 'Let me guess, wife of mine. You're here to tell me that it is your intention to dump Roger the Codger and come back to me, bringing with you our darling wee girl?'

Better to start with the unbelievable, unreasonable, unlikely and work downwards.

'No, Tom, don't be daft… I want to…'

'Okay, then, you're paying for this lot.' I nodded to the waiter and held my thumb up. Cue for a double whiskey. Mairead gave me a dirty look when it arrived. No problem, I was collecting them. I gave her one back and downed the liquid in one go, my head shaking with the shock.

She fiddled nervously with her hair, then rubbed her eyes. 'Tom, before you get too drunk to remember, I have something I want to tell you.' She looked increasingly uneasy.

That pulled me up.

'Okay, what is it?' I had a feeling temporary deafness would be welcome just then.

'Well, for a start, you could be a little bit more civilised towards Roger,' she said, suddenly thrusting forward that fiery look in her eyes.

Mistake, girl. Mis-fucking-stake. I slammed my fork down, covering the white tablecloth in curry. 'Civilised? You want civilised? Let me tell you something, Mairead Dooley. Yer man is civilised enough for the both of us, for the whole country, for a frigging continent, even. Civilised, did I say civilised? I meant boring.'

Mairead stared at the floor. I stared at my half-empty pint of lager. She offered me the rest of her curry, not to fill me up; more, I think, to fill the awkward silence. Bollocks, let the silence reign.

'He's just different, Tom, different to you. Why can't you just accept that? It would make life easier all round,' she said, staring hopefully at me. I looked at her, then at a couple giggling near us. A too-hot curry causing the amusement.

You want to know, then, eh, do you? You want to know why I can't be more civilised to Roger. Well, I'm not going to tell you: let myself down; let you know my true feelings. Yeah, right.

'Because I can't accept it, okay?' I've started so I'll finish. That's it, Dooley boy. Bollocks to the pride! Hold nothing back. 'I can't accept him 'cause he wakens up beside you every day; 'cause he's with my daughter all the time and 'cause he's frigging twenty years older than you. And he's a boring bastard as well. What the hell do you see in him?'

I looked up to find her eyes on me. In a second, they fell as sadly and reluctantly as early autumn leaves. She looked up again, her eyes now reflecting pity.

'Because...' I added. Yeah, so what if I sounded like a wee boy lost? I had tried everything else. We played with our napkins while the waiter cleared the table and I looked at those around us, seeing nobody really.

Might as well go the whole insane hog. 'Are you coming back to me or not?' Mairead shook her head.

Objection, your honour. Witness didn't take time to consider question.
Objection overruled.

I was about to put my thumb in the air again when she grabbed my hand. 'You're being childish,' she said observantly.

I made a sound on my lips with my fingers. 'Really, am I?'

Move to strike, your honour. Defendant not fit to participate in adult debate.

I relented. 'Okay. Look, I'm sorry. What is it you want to tell me?'

She just came out with it. Her gaze switched to across the restaurant. Without looking at me she announced, 'Roger and I have decided to send Siobhan to a different school. To St Theresa's. It's a fantastic school...'

I just managed to get to the Royal Oak in time for a lock-in. Jesus, I was fuming. Mairead and lover-boy knew I couldn't chip in with the fees. Bastards, the two of them. That Mairead one is going to have a fight on her hands.

'What, what did you say?' I turned to Cathal who seemed to be mumbling something. It had better be good, I was in full rant mode.

'I said did you have the Onion Bhaji or the Tikka to start?' he asked.

'Did I have... ye bastard, ye?' I could feel my anger giving way and I felt the beginnings of a grin. I sighed deeply. 'Here's me pouring my heart out...'

'There's only so much I can take. Anyhow, how come you're so wet?'

'I paid for the meal, didn't I? Had to show her I could still pay for some things.'

'Left yourself with no money for a cab?'

I nodded.

'Pride is a wonderful thing, Tom. Aye, you and some bronchial drug company are going to be so happy together.'

About a month later, after Siobhan and I had been to Southend for the day, I brought her back to Mairead who informed me Roger the Codger had been offered a new job. 'Oh jolly good,' I said. 'Now why not tell someone who gives a damn?'

Turned out he had been offered promotion. 'How can you be promoted in dental hygiene?' I asked. Mairead didn't rise to the bait, informing me that he had been offered, and had accepted, the position of Head of Orthodontics and Oral Surgery in the Northern Ireland Health Service.

Whoopee! Well, you could have knocked me over with dental floss. I was *so* not interested.

He was to be based in Belfast. Imagine that. Oh, hang on a minute. So, he'll be living over there during the week and coming back at weekends. My mind was working overtime now. Leaving my wife at the mercy of a husband who has designs on her. Loco move, Roger, me old son. Roger, with your clipped Sussex accent, I'd like to rearrange your teeth for you and see how good a dentist you *really* are.

The bitch saved the best for last. Didn't even tell me to sit down.

'No fucking way,' I screamed. I went mental, smashing a glass against the wall. I grabbed a bottle. I could see, *feel*, the fear in her face. That seemed to bring me to my senses and my rage subsided.

Why the hell was I getting myself into such a state? It wasn't going to happen, no way. We made a pact, bitch. We agreed. I have rights, I told her. She just stared at me. God forgive me, but I had been inches away from lashing out at her. I slammed the door. I could hear Siobhan crying from another room. Just as well Roger was out. I would have had the bastard.

She was not, I repeat, not, going to take my daughter to live in Belfast. We'd made a pact not to go back. Never.

What part of the word NEVER was she having difficulty with?

Cathal allowed me a few minutes of self-pity as I stared despondently into my glass. I needed a good drink. Like never before. Even then, though, I felt the weight of crushing inevitability. Invariably, Mairead Dooley got her own way.

But Belfast? How can I save my seven-year-old from that bastarding city?

'Twenty years ago, Mairead and I left Belfast, Cathal, and swore we'd never return.'

Cathal let out a big sigh, audible even over the bingo caller. 'Aye, so you said.'

I looked over at Wee Hughie limbering up for the Karaoke later on. Ronnie Corbett doing *Jumping Jack Flash*. I tell you, it was the stuff of legends.

'I made a pact once,' announced Cathal. 'It was with Rita Sweeney. I was six; she was six and three quarters. We promised we'd marry each other when we were twelve. Come twelve, she was appearing at the *Lido* in her father's knife-throwing act. Don't talk to me about pacts. Fair put me off, that did.'

'But we swore. I can remember us hugging each other and crying; we swore we'd never go back; and now this.'

I was wallowing in it, hardly listening to Cathal. 'I swore I'd never go back to my Uncle Charlie's.'

For whatever reason, I began to listen as Cathal continued. 'In those days it carried a stigma, you see. Less tolerant times in Liverpool then. Thankfully, for some, cross-dressing is more acceptable now. And as he said himself, how would he have fared at the Embroidery Guild dressed as a man?'

I tapped him on the shoulder. 'You're not taking me seriously, are you?'

'You don't really want me to, do you?'

I shook my head and there and then we made a pact: to get rat-arsed, a noble, traditional intention in itself. But first we watched as Dotty also limbered up for her performance. Her chosen number, *I Will Survive.*

A singing prostitute. Dotty's range of services seemed limitless, and so varied. In some Middle Eastern countries, she would undoubtedly have been classed as sacred.

The evening slithered by in a comforting haze of alcohol. Undeniably, alcohol does have the ability to throw not just caution, but also reason and common sense, to the wind and, boy-oh-boy, does that wind have a lovely scent at times!

Why one of us hadn't thought of it before was truly baffling. Cathal just seemed to pluck it from nowhere. I suppose it's down to the power of positive drinking. It was, without a doubt, a brilliant idea, one completely and utterly devoid of obstacles. All my problems about to be plunged into the quagmire of the unimportant.

'I think it is a wonderful idea, Cat,' I slurred. I could see he needed a reassuring response.

'Don't call me Cat. You always call me Cat when you're drunk.'

I grinned from ear to ear, awash with optimism. 'Why did we not think of this before, eh? As you say, we get enough money together, kidnap Siobhan, fly in our new three-seater plane to Spain, marry two women…'

Cathal interrupted; he was repeatedly insistent on this point. 'Marry two women *descended* from Spanish aristocracy.'

I nodded in agreement. Of course, Cathal, of that there would be no doubt. Sure it will be in keeping with our imminent involvement in the social strata of the Catalan district.

'And when Siobhan grows up, she will become a doctor and look after us, for we're not getting any younger,' I suggested, imagining the wonderful villa we would live in.

'Yeah, but not our teeth,' Cathal was in there quickly. 'We don't want her showing any aptitude for dental care. Roger the Lodger must not have had any influence on her.'

I could feel tears in my eyes. I was about to wrap up all my worries and label them discarded. Life was going to be great. I suddenly felt the urge to hug Cathal; he pushed me away. However, I sensed he, too, was on the verge of a deluge of happy tears. Neither of us could believe how simple it all was. Cathal was not resting on his laurels, though. Half an hour later he stood up, cleared his throat, threw a disinterested glance towards a feuding Dotty and Hughie, dusted me down, and announced how we would obtain the required amount of money. Once again, I could have wept. A sure-fire plan.

Belfast, my arse! As he spoke, the certainty that Siobhan would live with me for ever and ever became real. I hung on to Cathal's sleeve. He stared at me. I swear he wiped away a little droplet of intense emotion. With a raised hand of triumph, Cathal gave it to me. Straight.

We were to become male escorts.

'We'll make loads of money,' he said earnestly. 'You're not a bad-looking bugger. I'm sure there must be one or two women out there willing to pay for your company. And as you quite rightly pointed out, there are a number of women sitting at home, as we speak, stuffing themselves with sweets and watching telly. They need a good night out.'

'The Teletubbies?' I said

'Exactly. The Teletubby market for me.'

Whoever said there is no time like the present could perhaps be accused of a decidedly misplaced notion, for as Cathal and I left the pub, arm in arm, that unbreakable bond, which drunks share, tossed us out into the night to try out our infallible plan. A practice run, you might say. As we turned the first corner from the pub, I steadied Cathal. We both stopped and looked down the darkened street like a plane ready on the runway. Inhaling deeply the choking fumes of a London night, we progressed slowly, fuelled by this most wonderful plan. On hearing the muffled, but telling, sounds of high heels on tarmac, we once again stopped and looked at each other. Like two fighter pilots about to go into action, we gave each other the thumbs up and winked.

Neither of us felt the need to speak as two women came into view. It was as if we had been rehearsing for this all our lives. Cathal did, however, grab my shoulder; could have been to steady himself, but I felt, at that moment in time, it was a signal of our emerging bond to go forth and slay the world.

The two women stopped. Right there in front of us. They had little alternative; we were somewhat blocking their path. They were both blondes and skinny.

Tally-ho, said one pilot.

See you back in Blighty, old boy, shouted the other.

'Excuse me,' I stammered. I was not directing my words at either of them in particular, more targeting the middle ground, somewhere between their fake-fur-entwined arms. 'Excuse me, ladies, if I might call you that. Would either of you pay, money that is, for our company? Him or me, eh?'

I thought Cathal held up his end in style. 'For a period of time or longer. What do you think?' he politely slurred.

To their credit, the two women didn't react immediately. They took time to look us up and down, and then, licking their lips in exaggerated thought, they glanced at one another. One spoke, but you got the feeling she was speaking as part of a double act. 'We wouldn't even pay the binmen to take you away. Look at the state of you.'

They knocked against us as they passed. I exhaled loudly as I spun round. 'Boy, that was some put-down, Cathal.' I looked Cathal up and down. 'Right enough, now, I couldn't see myself forking out for you.'

Cathal was most magnanimous in rejection. 'Well, I would for you; no question. But only for a short period of time.'

I told him that had always been his problem. He should learn to be more choosy.

'Binmen?' Cathal suddenly shouted after them, seemingly wanting the last word. 'I'll give you binmen. Refuse disposal operatives, they are. Jesus! Don't people ever read council literature?'

Funny, the things requiring Cathal's clarification at times. I stood still, glued to immobility by sudden uncertainty.

'Cathal, we are cut out for this sort of work, aren't we?' I needed reassurance.

'What, the old escort business? Aye, of course. Don't let those two put you off.' He puckered his lips, turned round and looked me deep in the eyes. He grabbed my hand and let it drop just as quickly. I feared he had lost his train of thought. I was of little help.

'We are fine figures of men. Look at us,' he said. I was completely bowled over, and indeed encouraged, when he threw into the arena his proposed name for our business.

The Tomcats.

I was, as usual, reassured by Cathal's undoubted belief in the project. I suppose this rigid faith in all things hopeless comes from a lifetime of supporting Tranmere Rovers.

An idea suddenly struck: why not go the whole hog?

I asked Cathal his opinion. He could see I was deadly serious, so he did give my suggestion some consideration as cars sped by us beeping their horns to get us off the road. Such is the modern-day road user's impatience with genius.

Logic, however, fed his response. 'I can understand you wanting to kidnap Mairead as well, Tom, but remember, we only have a three-seater.' As usual, Cathal was in there sprinkling reasoning on my overly optimistic thoughts.

Later in the chippie, we continued our perusal of the idea and were not deterred by the odd looks we were getting. Cathal's face was determined. 'I want to make one thing clear at the outset,' he said as we neared the front of the queue. 'I am not, I repeat, *not*, dressing up in any uniforms for any women. Got it?' In the flickering neon lights of the chippie, he looked perturbed.

At first I thought this comment a little adrift of reality, but I then realised what he had in mind. 'Oh yes, I see what you mean now. A uniform, like a… like a… postman, maybe?'

'Exactly,' said Cathal as he ordered fish and chips twice, even though I wanted a saveloy. I took the fish, for he looked more at ease now that I was following his path and I didn't want to disturb the moment.

A sudden thought, however, made this path treacherous. 'Imagine, Cathal. Imagine if they requested you turn up for a date as a, say… a Lighthouse Keeper, eh?' Cathal screwed up his face and looked at me open-mouthed. I felt he was looking to me for guidance. 'I know, I know, Cathal. Imagine the indignity, not to mention the waterlogged boots.'

As we walked away from the chippie, Cathal blew on his chips. 'Waterlogged boots?' he asked, dropping a piece of cod. 'I don't follow.'

'Oh aye, we would have to wear Wellingtons. If we're going to do this, we'll do it properly. Be authentic, suffer for our art.'

'London, Paris, Milan, eh?' Cathal was way ahead of me, off setting up branches throughout Europe.

I felt he needed reeling in. 'First things first; we would test the waters, so to speak, in, say, Cleethorpes. Agreed?'

A compliant smile from Cathal confirmed another small business detail.

I don't know why, but it was at that particular moment we both burst out laughing. Perhaps fish and chips act as an antidote to the bullshit alcohol induces. The ridiculousness of the whole idea echoed all round us. We could hardly stand up, such was the force of our convulsive laughter. I was doubled up. My mobile phone rang. I could hardly retrieve it from my inside pocket. Oh God! My stomach ached.

'Oh Jesus! It's my mother. Here, Cathal, take it.' Cathal licked his fingers and wiped them on the chip paper. He nodded for me to hand the phone over.

He checked out the number before answering. 'Ah, Mrs Dooley. How are you?'

How does he manage it, to sound sober when he's pissed?

'Oh yes, sorry. Of course,' he said. He handed me the mobile. The air suddenly went cold. Take that serious look off your face, Cathal.

'Tom, it's your Uncle Richard.'

Later, I sat in Cathal's flat, staring at the walls, a cold cup of black coffee still in my hands. The TV flickered its late-night offering.

I wanted more alcohol; a mountain of the stuff. I wanted a drink with the word 'oblivion' written through it. My mind was racing, yet in slow motion.

A flashback came-a-visiting.

Belfast.

All I could think of was that I would have to return to Belfast.

I had to go.

My mammy was dead.

Chapter Three

I fell asleep on Cathal's sofa and woke in that twilight zone between fact and fiction. A gnawing feeling was mercilessly trying to penetrate my senses, but I could not as yet feel any pain. My head ached; my mouth was bone dry. It was sudden when it came.

Oh fuck! No way. Oh fuck! No. Please, no. Not my mammy.

Cathal came out of the kitchen with a cup of tea. I couldn't touch it. He told me he had called Mairead while I slept and she had come round to once again see me sprawled drunk on a sofa. Apparently, before she went back home, she had kissed me on the forehead. Cathal knew only too well that my mother had always wanted Mairead and me back together again.

Mairead was coming with us to Belfast for the funeral. Cathal mentioned that Mairead's last words before she left, drenched in sorrow, were that Thomas Dooley and Mairead Canavan were finally going back home, home to Belfast.

Christ! I couldn't get over the changes at Aldergrove airport – well, the International, as it was now known. Despite the tragic reason for our return, I couldn't deny a feeling of excitement as we landed. We were home after all those years. During the flight, however, I felt numb and, God forgive me, had I been given the opportunity to miss my own mother's funeral, I would have grabbed it with both hands. I didn't want to be in Belfast, I didn't want to see my mother in a coffin. I would have given anything for the chance to turn back, back to safety.

My mother was now gone: my only brother had died years ago; my father when I was just a child. I now only had a sister to whom I never spoke.

The weather in Belfast was cold but cheery. It was nice to hear so many Northern Irish accents again. There were one or two from Tyrone, a couple of harsh Belfast ones, and at check-in, we had chatted with a man from Fermanagh. We got into a taxi, Cathal sitting in the front.

'Where are youse off to?' asked the driver, a stout man in his fifties with a weather-beaten face. It was warm in the cab. He told us that all his windows were stuck. His blue shirt was buttoned up to the neck. I told him Corsta Street, North Belfast. Christ! It had been a long time since I had said that to a taxi man, to anyone, in fact. Mairead asked was I okay. I nodded. I could only assume that, like me, there was more filling her thoughts than just my mother's passing. We were back, back in Northern Ireland and on our way to Belfast.

Home.

It was… oh… I don't know, it felt, it felt like your first day at school, sweltering in the fear but reeling in the excitement. Belfast was up there on stage, in the spotlight once again.

And all for us.

'Home for a wee visit?' the taxi driver asked, pulling out into traffic.

'A funeral,' Cathal said, helping me out.

'A funeral? Somebody dead? Ah, sure that's sad.'

'Aye, it's my mother,' I said.

'Oh, sorry to hear that, son.'

I felt drawn to the man. I didn't know him from Adam, but he was Irish. I was home. I was in among my own. I struggled with that feeling. I had such hatred of everything Irish once. In time I had packed away that hatred, wrapping it up in indifference.

'Sure you only have the one mother, so you do,' he said, giving the fingers to the driver of a big truck sucking up the decaying autumn leaves who cut him up. 'Unless, of course, there are step-mothers involved like in my own particular personal circumstances. Oh, she was a right one! And then there were her pen pals in Venezuela. I don't know how I survived it all, so I don't. But I'm here to tell the tale, thank God.'

The three of us laughed, but he was deadly serious. Cathal continued to chat as I asked Mairead what she had told Siobhan. The truth, she said, and added that she thought about bringing her over for the funeral. No, I said. I wanted Siobhan to remember her granny as she was. She's too young for this sort of reality, I said.

Siobhan was staying with a friend of Mairead's as Roger the Codger was away at a conference. I didn't think it right that Siobhan was being left on her own without her mother or father at this time, but I was so grateful for Mairead's presence. I appreciated her doing this for me. We stopped talking and turned to look out the window as Cathal and the taxi man chatted away. Cathal was told he looked like John Lennon only a bit tubbier.

'Do I indeed?' Cathal said, feigning surprise. 'Never heard that before.' The taxi driver told him he had an eye for things like that.

Mairead and I watched the countryside pass by. Once or twice we caught each other's eye and smiled, not saying anything. Unwilling to actively revisit the past, perhaps. That past: it had, of course, touches of genuine warmth, but the iciness of its reality was constantly there.

'So, do you support Liverpool or Everton?' the taxi driver asked.

Cathal hesitated and then sighed; he knew he was in for the usual response. 'Neither. I support Tranmere Rovers Football Club.'

'Jesus, son! Are you wise or what?'

I think it was the Belfast accent, laced so heavily with incredulity, that made us all burst out laughing again. The driver then asked when was the last time we were home. When I told him, he glanced in the rear-view mirror, his suspicious eyes seemingly asking where have you been all this time?

As we neared North Belfast, I could feel the butterflies in my stomach grouping, the instantly familiar, yet oddly alien, streets coming into view. Vivid memories becoming punctured by realism. The little corner shops – where I once bought my penny bubblies, liquorice sticks and, later, a couple of Number 6 cigarettes – were now gone, steel shutters presenting a scarred face.

Had the newspaper reports of a changed Belfast been nothing more than rumours?

The taxi pulled up. 'This is as far as I go, people,' the driver announced with a warm smile. 'Corsta Street is down on your right there.'

'What?' I said, looking at Mairead, who glanced curiously at the driver. 'Are there still places you taxi men won't go?'

'Oh no, not the way you think. It's just I wouldn't go in there, like. It's too depressing; reminds you of the past too much. We in the North, we're moving on, son, looking to the future, like. In there,' he shook his head, 'in there, son, is the frigging past.'

We got out of the taxi, understandably a little mystified. The driver also got out and lifted our cases out of the boot and placed them on the ground. I paid him. He drove away, maniacally beeping his horn. It was a poor attempt at the theme tune from *Bonanza*. It wasn't that far to walk. Mairead said he was probably a lazy sod and didn't want to go off the main streets.

As we walked, the sun seemed to dim, projecting a feeling that it, too, had accompanied us far enough. Had I not seen it with my own eyes, I really wouldn't have believed it. I know it was probably only a freak of nature, but a mist suddenly appeared as we entered Corsta Street. Cathal looked a bit worried. We continued on through the descending gloom, and in a few moments it cleared as swiftly as it had descended.

We stopped, put our cases on the ground and looked round. With darting eyes, Mairead and I nervously took in our one-time home, the place in which we grew up, the place where we made friends. And enemies. We were savagely struck by its total dereliction. I couldn't believe what I was seeing.

Cathal broke the silence. 'This is still Belfast, isn't it?' I nodded. 'Makes Gracie Street in Liverpool look posh.'

Rubbish appeared to be the main inhabitant of the area, and a greyness covered the streets as I watched an old couple walk into what once was Maggie Smith's all-purpose shop. The windows were now made of cardboard and the once-white paintwork was both peeling and dirt smeared. A dog tried to balance on an overflowing rubbish bin. Maggie Smith must be turning in her grave; she wouldn't even have let you into the shop if your feet were muddy.

'Look!' I shouted, pointing to the gable wall of a now derelict house. 'I don't believe it. Look, Mrs Dooley. Can you see what's written there?'

Mairead looked puzzled as we walked over to be confronted by black lettering, withered with time, but still just, just, poignantly legible. Aye, even after all those years – MAIREAD CANAVAN LOVES THOMAS DOOLEY.

Mairead seemed pleasantly shocked, 'What, after all these years?' she grinned.

'As they say, Mrs Dooley, the walls never lie.' I laughed.

Tom stopped swigging from the cider bottle as she approached. He brushed his hair back with his hand and straightened the lapels on his jacket. One of his mates nudged him and pointed to her.

'Here, Thomas Dooley,' the young girl shouted across the road, a Brit personnel carrier whining its way down the brick-strewn Corsta Street. Another girl, wild red hair flicking at her freckled face, grabbed her mate and tried to shut her up. 'Thomas Dooley, Mairead Canavan fancies you, so she does.'

'I do not,' Mairead squealed, her face aflame. Thomas Dooley turned round, hands in pockets, flicked his head back…

Mairead didn't limp back then.

I watched Cathal take in the surroundings. Of course he had heard me talk about my home often enough. But he looked shocked at the state of it.

'What's that mean?' he asked, pointing to a large scrawl on a wall. 'Can they not spell in this place you call home? Shouldn't that be IRA RULES? What does IEA RULES mean?'

I paid little heed to Cathal, noticing Mairead's sudden ashen face, as if she had just seen a ghost.

'Mairead, I just want to tell you…'

She pressed her hand to my lips and shook her head. 'We're here for Molly. Leave the past. Please.'

I nodded. I had a fair idea what was going through her mind. I'm sorry, Mairead. *I'm so sorry.* I wanted to say it to her. Here and now, where it happened all those years ago. I had said it often to her in England. Aye, more often than not after a night on the drink when the old conscience gets a good lubrication, oiling the feeling of self-pity. I needed her forgiveness. Time and time again.

Really I shouldn't have allowed her to come home. But I needed her. Now, more than ever.

My mammy's house came into view, the last one in a row of red-bricked terraced houses. A big, almost naked, copper beech stood beside it. Number forty-eight Corsta Street. Smoke billowed from its chimney. My first thought was that my mother had got a good fire on for us coming home. Our front door was a vibrant navy blue.

Most of the houses looked pretty-well kept, but it was still noticeable that the new dawn that had visited Belfast, well, parts of it, was still strangely absent from this area. Peeling, half-torn photos of the Hunger Strikers clung hauntingly to life next to a clean whitewashed wall, proudly showing a beautiful mural depicting a British soldier walking away with the words BRITS GO HOME trailing him. Rubbish had gathered at the top end of the street; dogs walked around in pairs, seemingly eyeing strangers.

Where was the pride?

The pride we all used to have in this area. We may have been poor, but my mother would not have allowed a piece of paper to lie on the street, and neither would any of her neighbours. Mrs Murphy; old Mr Keenan, the watchmaker; wee Mrs Donnelly and her alcoholic husband; my best friends, two doors up, Paul and Christopher Nugent. All now gone.

A number of people were standing outside our house, glasses in hand. I pushed open the shiny black wooden gate and spotted one or two faces I recognised but couldn't put a name to. They nodded at me.

'Sorry for your troubles, son.' Open hands were offered, the beginnings of the handshaking ritual. I took the offer, then turned to look round the area again, aching for the past. The familiar past. My mind's eye sympathetically conjuring up the football pitch opposite our house where local teams fought for victory, cheered on by street-divided loyalties. It now played landlord to tired, cheap abodes, settled in the gloom.

I could almost hear my mother's urgent voice calling me in for dinner. Mairead must have sensed something, for she grabbed my arm and smiled warmly. I could have kissed her then, I *so* wanted her and Siobhan back.

My mother's words came crashing into my mind. 'If you don't buck your ideas up, my boy, the only time you and Mairead will get together will be at my funeral.'

My Uncle Richard came to the door. He was seventy-four, but always looked much younger. He and my mother often visited us in London. Oh God! I felt sick. I sucked deeply for breath, my mouth tasting sour. I had a sudden, all-consuming longing for the Royal Oak. Where nothing was expected of me.

'Good to see you, son,' Uncle Richard said, grabbing me gently, and touchingly, by the arm. Richard was normally not one for showing his feelings. 'Your mammy's at rest now. Your Uncle Pat's inside. Come on in.' He kissed Mairead and shook hands with Cathal. I took a deep breath and walked into the house. The hall wallpaper was green; I remembered it blue. The brass bell and elephants were still there on a ledge. The living room door was open. I walked through. I spotted Pat standing near the coffin. He winked warmly at me. Pat was four years older than Richard and was as big and broad as Richard was small and wiry. They lived a simple life together and both sported heavy jackets, with Richard favouring dark-blue working men's jeans, and Pat, brown trousers. As we moved more into the house, the gentle hum of mourners greeted me, reaching in seconds, to me, at any rate, a crescendo of accusing voices.

Eh, Dooley boy, eh, got nothing to say for yourself? Never came home to see your ma…

I recognised only a few people. I wanted to run, get the fuck away from here, but I tried to smile and introduced Cathal to some and Mairead to everyone. I had no idea who knew her, who knew us. Some just stared at me. Were they the ones who thought they knew me? Who the fuck did they think they were, judging me?

Slowly, people introduced themselves to me. I shook hands with Billy Turley and Sean Judge; Jesus! They'd aged! The three of us had this great idea to form a band; we used to stay awake some nights tuning into Radio Luxembourg. A small, fine-featured woman introduced herself to me, teasing me 'cause I couldn't remember her. Oh God! Yes. I went out with her for a week when I was fourteen. Went to the cinema twice, she reminded me. I recalled her warning words in the back of the cinema: 'No funny business, Thomas Dooley.'

Billy Doyle had put on so much weight and looked uneasy in an ill-fitting blue suit. His black hair was plastered to his head. He was so skinny back then when we struggled to climb Cavehill Mountain. His brother, now dead, used to sneak a bottle of Clan Dew on board when we took the train to Bangor. Admittedly, their faces were filled with warmth, but I still felt out of place.

I looked over at Cathal. He was chatting to a couple of older men, their shaking hands almost spilling their drinks. Cathal gave me a reassuring grin.

Get the pints in, Cathal. Get off your stool: give me a lecture; tell me it's time to go; leave here. We don't want to miss Dotty; she's about to sing. Just get me out of here.

I gulped for nerve-calming breath as people moved aside to allow me nearer the coffin. My hands shook. Mairead held them. I didn't… Oh Jesus Christ! I didn't want to see the coffin. My slow steps took me ever closer.

I was beginning to see my mother's lifeless face. If I don't look closely she won't be dead, that's how it goes, doesn't it?

Don't you be crying at my funeral, she'd once scolded me when I got a bit maudlin about her. Having consumed a few pints, I was questioning her mortality. I'll cry if I want to. I felt a coldness making deep incisions into my guts.

I would never, ever, hear her voice again. Why the fuck hadn't I come home? She never really mentioned it, but I'm sure she would have liked it had we come home. Even though she insisted it was best we didn't. Who was I to expect her to come to London all the time?

Only once, I remember it clearly, did she ever go into any detail. We were sharing a cup of tea in the flat; Mairead was putting Siobhan to bed. My mother just looked at me, and out of the blue, and with a sage-like calmness, announced that one day I would indeed return to my birthplace.

I laughed. Yes, she'd added, and it will be the making of you.

Mothers, eh?

'What happened, Richard?' I asked as I looked down at her small, frail features. I had listened to the standard, brain-numbing, religious-based bullshit echoing all around me: 'She's at rest now, son,' or 'She looks so peaceful.' She looked dead to me. I don't call that peaceful. I wanted her to smile at me again, shout at me; see her face light up when she hugged Siobhan; laugh out loud when she watched *The Good Life*; giggle red-faced when she had a sherry or two. I needed to hug her one last time. One last time; let her speak to me; let her tell me she's okay.

One last time? Yeah, even then I realised it would never be enough.

'If you had bothered to come home you would have known how ill she was.' The unmistakable cutting tone of my sister, Carmel. She had been in the kitchen preparing the food. Always doing the right thing was our Carmel.

'Good to see you too, Carmel,' I said, determined not to rise to the bait.

Richard wasn't so sure. 'Now, please, you two, not now.' He looked at me and nodded towards my mother. In that moment he aged considerably. I had forgotten. I had selfishly forgotten his pain; this was his sister.

I spotted a priest whom I assumed to be Father Rice. My mother had told me so much about him. I really wanted to chat to him. Hopefully, at some stage I would get the chance.

In no time, the mourners got the hang of the script and settled down to consuming the enormous piles of food and bottles of alcohol. Our long-awaited grand entrance now over, I slugged a good measure of whiskey; Mairead had a smaller version of my tipple. Cathal was on brandy.

'She didn't want you knowing she was sick,' Richard began to tell me. 'I mean she wasn't too bad for a good while. It was about a week or so ago when she really took bad. I wanted to phone you, but she said she would be okay. You know your mother, never made a fuss. Sure the other week we were talking about going over to London. She lived for those visits. It was quick in the end, son, have to be thankful for that.'

All I could think of, God forgive me, was when my mother would be buried so I could get the hell out of here. I was in no mood for the traditional wake.

From out of the corner of my eye, I noticed a man approaching, knocking into one or two people. He took faltering steps aided by a walking stick. I'd put his age at about sixty or so. He moved awkwardly in a seemingly seldom-worn brown suit. He shook himself spasmodically as if his back was itchy and pulled aggressively at his sleeves. A bright white hankie jutted out from the top pocket of the jacket. His black hair, which looked dyed, was short with a middle parting.

He threw his voice ahead of himself. 'Oh Jesus! I loved your mammy, Tom, so I did. Anyone will tell you that. Oh sure, she was one fine woman. Me and her were like that,' he said, crossing two fingers of his right hand indicating a firm relationship. 'She reminded me so much of my sister Marie, God rest her soul; she was a kind one as well.' He was beside me now but didn't feel that such proximity should require the lowering of his voice. I offered him my hand; he shook it and just stood there, looking at the floor, his head bobbing up and down. A tubby little woman, her face clenched in a red scarf, took him by the arm and led him away. She smiled at me apologetically.

'Who was that?' Cathal asked.

'Tom will know,' said my Uncle Pat.

I shook my head. I had no idea, although when I looked again, there was something vaguely familiar about him.

'You mean you don't remember Sammy Devine? He was in your class at school. Remember? He loved to play handball.'

My eyes widened. 'Jesus! Sammy Devine? He looks near sixty. Oh, of course. Oh God! I remember now what happened to his family. Jesus! Not a bit of wonder he looks the way he does.'

'Oh aye, that was shocking, so it was,' said Richard. 'And sure hasn't he had more bad news. He's been turned down for the IEA. As your Uncle Pat says, the only luck Sammy Devine has is bad luck.'

'The IEA?' Cathal spoke, but before he could continue, a deep voice alerted us to the appearance of a tall, very well-dressed man coming into the room. He looked about forty or so, a wide smile nicely complementing his tanned complexion. You didn't see many suits like that round here. Beige, seemingly tailor-made. The man shook hands with a number of people. Respect for him seemed to flood the room. Voices seemed to drop to a whisper as he walked over to my mother's coffin, said a prayer, blessed himself and turned, walking slowly towards me. He offered his hand, nodding at Pat and Richard. I shook it. His dark wavy hair looked dyed. He wore fashionable rimmed glasses and twiddled with a silver ring on his left forefinger.

'Sorry for your troubles, Tom. Your mother was a fine, fine woman. I wouldn't be where I am today without her.' He introduced himself as Emmett Burns. I thanked him for his kind comments and introduced him to Cathal and Mairead. He told her he had once gone out with a second cousin of hers. He said he'd see me later and moved away to natter with an old couple.

I grabbed Richard. 'Who's this Emmett Burns, then?'

'Emmett Burns? Oh, did your mother never tell you about him? Emmett got the IEA, top rate and all. And… a wee car. Never been heard of before. Emmett's a hero around about these parts.'

'What *is* this IEA?' asked Mairead. 'On the way here, we saw it written on the walls.'

'Aye, Cathal here thought we lot can't spell,' I laughingly spilled the beans on the Scouser.

'Oh aye,' said Richard, taking on the tone of the aggrieved. 'This from the boy who supports Tranmere Rovers?'

We laughed, all of us. It was such a relief.

Pat and Richard between them, and between slugs of whiskey, explained to us exactly what this mysterious IEA was.

It was the beginning of a fairly long, sometimes meaningful, often frustrating, relationship.

Chapter Four

So, that was what it was all about. The IEA was an allowance granted by the Department of Social Security. It stood for the Incapacity Existence Allowance. People round here would apparently kill for it. I then remembered the guy in the flat above us in London who had that run-in with a prostitute with a liking for kitchen knives and knobbly knees. He got something similar. It was granted to those who, for whatever reason, were incapacitated and were therefore unable to work. It covered all the basics plus quite a bit extra for any additional expense associated with the incapacity. As if by way of an advertising slogan, the extras on offer were reamed off to us with gasping enthusiasm: you could get a car; sun loungers in the summer; a choice of three heavy coats in winter, real or fake fur, and there was talk of massive discounts on holidays abroad or in Ballybunion, even. That was the theory anyhow.

Pat explained the locals' more pressing need for it. 'You've been out of here a long time, son. Notice many changes around here, eh? No, not exactly. This place is still a ghetto, a working class den, but without the pride we all used to have. People don't care; there's little work. No investment here. Big changes in the North? Look around you, son. There are no changes here.'

Richard took up the mantle. 'See the Waterfront, with its ballet and concerts, like. And the Odyssey, cinemas, exhibitions; apparently they have this big state-of-the-art venue for sports and that. Sure what use is that to us up here, eh? What's being built for us? I'll tell you: nothing. We don't go into town to them fancy bars and restaurants. We haven't even got a child's play area here, for God's sake.'

In quite an enlightening tale, Richard explained how an addendum to the Good Friday Agreement, seemingly recommended by Civil Servants and endorsed by Ministers, contained a reference to areas such as ours and introduced the allowance to, well, basically, keep the natives quiet. The ghettos were sacrificed for the bigger picture. It seemed the politicians thought that because many in these areas were on benefits anyhow, they would be happy to remain on them, but would relish the opportunity to obtain a more lucrative one. Hence the IEA. This, Richard said, meant the government could get away with not investing in certain areas. The Yanks weren't interested. They only wanted their names tagged on to success stories. A new library, a playground, a new shopping centre in Corsta Street? No chance! Little kudos for them here. The problem being that the DSS bastards were withholding the allowance. The addendum gave them sweeping powers. Genuine claims were being rejected on mere technicalities.

I have to admit that my first thought of sympathy for the people was soon replaced by the accusation that had often been laid at the feet of many around here that they took from the State and contributed little. Knew all about their entitlements but little of their responsibilities. I was to discover that fair means or foul were used to get the allowance. It was substantially more than any existing basic benefit, was for life and was index-linked. I could see its attraction.

Later on that evening, we took a stroll down to a local club. The number of people in the house was getting to me, so Mairead, Cathal and I joined Pat and Richard for an hour or two, just to clear our heads.

We sat at a table in the corner away from the few men standing at the bar and the young mother at the fruit machine who, I was told, came in most days to gamble her child benefit.

Cathal got the drinks in. It appeared the hardest part of actually obtaining the IEA was getting through the interview with the investigating doctors. Tough, uncompromising individuals, their bedside manner extended itself solely to shoving bed-ridden applicants out from under the duvet to check for genuine expressions of pain on hitting the floor. The nervous applicants had to go to quite unbelievable lengths to convince the GP of their genuine incapacity or, failing that, have spent a month or two at RADA.

That was, of course, if you managed to get that far. The form-filling alone was a nightmare.

Detailed questions requiring intimate information surrounding an ailment. For instance, one had to describe in one's own words the problems you had in, say, getting in and out of a bath or bed. Did you need assistance in getting dressed and undressed? Could you cook your own meals? How many days of the week did you experience problems with mobility and for how long? Did you need constant supervision and were you a danger to yourself or others?

The list was endless. I could see why some just gave up.

I was more than happy to keep chatting about this. It took my mind off my mother lying there with all those people around her. She wouldn't have wanted that; she never wanted a fuss. I should really have been back in the house looking after her, but I couldn't. I couldn't just stand around watching her lifeless form. I rang Siobhan; she was very upset. She said she wanted to see her granny. I tried to talk her round, but with little success. Mairead spoke to her and explained that her granny was now in heaven and watching over her, making sure she was safe and behaving herself. I heard Mairead tell my daughter that yes, her granny was looking after her mummy and daddy as well.

Pat told us there had been seventy applications for the IEA from the area in recent months: not one was approved. Emmett had been the only success story to date. Samuel Devine was their last hope. A car crash a while back had injured Sammy's neck, not badly, but enough for the locals to encourage him to go for the allowance. After all he'd been through, they reckoned he deserved something.

'The DSS are getting worse, so they are,' said Pat. 'They are answerable to nobody. You can't even complain to them. See if you do, you'll get a visit, a warning, like, from one of their officials. Any more trouble and they'll cut all your benefits. And, as you can see, most of us survive on benefits here.'

It was a sobering thought, this incursion into the daily lives of certain Belfast people. My mother had mentioned the odd aspect of life in our part of Belfast, but I hadn't realised it was this bad. Or, perhaps, I hadn't been listening. Perhaps I didn't really care about the lives of Belfast people. They were nothing to do with me. It appeared, however, that whatever peace dividend there was in the North, little of it had matured in this area.

I just wanted the funeral over. Mairead and I did get the chance to chat about certain parts of the old days, the good parts. We made Cathal laugh as we told him what we got up to on these streets as teenagers.

I have to say that on the day of the funeral, Mairead never left my side. As I stood in the City Cemetery, beside my mother's grave, I watched many make their way home. A mound of soil pushing my mother into Irish earth. Alongside my father. I wondered was she with him now, with my brother? That's what she believed in.

I felt such a bloody failure, though. I had let everyone down. I should have made my mother proud, done something for her. Instead, she spent her life worrying about me 'cause I was so self-absorbed.

I knew deep down I hadn't a cat in hell's chance of getting Mairead and Siobhan back. No chance. Of course, I still wanted her back. But she wasn't prepared to give me another chance. And why should she? Old dog; new tricks.

If I could have jumped on to a plane and set off there and then for England, I would have been happier. I could hide my failure there. In Belfast, it seemed so much more vivid. Jesus Christ! I couldn't get away from it; it had all been my fault.

'Fucking do the wee bastard now,' screamed the sweaty one with hands like shovels, the veins in his neck bulging as he tried to hold on to the struggling Tom Dooley. The other one, fat and pimply, held Mairead on the ground as she fought to save Tom. Amid the rubble of Belfast waste ground. An army helicopter floated off somewhere. 'This will teach you to fucking joyride, Dooley, ye wee shite.' Boom! Boom! A scream. Agony. Blood pumping. Squawking crows scattered. 'Oh fuck! Ye stupid bastard. Ye fucking got her. Do him! Do fucking him! Come on!' Gun jammed.

I thought I knew everything about traditional Irish funerals, but that night, in the local club, was off its head. Jesus! What a session! And just what was needed.

Oblivion with a happy taste. People came up to me, offering to buy me a drink, and talked about my mother, told me about what she had done for them. I never knew. A warm feeling of pride struggled valiantly with my feelings of deep loss, and as the alcohol took hold, I looked round the club seeing many faces who genuinely admired, even loved, my mother. Propped up by the booze, no doubt, I felt that maybe I could be at home here once again. These people were nice; they were so friendly. Boy, did I give the booze a run for its money.

Mairead, she pissed off back to England, catching a flight after the funeral. Roger the Codger was back from his conference. I knew Siobhan needed her, but so did I. Mairead hadn't even bothered to go and see her brother, the only one from her family who came to our wedding. He was all the close family she had; her mother died four years ago. She never knew her father.

Piss off then, Mairead. There was me having a post-mortem on myself, taking the frigging blame for everything. My mother would have understood. I decided I wasn't going to continually beat myself up over Mairead Canavan. I told Cathal.

'I knew you'd come to your senses one day,' he said.

'Did you really? You knew that one day I'd say, sod it, Mairead, I can't be arsed anymore, eh?'

He looked mystified and nodded towards my pint. 'No, no, not that. I knew one day I'd get you drinking Guinness.'

From the outside, the club was a mere hole in a stained, fragmenting wall. Inside, it fared better. Red leather seats, red and cream carpet, fairly new, by the looks of it. Pictures of local Gaelic Football teams adorned the walls. Generations of grinning faces in green-and-white hooped shirts. I found a picture of the Under-12 team in which I played. Collectively, we looked like eejits. Thought I must see if I can get a copy to show to Siobhan. The door hung off the Gents. When I was young, clubs like this, and indeed many homes, had framed pictures of three men: Pope John Paul II, Pope Paul VI and JF Kennedy. I noticed Pope Paul had been replaced in some by Martin O'Neill.

'Your ma was a saint, Tom, I'm telling you.' Emmett had been sitting beside me for most of the evening. He was good craic and a generous man. Despite our protestations, neither Cathal nor me had bought a drink all night. Cathal was up at the bar chatting and laughing with two women, one of whom I'm sure I went to school with. He seemed to be trying to teach them a Country and Western song. Either that or he had an itch somewhere he didn't think it polite to scratch. I fervently hoped he wasn't trying to push that Willie Nelson versus Elvis crap of his. Jesus! Maybe he was trying to push his JR suicide theory!

'I'd never have got the IEA if it hadn't been for your ma, you know that?' Emmett continued, his face creaking under the weight of a double whiskey. 'Just like Sammy there, I was turned down twice before, but your mother told me to keep at it, helped me fill in the forms and all. Oh aye, many's the night her and I would run through the questions the doc would ask. I had my answers off by heart and the old confidence was sky high. That's half the battle, you know: confidence.'

I nodded. Jesus! This IEA was some game!

Later that evening, as the haze of alcohol managed to numb the senses, Emmett made a grand gesture to me that left my uncles gasping in astonishment. The ultimate accolade, it seemed. Emmett stood up, cleared his throat. He was about to speak, but was interrupted by the unexpected and sudden arrival of a middle-aged woman in a green dress, her black hair wrapped up in a bow. Moments earlier, she had been dancing safely somewhere off in the distance. She was now, however, crashed out amid our table and chairs. Her flushed face looked up at us as if to ask, Who put those chairs there? Such is the brain-numbing power of the tango to people of a certain age. Her literal downfall was due, in no small way, to her including the not-so-Latino Splits in the famous Central American dance.

I helped Emmett lift the chairs and turn the table up again. I left him to point the tango lover in the right direction. Emmett was all smiles, but there was a look of pride on his flushed face.

'Tom, in recognition of your mother's help in beating the DSS bastards,' a big cheer went up, 'I think it only right and fitting that you, and a partner of your choice, accompany me tomorrow when I choose my wee car.'

Fuck, someone said. Lucky bastard, another uttered.

'He's an outsider, Emmett, why him?' came the less-than-friendly voice of a woman just off to my right.

A youngish bloke added his comments in a rather too loud a voice for my liking. 'Sure he never even came home to see his ma. We're not good enough for him here, so we're not.'

To some Irish people, I had committed the unforgivable. I had lived in England. Shit, you could live in Boston, New York, Outer-fucking-Mongolia and they'd treat you better. But England?

Mixing with the age-old enemy, see.

In a second, I was up and at the young bastard, grabbing him round the throat. 'Don't let me hear you speak about my mother again, ye backward bastard.'

If it hadn't been for Cathal, who abandoned his romantic entanglement with an agility I'd seldom seen, I would have mangled the wee bastard's face. Cathal grabbed me and pulled me away.

'Calm down, everyone,' Emmett said, holding his hands up and open. 'Come on now, this is not what we want.'

I did feel an easing of my temper when I saw my Uncle Richard's pleading eyes. Oh sod it, I've done it again. I sat down. I gulped deeply in an effort to calm my breathing.

'Tom Dooley is Molly's son and that's good enough for me.' Emmett was at my side again. There was anger in his voice. He pointed at the woman who had spoken. 'And you, Kate Thornton, just you remember Molly Dooley helped you out many a time when you hadn't the money for the milkman.'

The woman looked abashed 'Aye, did you think we didn't know? Look, Tom is one of us. Ignore these gobshites, Tom. Will you come?'

Cathal was all beams; I don't think he had a clue what was going on.

It had been a strange day.

I'd buried my mother; I'd come home for the first time in twenty years. I thought I hated everyone; I couldn't. I wanted to, mind you; it would have been easier. Whatever, these were my people. Maybe not exactly in thought and outlook. The important thing, though, was that they knew me. Nobody in England really did. Apart from the Scouser, that is.

I had grown up with this lot. For better or worse. I nodded at Emmett, who smiled and grabbed my hand, almost crushing it in a shaking frenzy.

'Oh, by the way, Emmett, what exactly is the matter with you? How come you got the IEA? You look fit and well to me.' I felt the need to ask.

Emmett looked round as if to say, stupid bastard has been away too long, doesn't know the way of things. 'Oh, I have trouble, Tom.'

With that, he stood up and with great assurance assumed the role of a ninety-year-old arthritic sufferer.

'So, you actually have back trouble?' asked Cathal, sipping from his pint and glancing at the guy on stage doing Elvis dressed in a loud blue shell suit. Somebody mentioned he was the local coalman.

'The way of it, Tom, is that sure when I was pretending the role, so to speak, I put so much into it, I put my back out. Oh, it gives me some quare jip at times, but thank God it doesn't affect my enjoyment of life.' He drank deeply from his whiskey and sighed contentedly.

It was a logic with which I found it difficult to argue. But then, it was Irish logic. Emmett started to chat about Sammy and his IEA rejections. He insisted, and many near us nodded, that Sammy's downfall was his two-point turn.

'What, do the DSS get you to take a driving test just in case you got a wee car?' I asked.

'What's he on about?' a man asked Emmett.

Emmett grinned and rubbed his face. 'No, Tom. You see, as I explained to Sammy, what, with his neck problem, his upper body movement was so vital. You see, these doctors, they know all the wee tricks, like, so you have to be ahead of the game, so to speak. I told Sammy the doctor would twist him in movement and in questioning. The doc asked Sammy to turn to the right. That was Sammy's mistake. You see he did it all in the one movement. This, despite your mother telling him often enough that you first feign to the left, slowly turn your head to face the middle and then, only then, do you slowly, at snail's pace, turn your whole body to the right. Sammy's nerves got the better of him. Like it does with most people.'

I laughed. 'Jesus! You people, you know all the scams, never mind the doctors.'

Emmett's face fell to serious mode. 'Let me tell you something, Tom. See most of the people in this area, they're on some sort of medication since the Troubles began: Prozac, Cipramil, Valium, the lot. They don't give a shite about us, the authorities. They owe us, and so what if some of our claims aren't genuine? I'll tell you something for nothing: our needs are. And anyhow, if they pay up, we'll live a more relaxed life and most will come off the medication. So that will save them a fortune, eh?'

'Oh, I wouldn't come off my Prozac, Emmett. It's a wee lifesaver,' one woman with a nervous tic said.

'See those Cipramil tablets? If it wasn't for them, I'd be away with the fairies, so I would,' added another supporter of Western medicine.

Near the end of the evening, I was chatting to a woman I remembered from my teenage days: Gemma Murphy. Tall, striking looking. Blonde. Nice tan. Been to Spain recently. Separated from her husband. Children with her mother for the night. Lived nearby.

Bingo!

My numbers had just been called. I left the club as Cathal was getting into a rather heated conversation with a few Celtic fans. 'There's nothing wrong with Tranmere Rovers; winning isn't everything,' he pleaded.

'No, but there's something wrong with you for supporting them,' a green jersey spoke.

God, my mother would never have set foot in here. Hardly drank. Would have a wee sherry at Christmas or a wedding or when she was over with us in London. Face would go bright red. I got my drinking from my father, one Benny Dooley. Legendary waster, God rest his soul. Neither worked nor wanted. But he could charm the birds off the trees and, legend has it, could, on occasion, hand feed them. Vague memories propped up with black-and-white photos of the man they call my father. That's all I have of him. Some might think it strange, but I don't ever really recall wanting more.

I think I had too much Guinness, for I spewed up when I left Gemma's house in the early hours.

I felt a sudden urge to talk to my wife. Roger answered the phone. Seemed to have woken him from a deep sleep. I switched off. As I walked down the street, careful not to fall too often against the wall, my mobile rang. It was Mairead. I expected her to give off to me, as it was three in the morning. I was ready for her.

Boy, was I ready.

My mother has just died, ye bitch.

All I asked was for you to stay with me for a few days. I needed you. But oh no, you had to be away back to Roger the Codger.

She asked me was I all right. I didn't get the chance to rant and rave.

'My mammy, Mairead. Ah, Jesus! My mammy.'

'I know, I know,' she said, and her voice was soft and soothing. She made me feel calmer, for traipsing along a Belfast street at that early hour suddenly made me feel uneasy. God, I *so* needed her. I *so* needed to be with someone who knew me, really knew me and accepted me for what I was. When you're on the piss, anybody vaguely familiar fits the bill; first-stage sobriety is choosier.

My mother was gone and Mairead was like a ghost. Vaguely there but untouchable.

I suppose I could have imagined it, but I could have sworn Mairead blew me a kiss when she signed off. When I got back to the house, Cathal was snoring away on the sofa, his legs sprawled, his face contorted into a drunken grin. The lights were still on. I slithered into an armchair and listened to the ticking clock. Cathal woke up momentarily and asked after my health. I nodded a couple of times; he was off again after the second nod. I shook my head trying to fend off the advances of sleep. It was the first chance I had to look round the house. To really look round.

And remember.

I recognised a lot of the changes my mother had made to the house from photos she used to send over. She still had that china cabinet stuffed with various ornaments and trinkets collected over the years. Behind an extravagantly green Irish doll, stood a small snow dome I had bought her in Dundalk while on a school trip. On top of the TV was a picture of her and my father, taken on a day trip to Newcastle, the majestic Slieve Donard hotel in the background. A picture of Kieran and me sat next to it. I wondered then what might have become of the brother I really didn't know, or the father I had few memories of.

I noticed two record sleeves sitting on a table; I never knew she liked Howard Keel. I knew she loved James Young. The perfume Siobhan bought for her last birthday still clung to the air, and a vase of artificial carnations, her favourites, sat in the window. I'd never been in this house without my mother. All the memories of childhood came flooding back, although in my inebriated state they became fuzzy with time. My drink-laced brain remembered when I was six, my mother crying when I had to go into hospital to have my tonsils out. I had never seen her cry before. Or since.

Not even that night.

I tried so hard to remember just the good times, but all I was getting were visions of that night. Visions that over the years had leapt out at me, dragging me back, back to a time I tried to bury. Often, through alcohol, I sought darkness, obliterating those thoughts, but there were always shadows. A pint, a wee half 'un usually had a nightmare chasing them.

The past, the present, the future – no order, no rationale.

Just potency in numbers and they finally got me. I would sob like a good drunk, pity topping it all up. I stared at the contented face of Cathal and remembered that night.

I remembered it in all its cold-blooded vividness.

It was warm. I was due to pick up Mairead; we were going to a disco. She was going to wear her new jeans. Two of my mates called round. Asked if I fancied getting a car and going for a spin? I said no, I was meeting Mairead. 'Fuck, married already, Dooley?' I loved the thrill of the car rides, tearing round the streets. Sure I could see Mairead later. White Cortina, just right. Jimmy cranked the door open, hot-wired the car. Revving, revving, revving! We were whistling and stamping our feet as Gerard raced through the gears. 'Get some fucking speed on it; it's not a hearse,' I shouted.

Metal smashing into metal; hissing steam; boke filling my mouth. Ah fuck, lads, we've hit Paul Canavan's car. Mangled thoughts unravelled. Run, run, for fuck sake run. Fuck, if he recognises us. Couldn't have seen me, the fucker.

Laughed our heads off at the disco. 'Paul Canavan's in the IRA, the IRA, the IRA – Paul Canavan's in the IRA but will they do his re-spray? Paul Canavan's in the IRA, in the IRA…'

Dragged out of the disco. Told Jimmy to fuck off. His cousin's connected, see. Gerard fell; they kicked him. Told Mairead to get away on home. Waste ground. 'Fucking do the wee fucker now,' screamed the sweaty one with hands like shovels, the veins in his neck bulging as he held on to me. The other one, fat and pimply, held Mairead. Boom! Boom! Scream. 'Oh fuck! Ye stupid bastard! Ye fucking shot her…'

Next morning, Emmett came round bright and early, a tad too bright and certainly far too early for me. Somehow, and outside my memory bank, Cathal and I managed to get upstairs and into our beds. The door knocker woke me up. I looked out the window.

'What? What is it?' I slurred through a closed window and a furry tongue. Swallowing deeply, I shook my head to disperse the effects of overindulgence.

Jesus! My head. Guinness, ye bastard, Cathal. I don't drink frigging Guinness. I walked into Cathal's room. There he was, fully clothed, sprawled across the bed. 'Cathal, ye big bastard, Emmett and a crowd are at the door.'

Cathal seemed less concerned with personnel than he was with location, judging by his quizzical glances round the room.

'We're in Belfast, ye stupid bollocks. Remember, my mother's…'

'Ah, Jesus! Molly…'

'Oh don't start that. I haven't the head for it. Guinness?'

He dragged himself up into a sitting position. 'Yeah, you said you were probably the only Irishman never to have drunk a pint of Guinness. So where better to put that right than here in Belfast?'

'So, you do remember last night, then?' I asked, trying to ignore the rapping on the door.

'Last night, did yesterday have a night? I remember only drinking copious amounts of Guinness. I remember nothing else.'

'Ah, you're suffering from Irish Alzheimer's,' I diagnosed.

I dragged on a pair of trousers and hastily buttoned my shirt before opening the door to the smiling Emmett

'Morning, Tom, and isn't it a lovely one?' Emmett looked fit and healthy as he strode past me. His alcohol consumption was at least ten times mine last night, but once again, he looked dapper. A smart grey suit, muted pink tie and a grin so wide, revealing teeth so gleaming white, he could well be the mouth of Colgate's next ad.

But best of all was his entourage. There must have been about fifteen of them: women, men –including my two uncles – children and the odd dog. One had to assume that this was the IEA delegation, hand-picked and ready for action. They all came in and waited while Cathal and I got dressed. Richard was busy cooking up breakfast, and the greasy food at least attempted to mop up the previous night's excesses. The whole lot of them watched us eat, nervously checking their watches, egging us on with impatient looks.

'We need to be away on, lads,' Emmett said, allowing us to swallow the last pieces of fried soda. And soon, away on we were, with Cathal and me taking up the rear as the group marched up Corsta Street, out on to the pot-holed Ariel Street. Most houses had someone at the door, waving us on with the odd word of encouragement or cheering and clapping. A banner or two wishing Emmett GODSPEED AND GOOD FORTUNE fluttered from upstairs windows.

And then a more personal banner, hanging, as it was, from Emmett's house. He gave a thumbs up as we passed it – YOU'RE A JAMMY BASTARD, BURNS

I sensed, however, that there were one or two accompanying us who were less than pleased with our company. Dirty looks still surfaced. Sod them.

We were heading for Morgan's car showroom, run by one Joe Donnelly. I remembered him from school. He had married into the Morgan family and, therefore, into the family business. He was still a wee shite, according to popular opinion; had ideas above his station. Thought he was yer man in the big picture, as my mother would say. Oh aye, he went to school with us, no arse in his trousers like the rest of us. Now looked down on the locals. Some had sympathy for him on account of marrying Maura Morgan; we used to call her Bessie Bunter at school. Lost a lot of weight since then. Put it all back on, though. On her tongue. Oh, they say the nagging she gives Joe is something terrible. It seemed, however, that everyone was looking forward to meeting up with Joe.

And there he was on the forecourt, king of all he surveys. A double-breasted beige suit, trousers at less than half-mast and a green, orange and red, tightly knotted tie, all gathered together to give him a more than convincing look of a strangled eejit. He quickly donned a pair of glasses when he spotted us. Joe Ninety rides again. A look of horror plastered on his ruddy features turned to a sneer when he seemed to recognise us. He knew it wasn't a social visit. Wee Joe Donnelly, all five foot two of him. Only lad I ever had a fight with at school.

'Yes, gentlemen. What can I do for you?' he asked as we approached and stopped, forming an orderly queue behind Emmett. We then spread out. Joe looked anxious.

'What can you do for us? You could change that hoor of a tie for a start,' said Emmett to roars of fashion-awareness laughter. 'I've seen gay boys dress quieter.'

Joey loosened the knot on his tie.

'We've come for a car, son,' said Emmett, and the rest of us nodded as we looked round eyeing

Joey's range of vehicles parked erratically in the forecourt. If we had smacked Joey in the solar plexus, I don't think we would have knocked the wind from his sails so swiftly. He recovered, though, and cleared his throat before taking a few swaggering steps towards us.

'You do realise, Emmett, that my cars are…'

Emmett didn't give him time to finish his sarcasm. 'Aye, your cars are grand, so they are. You can see that, no question.' Joey looked at the rest of us. To a man, woman, child and dog, we had grins on our faces.

'Now, Emmett, I only take cash. Cheques, credit cards, sure. No disrespect, like, but none of you have any anyhow.' Nobody seemed insulted by the comment. 'Again, Emmett, no offence, but I don't think you have the means. I really don't have time for all this. Whatever your game is, I'm not interested.' With that, he nodded and turned his back to walk away.

'Ye wee shite ye, Donnelly.' It was Sammy. 'Do you know who you're talking to?' Ah, the name game. Sammy felt the need to verbally collar Joey. I thought he was going to throw his walking stick at him. Emmett told him to calm down.

There was no placating Sammy. 'That wee bastard gets on my nerves, always has done. Remember in school he used to keep his packets of crisps and sweets in his pockets and munch them from there? Wee shite wouldn't share.' There were nods of agreement from those of us who had witnessed Joey's shameful antics and, from those who hadn't, a suitably supportive comment: The wee bastard.

Through all this, Emmett stayed cool and collected. Like a confident town sheriff awaiting the arrival of one of the Calhoun gun-slickers, Emmett stood with his hands inches away from his inside jacket pocket. He winked at us. And with an exaggerated ease, his right hand slipped into his pocket. Like a magician, he pulled out a card, bright blue in colour.

'Joey?' Emmett called out.

Joey turned round, boredom scarring his face for but a moment. His eyes soon lit up though. 'Ah, Emmett, so it's you,' he said, rubbing his hands together, then came running over to Emmett, his hand outstretched. 'Why didn't you say something before? IEA, Emmett, it's you who's got the IEA. That *will* do nicely, *sir*.'

Emmett raised his eyes in mock pride as Joey bestowed upon him the respectful 'sir'.

What happened next must have had some rehearsal, if not detailed research, but the sheer unexpectedness of it all floored me. Joey did a two-fingered whistle towards his office.

'I knew somebody from the area had got the IEA. I just didn't know it was you, Emmett.' He was beside himself with excitement. Seemingly, a big day for him too.

The portakabin door burst open and, with the unsteadiness which a collective age of about three hundred and three brings, out came three women of various sizes, all in black dresses, erratically waving raggedy pink feather boas. And from the rear came a man, bald, in a pink shirt, open at the waist and buttoned at the neck. He pushed one of the women out of the way and stood looking at Joey. Joey must have missed the last rehearsal, for he looked as shocked as we did.

'Let her rip, Simon,' he said quite tentatively, his eyes narrowing in doubt.

Oh, so that was Simon. With the elegant agility of an irate hippo, Simon trounced back into the portakabin and, within moments, our ears were treated to a form of music. It was a very bad recording, possibly Dickie Rock – more likely Joe Dolan.

HAPPY DAYS, OH, THOSE OLD HAPPY DAYS...

The three women were now lined up, arms entwined, fidgeting in their high heels. They mouthed the words of this happy little ditty as they fell, or were pushed, incredulity temporarily blinding me, into a tap-dancing blizzard.

'Who the hell are they?' asked Cathal, staring hard at the dancing queens.

To his credit, Joey was swift with an explanation. 'See the one in the middle with the long grey hair and slightly stooped? That's my mother. On her right, our left, that's the mother-in-law; she's plagued with corns, but she insisted.'

'And the one on the end, Joey, the one whose dentures have just hit the ground?' I asked.

'Oh, that's Miriam Donaghy. Miriam is their behavioural therapist,' Joey replied without a hint of disquiet.

Miriam's skills were quickly called upon as the mother and mother-in-law started to shove each other; and while little of it was in sequence, it did undoubtedly have an artistic quality to it. 'Now, ladies,' warned Miriam, leaning down to retrieve her molars, 'what do we do in times like this?'

It was spoken with such poise and determination. Joey's relatives and their therapist stopped and took deep breaths. We all just stood there, glued to the spot. Simon turned the music up. Definitely Joe Dolan. The women counted to three, and a semblance of the previous tap-dancing feast began again.

Accompanied this time by just the odd, slightly aggressive nudge, with clenched fists as an added bonus. Miriam didn't seem to pick up on them. Perhaps occasional self-expression was all part of the treatment.

'Beverley Sisters too expensive?' Cathal asked Joey as fatigue wilted their performances.

Joey just raised his eyes to heaven. You did feel for Joey; it seemed he had a lot to put up with. 'This is my first IEA, lads, I kid you not,' he announced, and in moments was on his mobile to the *North Belfast Chronicle* telling them about his good fortune. He turned to Emmett. 'You know you'll have all top of the range stuff, all the accessories. And you'll have to have it all changed every year in accordance with IEA regulations. And you know, Emmett, you can't use any other garage but ours. Boy, this is great.'

The three women stood, knees bent, gulping in air. It seemed the show was over.

And we hadn't applauded. We hadn't booed either, so, honours even. We left Emmett to the paperwork while we hung around waiting for the *North Belfast Chronicle* guys to arrive.

Richard slowly looked back at the women as they retreated to the portakabin. He shook his head wistfully. 'If only I was thirty years older.'

I had to admit to feelings of sadness when the next day Cathal and I sat in the airport lounge contemplating a couple of pints. He, too, looked less than joyous. Our flight to London was due to leave in an hour. After all, this had been my first visit home in twenty years. I now felt a certain coldness, like it was the end of something I had become quite attached to. My mother was dead; I still didn't get on with my sister. The past, therefore, was gone now too. I had nobody to share it with. But what about the future? I suppose all I could hope for was that the remainder of 2003 wouldn't get any worse.

Cathal asked if I wanted a refill. I nodded. Well, that was the future taken care of.

The Scouser had really taken to Belfast, I could see that. I also got the feeling that it wouldn't have taken much for him to stay. He didn't put any pressure on me. Just little comments made me aware. Had we been in the Royal Oak, I felt he would have been off his stool giving me a lecture as to the value of staying put.

'The craic's great in Belfast, eh, Tom?' was his summing up.

True. But the craic was experienced through the eyes of a visitor; the reality of actually bedding down in Belfast for the duration would be a completely different ball game. Christ! Even the thought of it made me shiver. I experienced periods of isolation in Belfast, just as I did in London and had ever since the first day I arrived. I felt nowhere was my home.

It hurts more, however, to feel isolated in one's own city. Yet, why was I surprised?

Sure the people were great, but I didn't really feel one of them; wasn't sure even if I actually wanted to join their gang full time.

'I could visit Siobhan at weekends and have her over at holidays,' I said, breaking the silence.

'So you've accepted that she and Mairead will be coming to Belfast?' asked Cathal.

I nodded. 'You and I know that Mairead one usually gets what she wants.'

'Do you really think that would satisfy you, seeing Siobhan so little? Out of sight, out of mind?'

Cheers, Cathal. Always a big help in making me feel better. 'I can't see myself living here, Cathal. I've been away so long, makes it hard to come back and stay. And anyhow, what would you do without your regular drinking partner and all-round mentor? Who would keep you on the straight and narrow, not to mention on your stool come Country and Western night, eh?'

'Oh, I could come over and see you all during my holidays, which are Monday to Friday on any given week, and alternative Saturdays.'

I was glad to see a big grin return to his face.

'Look, Tom, the one person you really give a damn about, I mean *really* give a damn, present company excepted, is your daughter. You have got to think seriously about coming to live here. Hey, maybe I might too, eh?'

Cathal seemed determined to continue, despite my thoughts drifting off elsewhere. Back to my job in the off-licence; my flat above the Indian; getting drunk in the Royal Oak; listening to Wee Hughie slagging off Ronnie Barker and wondering how many years it would be before I ended up chatting to Dotty for entertainment. And she'd be that much older: faded hearing, creaking bones. My street cred blasted sky-high. Cathal stressed it wouldn't do my chances with Mairead any harm if she could see I was making such a sacrifice for Siobhan.

I don't know if it was my mother's death that brought reality too close for comfort, but the increasingly sinking feeling that Mairead was drifting further and further away from me was staring me in the face. And it wasn't blinking. Yeah, she had offered me a closeness in Belfast, but that was grief laden, not the basis on which to resurrect anything.

Anything meaningful, that is.

They called our flight. A truly deep sadness grabbed me. My mother was gone and I was leaving her. I was not one for visiting graves. No matter what I did in the future, good or bad, I would do it without her hand on my shoulder. I would do it without the knowledge that no matter how bad things got, she would be there for me. Chastising, no doubt, but understanding. While my mother was alive, my father and brother lived on. They existed through our thoughts, our memories of them. Our laughter and sadness kept them vividly alive. My mother would often tell me of the days of her early marriage to my father and how he made her laugh; how, no matter what he did, she always forgave him. He used to bring her home ice-cream laden with tinned fruit from the local shop after a few jars down the pub. She told me how much my brother had loved the law and had intended training to be a solicitor.

My sister and I would never be able to re-create these memories; she was unwilling and I was unable. The past, the one certainty in life, was now gone. I felt so alone, but in many ways I always did. They called our flight again.

Goodbye, Belfast. I really didn't know you that well.

God bless you, mammy.

Chapter Five

We never did catch that flight. Oh, we intended to catch a later one, then the one after that. Cathal wanted to stay in Belfast, and it wasn't just the airport alcohol firing his enthusiasm. He genuinely felt he could be at rest here in Belfast. It seemed, however, that he required my backing and presence.

God! Could he not do anything on his own! I asked him what we would do. 'What do we do now?' was his answer.

'So I get a job in an off-licence, and you, you get a job…'

He didn't let me finish. 'I have a feeling about this place, Tom, I really do. You know how we always crap on about making something of ourselves, hitting the jackpot. Bullshit, that's just talk to dodge reality. Hey, don't get me wrong, nothing wrong with that. I've been happy to just dander through life, as you would put it. I like this place, Tom. I really think we could get somewhere from here.'

Such a serious face. If it were a library book, he'd be sent reminders for keeping it too long. 'We could get to Helen's Bay, for instance,' he said with an emerging grin.

That's better.

I, too, however, had a feeling, one that I dared not take too seriously, that maybe, just maybe, we might be able to do something here. But what? Could of course have been us trying to flag down another trolleybus to escapism, who knows. But isn't escapism just another way to lead one's life? Nothing wrong with that. I don't think it carries the death penalty. Enter nothing, take part in little, come out untouched. But what about the candle, burning it at both ends? Doesn't it give a lovely glow. From some poem or other. Mairead would know.

Ramshackle DSS Offices, Belfast, on a Monday morning as the mist came off the mountains and descended on the city centre. That was where we first met Cecil Gordon McGladdery.

Cecil was about six foot fourteen, looked less than comfortable in his wrinkle-doused three-piece suit and spoke softly for such a big man. His brown hair was short and he flexed the muscles in his plump face when he spoke. Sitting behind a glass partition, looking completely uninterested, his hands behind his head, he yawningly fired standard questions at me. I was trying to claim some benefits until Cathal and I thought of a way to get some money, something legal and not arduous. We ended up chatting about his job. I told him about my experiences in the DSS in London.

'Regular replacing of your Spar bag would count in your favour here,' he said with such a deadpan voice I didn't know whether he was being serious or not.

He told me how much the job bored the arse off him as he cleaned his nails with an official HB1 pencil. I complimented him on his ability to throw such a convincing disguise over his unrest. He grinned. It turned out he had been passed over for promotion in the previous three years. Twelve years as a Local Officer II, he informed me. Said his face didn't fit. I thought he would have trouble with his frigging frame fitting as well. Too much empathy with claimants, officialdom told him. Too much empathy with bullshit, he told officialdom via an anonymous e-mail. I liked the guy. He reminded me of me.

Now apparently, while the Civil Service didn't actually have the words "sod the bastards, they're getting nought" on their headed notepaper, Cecil insisted there was an unwritten rule ensuring that many, particularly those in the ghettos, got just that. He mentioned some Englishman's name who had taken over as Head of the DSS in Belfast. Out of interest, I wanted to ask him about the IEA, but my five-minutes allotted time was up, by about half an hour. I said maybe I'd see him again. He said he didn't deal with appeals. I grinned this time. I thanked him for his help. Cathal looked anxious when I met him outside. He had amassed a number of DSS leaflets.

'I don't know what I'll end up with. I had my interview with a Scottish woman; couldn't understand a word she was saying.'

'Scottish? Did she say where she was from?'

'I think she said Port- something. Portrush?'

'Oh aye,' I laughed, 'that's south of Scotland.'

As things turned out, we were to be in Cecil's company quite frequently and not at his place of work.

One night he was a little late for our pre-arranged meeting. He entered our local wearing his usual black duffel coat, buttons undone, and tottering on his Noddy Holder-style boots. The hood of his coat stayed up, even when he banged into tables and people as he moved through the bar. Cecil was mindful of protecting his identity.

'For fuck sake, Cecil, watch where you're going!' the barman shouted.

'Aye, Cecil, next time I'm down the Bru, I'll tell them to take them big shoes off you,' moaned a woman rubbing her leg.

Cecil Gordon McGladdery was our mole within the Department of Social Security.

As I watched Cecil approach, my mind re-ran the events of the last few weeks since I first walked into the DSS and set eyes on Cecil. Our decision to ignore all calls for us to board the flight to London that evening, and to fail to re-book, found us back in my mother's house with no idea what we were going to do.

It had been Cathal's idea to look into the Incapacity Existence Allowance, more out of interest than anything else. The more we looked into it, the more we were convinced that the reason so many claimants were unsuccessful was that they really did not put everything into the claims. Untidy completion of forms tends to annoy officialdom; that, and lack of confidence and knowledge of ailment, resulted in investigating doctors swiftly dismissing the claims.

Hey, I couldn't stand working in the DSS; maybe I would fare better as an opponent of their policies.

One night, tucking into a few cans and a stew I had made, which Cathal found to his liking but advised me to go easy with the pearl barley next time, we decided that, if we could, we would try and help the locals to at least have a chance of success against the DSS. God only knows, and time would only tell, whether we had taken leave of our senses. I must admit to having had feelings of excitement – and not a little trepidation – but, overall, a sense of adventure.

Running half-blind into unknown territory. The script was written for myself and Cathal. So what if we failed! No harm done.

I've always had this nagging urge to do something with my life, something worthwhile. In reality, I just couldn't be bothered struggling to find it. From the outset we knew this project would take quite a bit of effort. It was immediately clear that we required an in-depth understanding of the application forms.

Problem one: we needed to be able to coach applicants in how they should behave when suffering from a certain ailment – so many applications had been rejected by a doctor unconvinced by the validity of an injury sustained.

Problem two: could we engender enough confidence in the people, through our confidence in our own ability, that they wouldn't be intimidated by the medical men?

Problems three, four, five, six… could we gain the trust of the local people, Cathal being an Englishman and me, according to some, being a deserter?

My mind was brought back to the present when Cecil took off his hood. A recent visit to the barber was evident. His hair was short with the back and sides missing. He raised his eyebrows acknowledging the coiffure disaster with a violent rubbing of his head as if he were trying to dust off the evidence.

We decided not to say anything.

The DSS and their inflexibility, corrupt work practices and basic desire to do us down were formidable opponents. They were our immediate major obstacles, but undoubtedly, a bigger mountain to climb would be to prove our worth to the locals. We spent weeks poring over DSS literature; leaked memos, kindly supplied by Cecil, made unpleasant reading. That very morning, during a meeting between the IEA staff and Charles Fortesque-Smith, the Sussex man Cecil said had taken over, a heated conversation, mainly one-sided and with an English accent, saw a copy of the *North Belfast Chronicle* thrown on the desk.

There he stood, Cecil said, a raging bullshitter in his pinstripe suit, glasses in one hand, a clenched fist in the other. For four minutes, he ranted and raved at his staff, asking them why he had not seen the paper at the time of its issue some six weeks previously. At the time, he had been deeply unhappy that Emmett's claim had been successful, but was now beside himself with rage that such negative publicity could undermine his job, or rather his promotion prospects. Miss Webster, a career Civil Servant of some thirty years, and Cecil's line manager, assured her boss that everything possible had been done to thwart Mr Burns' claim. Within official DSS guidelines, she added, emphasising the word *official*, Cecil said. The Englishman gave her a dirty look. Cecil liked Miss Webster.

Fortesque-Smith stomped up and down the room, reintroducing to his now attentive staff the guidelines on the IEA. Drawn up by him. He reiterated, with a spitting tirade, that the target for granting applications had not been reached. Cecil said the Englishman pushed his face into his and asked Cecil what that target was. Fuck knows, ye English bastard, thought Cecil, but decided to keep his opinions to himself. Cecil's thought process always impressed Cathal and I. He then told us he stuttered to get the answer out and was saved by Miss Webster. None, she said. The target for granting successful claims was none.

'No successful claims, no successful claims,' shouted the boss. The DSS mantra at the time.

Cecil told us he had to stifle a laugh when he looked at the newspaper, for there, in all our glory, was the IEA delegation on our visit to Morgan's showroom. Emmett to the fore, shaking hands with Joey. The Beverley Sisters Tribute Band in the background, heads bowed, hands on knees, looking out of breath. Dentures all in correct location, though. The rest of us, taking up positions to the front, side and rear of Emmett, all declaring we had effortlessly passed the eejits' exam.

Cecil finished his pint. You could tell that morning's meeting had taken it out of him, for he was up for another pint, something he normally refused at these 'secret' rendezvous. I got him one. He downed half of it and looked furtively round him, wary of any strangers. One or two waved at him, an old man smiled, and two young lads shouted over to him asking how many hours a week they could work as astronauts before losing their benefit. Pat and Richard came in, Pat with his nose in some geometry book. The two of them came over and sat down. We filled them in on the developments.

'I wanted to walk out of the room there and then,' said Cecil. 'The Englishman kept saying that "none" was a fairly straightforward number, not easily forgotten. He had the facts and figures at his fingertips, I'll give him that. Reminded us that seven million pounds had been paid out the previous year across Britain and Northern Ireland – three million in the North alone. He

51

pissed us off by saying how people in England were being deprived because of the Irish. English bastard! Who did he think he was talking to! Of course, this was before I arrived, he said. A threat, like. And then the bastard raised his eyes and said, "Oh, we all know the problems the Irish have had in the past..." I was ready to clock him one.'

And then Cecil said my mother's name came up. It gave me a feeling of pride. To be honest, I think the main reason I decided to stay in Belfast was for my mother, to continue her good work. It wasn't some bolt of lightning revealing my true vocation. I didn't suddenly possess some deep-rooted feeling, although I dared to hope, that I could actually make a difference, not the way she seemed to, but I had a sneaking feeling that Belfast could well be the place I was meant to be.

As she had once intimated.

My mother had helped Emmett to finally get the IEA and she had given others hope, had helped them, made them feel there was someone to whom they could turn. She had helped people, not in any melodramatic sort of way, but mainly from a sense of duty. She could help so she did. Simple.

It seemed only right that I should continue her dream. I was enjoying the craic as well, the Belfast way of looking at life, finding humour in damn near everything. Something I had *so* missed over the years.

Her dream? She had told Pat that she wanted each and every genuine claim for the Incapacity Existence Allowance to be granted. As Pat said, she didn't actually define *genuine*. I don't think she ever envisaged taking on the DSS and its less-than-acceptable policy decisions and operational activities.

Cecil had hinted on more than one occasion that the establishment of a new Enforcement Unit for areas such as ours was being discussed in Whitehall. The PSNI, the Police Service of Northern Ireland, never called; there was no point in reporting anything to them. Like the taxi driver, they, too, felt that an incursion into our area was taking a step back in time. They had their new name sorted out, new uniforms, overtime payments, annual and sick leave was better than any "force" on the mainland. They were quids in, not interested in actual policing where it was needed. Cecil said that the new Unit could well be used to combat us. A policy of harassment could well break our spirit.

Oh yes, Cecil said, the DSS was well aware of us; not our names, as such, but they knew someone was helping the locals. Our success being measured in the couple of airtight applications that were recently submitted. As yet, however, we had not secured any grants. If there was one thing we did possess, it was potential, and that was something the Englishman was having difficulty with. Cecil said he was determined to take us out stressing that the DSS had more far-reaching powers that many foreign dictatorships would literally kill for.

'Were those his exact words, Cecil? He said he would take us out?' I asked, feeling a little worried.

Cecil nodded solemnly.

Cathal jumped in. 'Maybe it's like that time, Tom, when you were determined to take that nurse out, eh?' he said with that eejit look on his face again. 'Maybe this boy wants to take us to dinner and discuss things.'

'Don't think so, Cathal,' I said.

Cathal still seemed a tad adrift of Belfastspeak. 'So, what am I supposed to say if a woman says she wants to take me out?'

'If you're in anyway suspicious of her motives, decline. And if it's an invitation from Miriam or any of her patients, decline immediately.'

We were skirting over the main issue. We were genuinely concerned. Cathal and I had recently discussed the need for possible safe houses if this new Unit got up and running. We were well aware of the need to be one step ahead of the authorities. One of the more worrying aspects was the real possibility that just as we had a mole within the DSS, could they, too, have someone from our side working for them? Our organisation was still very much in its embryonic stage, but people round here get to know things very quickly. Yet Cecil had no evidence of this. Richard at one time suggested Cecil could well be a double agent. I discounted this immediately; I said his boots might well stand up to the strain, but I didn't think he would.

Emmett had been my mother's only success. We needed to build on that and quickly, both to impact on the DSS and, more importantly, to convince the locals that maybe we could help. It all sounded like hard work.

We met with Cecil again the following week.

'They're worried, Tom, about the success you're having,' said Cecil. 'I mean, those two apps recently submitted are almost perfect.' He again warned us of the imminent setting up of the new Enforcement Unit.

When we thought about it logically, though, we weren't overly concerned, for Pat told us that trying to get anything set up in the North, what with all sides shunning compromise, could well take forever. Cecil stressed that the one good thing was that there was little money available to fund the Unit. In inner circles, it had been suggested that the Unit would be manned by retired policemen and those constables who, in the old days, were transferred to South Armagh if they were, or appeared to be, less than establishment orientated. Numbers were to be made up by people from the locality.

Word on the street indicated that few would be interested. The DSS might have to look further afield. The uniform was causing problems and, as the Unit would be bullying in both Catholic and Protestant areas, a merging of the tribal colours of green and orange would probably be required.

And then there would, no doubt, be an argument about the shade.

'Hey, your bosses don't know about Tom, do they?' asked a suspicious Richard.

'Not from me, they don't,' replied the indignant Cecil. 'They did know about Tom's mother and they were making plans for her.'

'What? Why the hell wasn't I told?' I was up on my feet. 'I mean, Cecil, we don't pay you nothing to be told nothing, if you get my drift. What were they going to do?'

'They were going to blacken her name within the community, have the people turn against her.'

Pat and Richard looked stunned as if never in their life before had they heard anything quite so outrageous or, indeed, unlikely.

'That never would have happened,' said Pat, proudly. 'Nobody would have questioned the word of Molly Dooley.'

Cecil nodded his head. 'Yeah, you're right. I found out enough about your mother, Tom, to know that she was as straight as a die. But they were going to put it about that she was taking backhanders from the DSS. I told them there was no point. It just wouldn't have been believed. Straight as a die, your mother was.'

'And so is her son,' said Pat.

I felt ten feet tall. There were certain things I had done in my life in England I wasn't proud of, things that would have made my mother ashamed. But if nothing else, I considered myself honest. She would have been proud of that. I hope somewhere down the line she was proud of me.

Cecil twisted an empty packet of crisps with his hand and threw it on the table. 'As you all know, the investigations carried out by the doctors into each claim are stringent in the extreme.'

We all nodded. That was indeed a big problem for us.

Cecil continued, 'Fortesque-Smith frequently questions the loyalty, conscientiousness and efficiency of the doctors we use. Miss Webster sarcastically told him the doctors do what is required of them. The Englishman recently edged out a Dr Mullins who wasn't toeing the party line. We got a postcard from him the other day. He's running some Pitch and Putt Emporium in Santiago. Best thing happened to him, he said. The present crop just do what they are told. So it's a job to beat them.'

Little good news for us there, then. Cecil then told us the Englishman had instructed him to go undercover in our area, be the eyes and ears of the DSS on the street. Cecil felt he was trying to get him on his side by giving him a seemingly important job. Fortesque-Smith told him that should anyone be seen even looking at an IEA form, then he wanted to know. He tried rallying Cecil with a bit of old Civil Service rhetoric. We owe it to the taxpayers, he said, to protect them against the lower classes; we owe it to all that is right and proper in the world. We are the bastions of the taxpayers' money.

'Roughly translated,' Cecil explained, 'the bastard is after promotion. He kept saying that we must ensure that we pay out only where there is no other option. And, he stressed, there is always another option.'

I was so glad my Civil Service career was so short and so undistinguished. I considered it an achievement of sorts.

Cecil's face was suddenly like thunder. 'And then the bastard said to me, "I have something to tell you, Cecil." He smirked as he told me I had once again been passed over for promotion! "Must be a record now," he said.' Cecil bowed his head.

We were shocked. We honestly thought this time he would do it. Selfishly, we were only too well aware of the advantages of having someone further up the ladder in the DSS, but we also genuinely wanted Cecil to succeed for his own sake. We even set up a mock "Board" for him in the bar a couple of days before his interview. He did well. My immediate concern was, which I never shared with anyone, what real use was an angry mole? His guard might well be down now.

We would need to keep an eye on the big fella.

The Scouser and I had spent a couple of days sorting out my mother's things. It was painful, more than I could have imagined, but I didn't feel the pain would lessen if I ignored it. We carefully packed away her little personal things that she kept by her chair in a newspaper rack. Drawings from Siobhan neatly wrapped in Cellophane; murder-mystery books; a couple of IEA forms; a half-empty packet of Liquorice Allsorts; and a copy of *The Irish News* and *Ireland's Saturday Night* she'd had in an envelope ready to post to me. Something she'd done religiously each and every week I had been in England.

An unwelcome iciness now doused a once-happy house as I imagined my mother sitting in her favourite chair by the fire listening to the radio; she hated the TV, apart from *The Good Life* repeats. I looked at, and felt, things that made up my mother's life. I remembered her telling me how she and my father used to sit by the fire and plan their lives, what they were going to do. My father, it seemed, was a dreamer. Always on about some scheme or other that would take them away from here. A Belfast "Del Boy".

I wondered if she ever really got over the death of her first born, my brother, Kieran, killed in a motorcycle accident in Australia. He was eighteen, had married and left Belfast for a better life. I remember asking her why Kieran wasn't buried in Belfast. She said it was only right that he be buried close to where his wife could visit. Katy kept in contact. She remarried and had three children.

One evening, Cathal went out, said he was off having a few pints and to watch the football on the big screen in one of the clubs. I reckoned he was seeing this girl he had met. But he wouldn't let on. Maureen Doyle was considered an extremist around these parts. She was a vegan. For those with a less than full appreciation of that chosen lifestyle, they thought she went home each night with the Vulcans to the Star Ship Enterprise. And for those who knew that she shunned meat and dairy produce, she was still a weirdo and an extremist. You couldn't win in this country.

I squeezed into the loft and happily spent a couple of hours looking through old annuals which had been bought for me at Christmas; school photos; reports of my progress at school. I found one of Kieran's reports. God! She must have been proud of him. He excelled at everything. Nothing was ever said, but I always thought I never really measured up to Kieran. Not to what he was, but to what I thought he was. I figured I had a dual role in life: to be myself and also Kieran's ghost.

My hands then rested on an age-stained letter. With my handwriting on it. It was the letter I sent my mother the first week I was in England. The letter was worn. I wondered was that through reading.

Although my handwriting was dreadful, I managed to read through it and could only imagine what my rage-ravaged words must have done to her.

I blamed everybody.

I blamed her, for Christ's sake!

I blamed *all of them* for not making it possible for me to stay in Belfast. They could have helped us, Mairead and me. Why was everyone allowing thugs to put us out of our home? It was obvious the letter had been read time and time again. Why hadn't she just ripped it up?

Was she looking for something that wasn't there? Or maybe, just maybe, she was trying to discount something that *was* there. What right had I in making her feel she was in any way to blame? Always someone else's fault, eh, Tom?

I wished I had apologised to her.

I had forgotten writing the letter. I tore it up, there and then. I knew I would torture myself with it if I hadn't. As if I would ever have forgotten those crushing words. Oh God! I wondered did she ever show it to anyone. Nobody, but nobody, would ever get to see this. Ever. God! Each and every time she would have read that, the past would have reared its ugly head.

The past. I had my own nightmares to deal with. I now wished to God I had never read that frigging letter.

Over the next couple of weeks, we talked to people from the locality and outside of it who had submitted forms to the DSS. With little hope of success, as they admitted themselves. Cecil supplied us with a list of doctors who had once worked with his department and who had been removed because of their "leniency". We spoke to them on the phone. We contacted the maverick priest, Father Rice, who we thought could well be of use. We were slowly but surely building up both our knowledge and our contacts. I don't think either Cathal or

I ever imagined we would go into this in quite such detail. I thought we would just give it a go, help out with the completion of a couple of applications, as we had, and then realise that it really wasn't for us, despite our best intentions. We soon learned it was a minefield of official obstruction.

And still, totally against our surrender-type nature, we weren't put off.

Siobhan and her mother had taken up residence in Belfast. With Roger the Codger. It was inevitable, of course. It was, I had to admit, so comforting, though, to know that Siobhan was close by again. I spoke to Siobhan regularly by phone. I had to get to see her soon. Oh, it would be so good to hug her tight and give her a big kiss.

When Mairead had called to give me their new phone number she expressed amazement that I might be staying in Belfast. She thought I was remaining simply to sort out my mother's affairs. Her affairs. God love her, she had little of value. The Housing Executive house in which she lived should really have been returned to the "needy pool", but a few strings were pulled, mainly by Father Rice, who was encouraged by our intentions, and I got the rent book. Never in my wildest dreams did I ever imagine that one day I would live in this house.

Without my mother.

I didn't put a lot of store in fate.

Cathal flew back to London on a couple of occasions to sort out our flats and sell what possessions we had which could attract a few bob. We needed all the money we could get our hands on. I decided not to return to London, make a clean break, just like I had with Belfast twenty years ago. Uneasiness still prodded my thoughts, though.

This was a damned big decision I was making; the biggest I had ever made.

In addition, I felt I had let myself down, recalling the pact Mairead and I had made. Just like her, I, too, had returned in defiance of it. I berated her that night for even thinking about it, now I was an accomplice, albeit one branching out on his own. In the past when I had fleetingly thought about going back to Belfast, I thought it would be with my wife and daughter.

Life, eh, who plans it?

Cathal rang me one night from the Royal Oak. It was heartening to hear little had changed and I laughed when I heard that Wee Hughie was now using his likeness to the smaller of *The Two Ronnies* as a launching pad for a career in TV. Cathal said he had sent tapes off to some of the big production companies, claiming he could also tap-dance, recite poetry and, at a push, could show a degree of competence in the art of origami.

Don't you just hate the Jocks and their versatility!

The call made me genuinely miss the old place, and I knew if Cathal had said jump on a plane, I would have. I felt lost again, there in Belfast. It seemed to be okay going to the bars and clubs with Cathal. I didn't feel so isolated when he was around. I stayed in all the time he was in London. I felt unable to venture out alone. In among my own. I knew only too well by Cathal's animated attitude that he was up for our project in Belfast, but I continually had doubts. Some people were still suspicious of our motives. Cathal was English: why would he want to help them? I was, well, I was someone who couldn't be bothered to come home for all those years: so what was I up to? It seemed many of them were only too willing, and indeed able, to cast aside the reason why I didn't come home, return to the place where those bastards…

Ah, sure I was only annoying myself.

My sister was still sticking to her guns and ignoring me, more outraged than ever now that I was living in the family home. I felt continually ill at ease in the company of some of my fellow countrymen; even going into a local shop I felt on the defensive. I hoped it wasn't too noticeable.

When Cathal returned, he said he had been doing a bit of thinking, and suggested what we needed to do was to show the locals that not only were we on their side, but that we could genuinely help them with their IEA applications. Emmett was forever in our corner, and Sammy, God bless him, couldn't have been more supportive. We were being given some breathing space to build on our limited knowledge, thanks to Cecil sneaking out bits and pieces from general office memos, together with more detailed policy documents. We were becoming more *au fait* with IEA guidelines.

Initially, Cecil had been a little reluctant to come on board. We had to work on him for quite a time. He had been taught well by Miss Webster; like many Civil Servants with their eyes on an index-linked pension, and an extra day's leave on the Queen's Birthday, he was loyal to an employer that never felt the need to reciprocate in any way. In his DSS undercover work, he would drive around the area, visit bars and chat to people, all the while dressed in his uniform of black duffel coat, minus the platform shoes, which he didn't wear on duty. That would come later; his symbol of defiance was also a tribute to his hero, Noddy Holder.

When he got to know us better, Cecil would talk in great detail about his obsession with 1970s' Glam Rock group from Wolverhampton, Slade, and would, in particular, wax lyrical about the man himself, Noddy Holder. Cecil was an odd one, but sure that was what appealed to us. We identified with him. He, too, seemed to be struggling to fit in. He would sit in some back street for ages in his official-issue pale green – with rusty attachments – Ford Cortina, a scrunched-up figure peering out at the locals. Most people would nod a greeting; even the dogs on the streets knew Cecil. He would just stare ahead or make notes. Perhaps he was penning something to Noddy; we never did find out.

Cecil was now in deep as a double agent and didn't seem to know it. He would, on our suggestion, relay misinformation to his lord and master diluting the details of any IEA interest from the locals. Oh aye, we used him. Of course we did.

It was immensely gratifying when a further two people from the area allowed us to help in their IEA applications. Word of mouth really had alerted the locals to our intentions.

We put a lot of effort into securing as much inside information on the allowance as possible and any changing policy decisions. Cathal suggested we should perhaps consider holding a meeting. Invite the locals, let them know what we were trying to do. I didn't feel we were quite ready for this; I thought we were about twenty-five years away from that stage. It was not the time for a public parade of our knowledge and our ability to make a difference. I didn't feel our knowledge was up to the mark, and as for making a difference…

The encouragement I got from both my uncles, however, went a long way in making me feel we should continue, so I agreed to a meeting.

My Uncle Pat had been born and bred in the area. He left at the age of twenty and went to work in England like so many before him, and indeed since. Tradition constantly ferrying us from our shores. He sent money back home. Working on building sites, toiling the long, hard hours away, burying in the back of his mind his thirst for knowledge. Pat had an incredible brain, left unnourished by his circumstances and society's expectations. Aspirations in our area, during his younger days, stretched merely to securing a mind-numbing job in one of the mills. During his days off in England, where he stayed for ten years, he would be a regular visitor to the local library where he indulged himself, gorging on books, particularly ones on Russia.

Pat was a mathematical genius and lived a very simple life with Richard. It was without a doubt one of the most genuine, warm relationships I had ever encountered. They cared about each other. Pat hardly ever left the house. He hid away from a world he found no place in. Nothing but aggravation and agitation. He had felt like this on the first day he arrived back from England. He knew he didn't fit in. Richard would go to the library twice a week and bring him home books on geometry and trigonometry. He would spend hours on sides and angles of a triangle, and his enthusiasm went a long way in making a very boring subject rather interesting.

Pat was going to be of use to us because of his amazing gift with figures. They held no fear for him. In an instant, he was able to work out the financial implications of an application. The mind-boggling details inserted by the DSS on their rejection letters were dealt with by him with ease. The DSS tended to use the minefield of pages and pages of figures and policy decisions when turning down an application. Totally irrelevant to the claim, but, as Cecil told us, they treated people with such contempt they imagined they could baffle them into submission. Pat was currently reviewing several applications. We were going to lodge an appeal in one or two cases.

Richard loved singing and would, at the drop of a hat, launch his vocal chords into songs from the many musicals he enjoyed. Often criticising modern songs for their total lack of a tune, as he put it. Throw on a Rodgers and Hammerstein video or tape – he hadn't got the hang of CDs yet – and he would be in seventh heaven. The rest of us had no idea who the hell Rossano Brazzi or Mitzi Gaynor were. He could even tell you who did the frigging screenplays.

It didn't seem odd to see him on stage on a Friday night in one of the clubs, his hands deep in his jeans pockets, tweed jacket, one button only locked, as the microphone in his hand treated the audience to *I'm Gonna Wash That Man Right Out Of My Hair*. His voice was so good you forget about the implications of the words. Oh, and what a treat when the mother of Joey Donnelly, the car showroom giant, and he did a duet. *There Is Nothing Like A Dame* sounded great until Joey's mother-in-law nudged her way in. Her extravagant gesticulations caught Richard in the mouth twice and her adversary once.

It wasn't Richard's musical bent we were after, although it could well brighten up a dull day. No, Richard claimed to be a faith healer and a spiritualist. I say *claimed*, for there were many, myself included, who were sceptical about his so-called powers. In his defence, however, there were many who swore by him. His claim that he was in contact with the dead bothered me. I thought we could be burdening ourselves here.

If we had a claimant who didn't get the allowance before he or she departed these shores, I sure as hell didn't want any further contact from a heavenly address or, worse still, ranting and raving on singed headed notepaper with a set-of-horns logo. It was Cathal who first spotted a use for Richard's healing powers.

If, say, on the day of the visit from the investigating doctor, the applicant had the sniffles, bad throat or a bit of a cold resulting in nasal blockages, throwing up less than clear enunciation, Richard could use his powers to clear up any such ailment. We knew we were up against it without the nasal mutterings of some flu victim giving all the wrong answers. Applicants needed to be at the top of the game on appointment day.

I wasn't convinced by Cathal's argument. I felt a visit to Boots and a bottle of Benylin would be more helpful.

Cathal persisted. I told him to hang fire and not to mention this to Richard. I had this vision, you see, of Richard on his knees, the sleeves of his jacket rolled up, administering his *gift* to the affected parts of some fifteen-stone bugger who might not take kindly to being serenaded by:

I'm as corny as Kansas in August
High as a flag on the fourth of July
No more the smart little girl with no heart
If you'll excuse this expression I use
I'm in love with a wonderful guy...

Maybe I worry needlessly.

One night when we were in the house playing cards, my resolve to catch Cathal cheating fast receding, he suggested we go out some evening for a meal with Siobhan and Mairead.

'With Mairead? You must be joking!' I said, 'She wouldn't come out, not when she can cosy up to Roger the Codger.'

'I've already spoken to her. She says she will. Fancies a laugh.'

Oh, the weird and wonderful mind of the estranged wife. Cathal felt I needed to get out more; he said he was becoming increasingly concerned at my recent mode of dress. I was not conscious of it, but he pointed out that I was becoming more formal in my daily attire. I would iron my shirts and brush my jacket before going down the boozer, he said. The only time I ever did that, according to Cathal, was when I was meeting Mairead. Was I becoming respectable? I hoped not. I asked Cathal to keep an eye on me and inform me of any further incursions into conformity.

I readily agreed that a meal with Siobhan and Mairead would be good, a nice trip down memory lane, for all four of us had at one time spent a lot of time together. It would be a relaxing prelude to the following evening when we intended to have our get-to-know-you meeting with the people in the local primary school hall. We had stuffed a few leaflets through doors and put up a couple of notices on walls advertising the meeting. Hopefully, that would do the trick and we might get a full house. Cathal thought the leaflet should have been more eye-catching. I thought we needed a more serious approach. I suppose we compromised:

EVER GONE ARSE OVER? EVER THOUGHT YOU'D NEVER RECEIVE INCOME AGAIN? EVER FEEL NEGLECTED? LOOK AROUND YOU AND DON'T WORRY IF YOU BUMP INTO SOMETHING. INTRIGUED? COME TO ST GEMMA'S SCHOOL ON FRIDAY AT 8 O'CLOCK.

The table in the restaurant in Brunswick Street was booked for seven thirty. Cathal and I had a couple of jars in a bar in town before making our way over. We stood outside the restaurant at seven twenty, waiting for Siobhan and her mother. There was a definite chill in the air. A taxi pulled up. The driver, a man in his twenties with thick red hair and a kindly face, wound the window down.

'Connelly?' he asked.

We shook our heads.

He looked at the computer on the dashboard detailing the job and then looked up at us with an assured look. 'It says Connelly, Regent Restaurant, Brunswick Street, seven twenty.' He looked at his watch, then at us again, as if saying, Well, it's not me that's got it wrong.

I looked at Cathal; he stared at me then looked at his watch. He seemed willing to encourage the driver if not exactly be of any help. 'Well, indeed, it does seem you've got your first bit right. Now, much as the correct customer being here would complement your map-reading skills, not to mention your punctuality, something sadly lacking in many cab drivers, I might add, neither of us is called Connelly.'

'Where's he going, this Connelly boy?' I asked.

'Eh, it says here, the airport, catching a flight to Heathrow for onward travel to Barbados.'

Holy shit! Was this our opportunity to flee?

For a split second, one of those mad moments Cathal and I used to have in abundance presented itself for our approval.

We were almost in the cab.

Barbados? In all probability we would not have got any further than the airport. We were lacking such items as tickets, passports, etc; minor details at one time. At that moment in time, it just felt like the right thing to do. I knew by Cathal's wide eyes and expectant face that he, too, felt the opportunity was there for the taking.

Dispense with all the seriousness of recent times. Come on, Dooley, neither of us was designed for this sort of life. Bollocks to everything!

We wouldn't have thought twice, once.

A fella and his girl came out of the restaurant, followed by a crowd of back slappers. 'Cab for Connelly,' he shouted to the driver, who nodded and then gave us a "see, I told you" sort of look.

'Come on, youse 'uns.' The taxi man had the last word. 'Hurry up. You might be going to Barbados but I have to take the mother-in-law to bingo.'

Siobhan was in great form. It was obvious that Belfast was agreeing with her. God! She was looking more and more like her mother. And my wife looked terrific. I had to stop myself staring.

While Cathal and Siobhan fought their way through a shared banana split, Mairead and I engaged in a bit of small talk. She was telling me Siobhan had made two new friends, twins Katie and Gemma, with whom she had been horse riding. I tried to have Siobhan with us most weekends, but I had missed a couple, such was the pressure of our project. That was not what Mairead chose to moan about.

'I don't really like Siobhan staying with you in that area,' she announced.

That area?

You mean the place where you were brought up?

'Why not?' I asked, my voice a little loud. I could feel the hairs on the back of my neck rising.

'Don't make a scene,' she said, looking round her and smiling awkwardly at a young couple at the next table.

I did my ventriloquist act. 'Don't make a frigging scene,' I said through clenched teeth. I didn't really want to make a scene. I remembered the last restaurant argument we had in London.

She wasn't happy with Siobhan spending so much time around us when we were so involved with the IEA, she explained.

Apparently one morning recently, Roger was lying in bed and called Siobhan into the room, telling her he was going to pretend to have a headache so as to get her mummy to bring him breakfast in bed. Before Roger could even begin his sham, Siobhan was up on the bed directing operations, so to speak. She told him that if he had a pain in the right side of his head, he could make it sound more serious if he added that he had shooting pains and also an ache behind the eye. A little feeling of nausea would also help, she said.

It took her a while to pronounce it, but she eventually advised Roger the Codger to pretend he was suffering from a migraine. Roger apparently found it hilarious. Mairead didn't and said she didn't like Siobhan lying with such ease.

I didn't find it funny either. Somebody else's kid, maybe.

Roger and my daughter were seemingly now building a relationship. That was the sort of thing she and I would have done. I looked across at Siobhan and caught her warm, ice-cream-smeared smile. I hadn't noticed until then she was missing another tooth.

Mairead and my daughter were becoming more remote. I shook my head sadly, and in that moment realised that Mairead had in fact kept her promise, our promise. The pact we made all those years ago was for her still intact. We swore we would not go back.

She hadn't.

Oh no, Mairead hadn't gone back, she was now part of a new and noticeably more vibrant Belfast. *I* was back. I was *so* fucking back.

I was the one who had broken our promise. I was the one who had returned to the familiar back streets, I had returned to the ghetto. All those memories we had struggled to abandon, lest they destroy us, were now firmly embedded in my everyday life. The street where it happened, the people who had committed the atrocity, the acrid smell of the past still within spitting distance.

Mairead did not want Siobhan to be anywhere near that and I couldn't really blame her, for I had closed my eyes to it all. To the backwardness, to the filth, to the ever-present gloom. I had ignored it all in my desire to fulfil not a dream, to fulfil a pledge I never really knew I had taken.

To atone for my actions, to lay to rest the need to be someone.

I hoped it was worth it. No, damn it, I thought as I stared at Mairead. I was going to make sure it was. *I had to.*

It was irritating, though, to have so many positive vibes in my life and see them fade when I came into contact with Mairead. Purpose-built conscience pricker, that one. I suddenly remembered that night in the Indian when I told her that I was going to make something of myself and she would miss out. Didn't feel such a big deal now. Make something of myself? Holed up with a lunatic from

Liverpool in the back streets of Belfast, crossing swords with a government department in a vain attempt to wrestle from them an allowance which the rest of the country neither wanted nor needed!

Working class hero? Whoa! I really must be the envy of the world. In an instant, I felt the old doubts returning

I was going to throw away the waitress's phone number but suddenly thought better of it. Did I notice a slight, just a slight, look of jealousy on Mairead's face when she saw me chatting to her when I paid the bill?

I kissed Siobhan, grunted at her mother, and watched their cab disappear. Cathal and I called into a nearby pub for a few. He suggested maybe it was time for us to go on the pull again. On the pull? Jesus! We really must find a new term for it; on the pull sounded so dated. I didn't let Cathal see how pissed off I was. He seemed to enjoy the evening.

On reflection, we should just have gone home. The pub was packed solid, hardly room to breathe. We squeezed our way through the mass of bodies and managed to secure a small space at the bar, which Cathal enlarged with the use of his elbows and a steely stare or two. The music was louder here and Dexy's Midnight Runners were prattling on about a reluctant Eileen. The smoke-laden atmosphere made me cough as the explosion of excitable voices crashed against the incessant clinking of glasses. Right crowd in here, I shouted at Cathal, who just raised his eyes and held out his tenner to the harassed bar staff.

I was suddenly alerted to the proximity of a peroxide blonde by her advance scouting party – cheap perfume. She sidled up to me and smiled – smiled one of those smiles that would have been immeasurably enhanced by the presence of even one, just the one, tooth in her head. You've guessed it; we're talking real style here. To her credit, she seemed instantly aware of her molar deficiency, for she dispensed with any introduction and declared she could look better than this. She looked me straight in the face, at nose level. Look better than that, of that, I, too, had no doubt, for it would have been rather difficult to actually downgrade that look. She appeared to be on her own. Another surprise, for as I looked around for an escape exit, I was sure I would see a 2 FOR 1 WEIRDO NIGHT sign somewhere.

She seemed determined to explain further and pulled me by the lapels so I was even closer to her lisping slur. Her breath getting me in a stranglehold.

Pernod.

'I'm missing some teeth at the moment,' she said with a hearty guffaw that wouldn't have sounded out of place in a pub team's celebrations. 'That can be fixed easy enough, eh, handsome?'

Smooth-talking minx.

Cathal, the big Scouse bastard, had turned his back on me, but I could tell by his shaking shoulders that he was laughing his head off. And there was me, worrying about our forthcoming meeting with the locals. I had more immediate problems. I again looked for a way out, but it was denied me.

Perhaps a little *tête-à-tête* wouldn't do any harm. 'Oh aye, that would be easy to fix,' I said, trying to be helpful, diplomatic and, or, caring. She could take her pick. 'Sure dentistry has come on leaps and bounds. They can work wonders now, so they can. You'd have no problem getting that sorted out, love.'

As it turned out, less of a problem than I imagined, for she suggested I hail a taxi, go straight to her house, up the stairs, third door on the right and there, there, top left of the dressing table, were the two halves of a whole.

Her molars.

She looked expectantly at me. I reasoned she thought that as I was a potential partner for the night, she should at least make an effort to become the complete woman. How could you not be impressed? In the past I've bought women drinks all night, treated them to lavish meals; paid for taxis home, even. I drew the line, however, at locating and retrieving absent teeth.

Perhaps the art of courtship had taken on a new edge here in Belfast.

I saw an opening and grabbed Cathal as he began to cast his eye across the floor at a couple of women who definitely were offered, and took advantage of, the 2 For 1 Weirdo Night. The cool air outside hit me like a cold shower on a hot summer's day, refreshing and revitalising.

'Jesus! Even Dotty at the Royal Oak never came on to me,' I said, trying to hail a black taxi.

'Dotty, as you may recall, Tom, was a business woman, a lady of the late afternoon, early evening,' Cathal said.

'So?'

'Well, she was hardly going to bother with the likes of you. You never had any money.'

A cab pulled up, depositing some female revellers, one or two of whom looked distinctly attractive during my two-second glance. We jumped in. I really must get out and get at it again, so to speak. This abstinence from the fairer sex wasn't good for me. I now felt that my periodic faithfulness to Mairead was pointless. Oh yes, since we had separated, I still had pangs of regret and tried to behave myself.

No more, Dooley boy. As they say in polite company, It was the filling of one's boots time.

The cab pulled away and I breathed a sigh of relief. 'Do you think yer woman in there could have been a lady of the night, Cathal?'

He shook his head and looked out the window, then back at me. 'It would have to be a very dark, a very very dark night. Pitch black, in fact. No less than a blackout. Still, she saw something in you.'

Chapter Six

I was Molly Dooley's son; the locals had gotten to know Cathal. We bought our round in the bar. How could we fail to attract them in droves?

But fail we did. For whatever reason, only a handful turned up at the meeting. This was the school I went to as a child; Mairead also. God! I could smell the sickly odour of loose bowels, underdeveloped bladders. Residues linking successive generations to their schooldays.

It was not as if we hadn't shown willing and helped out with those two IEA applications. We had also been getting some general enquiries from the locals, but it appeared that apathy was still flying from the flagpole. The school hall had a small stage on which Cathal and I were joined in the spotlight by my two uncles. Pat coming out in support, even though he was immersed in a number of geometry problems and the maths book was overdue at the library. Steel back chairs were scattered at angles about the hall in no particular order. The audience, if you could call it that, comprised an equal measure of male and female and amounted to eight. They observed us from various sniper-like positions. Stern looks abounded. A depleted jury they might well be, but they looked the type to side-step evidence and press for the death penalty.

They sat motionless and silent, waiting for things to happen, I suppose. It was comforting to have Emmett sitting near the front.

We didn't envisage anything terribly significant coming out of this get-to-know-you meeting; a few questions asked and hopefully we might offer a round or two of adequate answers. Beforehand, Cathal and I decided the best way to approach this was to emphasise how much we cared about the rights of the locals, how we wanted to help. If they were willing to give us a try. We needed to stress how we felt this area had been neglected for long enough.

With an uncharacteristic use of profanity, Richard told us that was a load of old shite. Tell them you're taking on the establishment. That works round here, he said.

Just as well we knew our lines before getting on stage.

I knew I had been away from the country for a long time. Had to appreciate that perhaps certain traditions had changed or new ones had been introduced. But surely a certain protocol should always be maintained in public meetings. We had barely started and the bastards were on their feet, seemingly on their way out.

A few minutes only had elapsed, and as one person got up, another looked round her and slowly followed suit. I couldn't help myself. 'For fuck sake,

Richard! We're trying to help these people. But look at them. Christ! It's not as if we're charging!' My temper was rising, but ebbed slightly when the exit became blocked as an old man, one I didn't recognise, entered the hall. He was dressed in a long, fairly modern-looking brown overcoat and wore an off-white baseball cap. Resting on his belly was a placard. THE LORD GIVETH AND THE LORD TAKETH AWAY, it proclaimed.

'Hey, boy!' I shouted over to him as he walked aimlessly round the room. 'The DSS giveth and we keepeth, okay? Christ! You've got me talking in a lisp now.'

He took a seat at the back while I watched an interest returning as seats were once again hesitantly filled. Could you imagine this lot at the theatre? Any delay in the curtain going up and they would be off!

Cathal grabbed me by the arm and shoved a copy of a recent claim into my hand. I hadn't a clue what he expected me to say, for he provided little by way of guidance apart from, 'For Christ's sake, say something!'

How could I go wrong, armed with that sort of encouragement? I flicked through the form and then, holding it in one hand, I raised both my hands as if a metamorphosis had taken place and Father Rice was now on stage. Armed with that pious look only the clergy can summon up, I moved to the front of the stage, all the while feeling my mouth drying up.

'Please, just a moment,' I pleaded.

I hadn't a clue what I was going to say. Say nothing, but often. Where had I heard that bullshit? It wouldn't work here. Something comprising sounds – words, even – was required. I opened the form again.

'Look, I have here a copy of an IEA claim form completed by a local person. I obviously cannot name names, but this individual, a male, was suffering from extreme lumbar problems, result of an accident on a building site. I think we could have helped this claimant…'

A man seated at the back prodded his neighbour. 'That'll be yours, Colum.'

Ah, so that was Colum McGeough. Even though he was seated he was stooped. He must have been about five foot seven or so, well built with straight black hair. He sniffed a lot. He had been slumped in his seat; he now struggled to become more upright.

Grab the moment, Dooley, grab the frigging moment. My inner voice out of control.

I squeezed my eyes shut and then opened them. My voice became stronger. 'It appears, and it has been admitted by the claimant himself, I believe, that his nerves got the better of him on the day of the investigation.'

Colum nodded.

I could hear children playing outside. Oh, to have no responsibility in life!

I continued. 'This is a common problem with claimants. Genuine claims are being cast aside simply because of inaccurate answers. Now, we would suggest…'

I looked over at Cathal. He looked more relaxed; that encouraged me. Same with my two uncles. 'We would suggest that Colum, here, would benefit greatly from some self-relaxation techniques. Yoga, maybe. Possibly t'ai chi...'

I looked for some sort of response. My throat was becoming dry, my lips about to seal, I licked them and swallowed hard.

Colum again nodded his head. There was no smile though. However, I took it as a definite sign of encouragement. 'I don't know what you're on about,' he said. 'But I'll give it a go. Go on, we're listening.'

Emmett gave me the thumbs up. For the life of me I don't know why, but the song, with those deep, meaningful lyrics *If you're happy and you know it, clap your hands* rushed into my mind and took up residence for the rest of the evening.

Applause was out of the question, but there was a definite change of mood.

Treat them carefully, Dooley, mind your step.

I shuffled quickly through some papers. 'We'll go into your case in more detail later, Colum, but I would like to refer to another case. A woman, sixty-three, extreme leg pains. Makes getting about, doing normal things about the house, very difficult. I would like to refer her to a chiropractor we know in Bangor. I have her x-rays in front of me.'

I held them up and tried to look knowledgeably at them. I referred to the notes again. 'The chiropractor has suggested different position you need to undertake. He also suggested moaning more and using the odd swear word in front of the doctor.'

A woman at the front of the hall stood up, dropping her packet of Rich Tea biscuits. 'Jesus Christ, I couldn't swear for no reason, so I couldn't.'

'Catherine McCarthy, is it?' I asked.

She nodded slowly.

She then looked round her, nodding at one or two, and, with a guarded voice spoke to her neighbours. 'Maybe these ones do know what they're talking about. Maybe we should give them a chance, eh?'

Another woman seated two seats behind her – and about the same age – stood up. 'It's been a long time since you, Catherine McCarthy, have been sixty-three.'

It was just the levity we needed, injecting a much-required relaxed atmosphere into the proceedings. Thanks, Assumpta Daly.

Like a supportive chorus line, my two uncles and Cathal joined me at the front of the stage.

For the finale.

Cathal opened a file. 'Vince Smith, back and knee-joint problems. Ah, he is still having trouble with his bowels. It says here that each and every time the doctor interviews him, he's off to the toilet. In the end, the doctor gets pissed off and rejects the application.'

'Irritable Bowel Syndrome,' I said. I had read his notes. 'Stress related, do you think, Cathal?'

'Most definitely. He has six daughters.'

Pat caught the baton and moved on. 'This will be Vince's third attempt. He needs help.'

'Our help,' Richard said.

I pointed at Cathal. 'Tomorrow, Cathal will get in touch with that Stress Management Consultant in Crawfordsburn. We'll also need to supplement his diet and introduce an exercise regime.'

It was as if the hall was suddenly full. People started to talk among themselves, some getting up to cross the room to chat. Nods and promising gesticulations were being aimed at us.

Dare we feel we were making some inroads? Would we be given the green light to further annoy and irritate, and finally defeat the DSS?

'We need Vince on top form if he's to stay long enough in one place to answer the questions,' I said.

Cathal remarked what a pity Vince wasn't with us tonight.

Pat said him and his wife had managed to off-load the daughters with various relatives throughout the city and were away for the weekend to a Joe Dolan concert in Skerries. I made a mental note there and then.

Self-help.

I felt like shouting with relief as my eyes darted around the room. Smiles, definite smiles.

To the pessimist, though, it could all have been down to wind.

The evening came to a close once we discussed, in a little more detail, Colum McGeough's case. In the absence of any natural or expected conclusion, other than we had made real contact, I felt a degree of contentment as we watched the audience leave the building, Pat and Richard accompanying them. Cathal and I sat on stage in a now-empty hall enjoying the wonderful silence.

God! One or two had actually waved as they left.

We weighed things up. Had the evening been a success? Realistically, it was probably more than we expected. At the end, at any rate.

'What do you think then, Tom?' Cathal asked, stretching his legs and trying to stifle a yawn. 'Feel tired all of a sudden?'

'About what?' I asked sitting back in my chair, resting my hands behind my head. I knew what he meant about the tiredness, though. I, too, felt a sudden releasing of tension. It was a nice tired, though.

'Do you think we are going to make a success of this?'

'Do you?' I threw it back at him.

'I do indeed.'

'That's not as encouraging as it might be, Cathal.'

He threw me a sideways glance. 'You don't think so?'

'Well, the thing is, Cathal…' I got to my feet remembering we had to put away the chairs and make sure all the lights were off before we left. 'You were the one, were you not, who thought we would make a great success of being escorts?'

He mused that one over as we walked down from the stage, down the rickety steps, accompanied by clicking light switches and emerging pockets of darkness.

'We would have been a success. We did talk about London, Milan, Paris and Rome. We did mention Cleethorpes, didn't we? I've rethought that one. We would have tested the waters, not in East Yorkshire, but in Catford. Yes, Catford.'

I flicked the last light switch, chucking both of us, and the image of offering our wares in South London, into the quagmire of darkness.

'Why Catford?' I felt obliged to ask.

'Can you imagine the headlines in their local paper, "Tomcats Run Amok In Catford"?'

Oh dear God! We needed something stimulating in our lives if only to improve our one-liners.

The weeks leading up to Christmas had been, in equal measure, both exhausting and exhilarating. The changes in my life had been many, and on more than one occasion, I questioned my sanity; best to get in before everyone else. Still do at times. My sister still wasn't talking to me. Not a great hardship in itself, but this continued animosity made me feel lonelier at times.

Christmas? Not much fun. Obviously Siobhan spent the time with her mother. And the dentist. We had her over a couple of days before Christmas. She was a dab hand at wrapping presents. Cathal and I spent Christmas Day on our own, although Pat and Richard came over in the afternoon. Cathal didn't even get to see his vegan friend, even though he said he wasn't bothered. I thought my sister would at least have invited us for dinner, but she didn't. And much as I tried to persuade my two uncles to do otherwise, they boycotted her because of her stance. Although I tried not to let it bother me, I hated being the reason for such unrest. Was I ever going to be forgiven for not doing what she thought I should?

January 2004 was a bitterly cold month and one Thursday near the end of it, as we sat indoors listening to a Country and Western compilation to which I was regularly subjected, Cathal looked a little coy, which was unusual for him.

We had been discussing money, or rather the distinct lack of it. He said that although he still missed Tuesday nights in the Royal Oak, he had taken to Belfast like the proverbial duck to water. He'd even managed to convert a couple of football fans to Tranmerism, a bit like hypnotism without the pleasure of coming out of it. Financially, we had reached an impasse. Even the basics, like telephone calls, were costing us a lot of money. Our benefits were hardly keeping us going. We considered having to charge our *clients*, but that was something for the future. Jesus! If we mentioned money to them at that stage, when we hadn't actually achieved anything, they'd have lynched us, no mistake.

The future: did we have one?

We did need money for bills; we needed premises if we were going to do this properly, and possibly staff – certainly a typist. We needed a job, both of us, but then we wouldn't have the time to devote to the project.

Neither of us had money in large bundles; in fact, even small bundles were in short supply. We were able to get by at a pinch. We didn't really want to rely on the State, seeing as how it was our intention to battle with it. Didn't seem right to oppose a regime while at the same time benefiting from it.

I had noticed a change in Cathal; it was subtle and not immediate, but it was there. Sure, he looked happier; so did I. But we weren't having the laughs we used to. Of course, we were finally doing something we both believed in and that in itself was fulfilling. The drinking sessions we shared in the Royal Oak were great craic and I wouldn't have missed them for the world, but this was a reality we could submerge ourselves in rather than avoid. I was beginning to feel more at home here at times too. It was a damn slow process though.

'I think this is the right time to mention this,' said Cathal, getting to his feet and turning off the tape. Thank God for that, I thought, there's only so much I could take of somebody called Lynn Anderson reneging on a promise to buy someone a frigging Rose Garden.

'Money's a problem, isn't it?'

I nodded.

'I have a bit put by,' he said.

I laughed.

Cathal having a bit put by? It was a bit like imagining the Pope rapping with Puff Daddy.

'I was left a few quid by my granny in her will.'

I remembered Cathal telling me his granny had died a good ten years ago, yet he never had any money. Not while I knew him, at any rate. Certainly, the Royal Oak was never treated to his supposed wealth. Oh, he always stood his round, don't get me wrong.

His eyes never left my face as he held up two fingers. Oh, I see. Now you've got money, you're off. I'm all right, Jack, eh?

He must have noticed my disquiet. 'Do you know what this means?' he asked, nodding towards his fingers.

'You've been left two quid. I get the joke, which I'm not finding that funny.'

'Two quid?' he laughed. 'Not exactly...'

His face then broke into a broad smile. As if to block any questioning outbursts from me, he drew from his pocket a bank statement. He handed it to me. It had that day's date on it. If this was Cathal's account, he hadn't even touched the interest. Twenty-three thousand, five hundred and ten pounds. Sterling.

What could I say? There were so many questions I wanted to ask: why, where, when? I settled for verbal conciseness. 'Fuck!'

He laughed, 'Fuck, indeed!' He walked round the room clasping and unclasping his hands. 'Dooley boy, this is the one. This is what we are meant to do.'

'All those times in London when we both pleaded poverty and there was you with all that money?' I challenged him.

He shook his head vigorously and pointed at the bank statement. 'No way was I going to blow this money. Oh aye, I wanted to. I wanted to travel, I wanted to get pissed in some of the best bars in the world, and as for the women… I didn't want to live the life I was living. I could have got out but when it was all over and the money was spent, I would have been back in it again. Now, that would have depressed me.'

My mind was racing.

'I wanted to keep the money for something meaningful,' Cathal said with a seldom-voiced deep sincerity.

'What if nothing meaningful came along?' I was intrigued.

'Well, I suppose I would have made a decision. I would have travelled the world, got pissed in some of the best bars in the world…'

I jumped in. 'Oh, and as for the women…'

Jesus! Did we have some piss up that night!

Meaningful?

What? Come on, tell me. What could have been more meaningful than the two of us swapping jokes, drinking ale and trying to focus on members of the opposite sex?

And talking enthusiastically, for the first time, really, about the future. God! Did the booze taste good that night! Celebration, a lovely mixer. At first I argued with Cathal, saying that I couldn't allow him to invest his inheritance in what was effectively my desire to help the locals. He said he wouldn't be offering if he, too, didn't want to help. I was so glad my half-hearted attempts to dissuade him fell on deaf ears. It seemed we were now in a position to bankroll my fantasy.

For that, I suppose, was what it really was.

It was such a good feeling being fired up with enthusiasm, just like that time when in an inebriated state, we canvassed the women of Camden as to our suitability as escorts. Our potential success then could well have been realised more easily than what we were about to undertake. On the way home, as Cathal tucked into a bag of vinegary chips, he let slip a past lapse in his desire to retain his inheritance for something meaningful.

'Oh, I did consider that night investing some of it in the escort business.'

'You never did!' I was shocked. 'Jesus! You're not fit to have large sums of money near or about your person.'

Scrunching up the empty bag, he made a direct hit on a wastepaper bin. 'You know something, Thomas Dooley? One day, you're going to find out that what we are about to embark on is the best thing you've ever done.'

Good to see Cathal back to norm. Bullshitting.

Oh, out of the mouths of Scousers…

Chapter Seven

Over the next few weeks, with the weather being unseasonable and therefore quite warm, we got out and about trying to locate suitable premises, buying office equipment and thinking about staff. I was particularly cost-conscious; it was, after all, Cathal's money. He was adamant that we get what was required. I was finally convinced about the value of having both my uncles on board. Pat, for his obvious mathematical prowess, and Richard for his healing powers and, at low tide, his melodious tones.

We rented a small office from the Church with a calming view of the mountains. It took us a few days to clean it up; its one time resident, an accountant of dubious qualifications, had left it in quite a mess. Soon we had a few filing cabinets in and up against a wall. A rubber plant was next and a couple of high-backed chairs as well as a hideous brown desk. An old Dell computer was our electronic friend. No fax, no landline. We bought the lot at a sale at McGiver's shop, where the old Fire Station used to be.

What a shop!

Fresh chicken at half price; Birds Eye chicken curry and Jammie Dodgers were all "Offers of the Week". Maybe one day we'd get him to sponsor us.

We could also have taken advantage of a good deal on Memory Cards but declined. We did, however, fall victim to Mr McGiver's persuasive tongue and bought a couple of easy chairs which, if you believed the proprietor, once had a place in Hillsborough Castle. A recommendation of sorts, I suppose. Injured claimants would feel more comfortable in these chairs. Hastily, we made our excuses and left when Mr McGiver pointed to a sign in the window: "Giftware Too Numerous To Mention".

We painted the walls of the office pale blue, the doors white and put up a blind of a colourful country scene. A couple of pictures of a calm sea and one of a field drenched in poppies would, we hoped, help in making people feel more relaxed. The second-hand PC was cheap and had a habit of cutting out whenever it felt the urge. Our own website, www.IEA-Rules.co.uk, was a long way off but still, we persisted. We would keep records on the system but would always have a manual back up.

We didn't, well, rather, we couldn't, advertise openly. No, to do that would undoubtedly give the authorities a head start on us. Clandestine was to be the key word. We continued building up contacts with medical experts, replacing some with others when we doubted their motives. We had been in touch with one or two counsellors if we needed an in-depth mental appraisal, and we had on our list some financial experts, just in case we were on the road to making millions!

We soon realised that before- and after-care were of equal importance. It was truly amazing to discover how many experts in various fields had fallen foul of the DSS. Seemingly, if the DSS approached you, and you were unwilling to go along with their way of doing things, they then went to great lengths to discredit you. Many of our "helpers" were found in remotest Kerry and in rugged County Galway. Forced out of the North by the DSS, unable to practise there. And no hope of return.

These people were the mavericks, the renegades, we needed.

We had to shell out for some basic medical equipment: a Blood Pressure Monitor from Boots and a weighing machine, second-hand, from the local Weight Watchers' Group. They said it didn't work; nobody had lost any weight. We were prepared to take our chances. We were hoping Cathal's dip into medical college would help, but he was adamant that he didn't want to get involved in that side of things. I hoped I could persuade him otherwise. Emmett would be of use for his calm, been-there-seen-it-all approach. Give the applicants hope. We were also pleased to have Assumpta Daly on board. Cathal had remembered her from that meeting in the school hall. She would deal with the administrative side. He said there was something in the appearance of that small, plump, auburn-haired woman that belied an inner strength.

Assumpta neither drank nor smoked, went to Mass every day and never watched the Soaps. What a woman! We would make use of her until the inevitable happened and she became the first female Pope. For some reason, her nose curled up when typing. She was a great ally to Cathal as he battled with *The Times* crosswords.

It seemed we were all set, ready for something or other. We all discussed our priorities the night before we officially opened the office:

a) ensure Incapacity Existence Allowance forms were correctly completed in black pen;

b) any appropriate supporting medical evidence properly attached to forms with paper clips, not staples (a reason for DSS rejection);

c) ensure that the applicant was fully aware of ailment and its effects on the body and everyday life; and, most importantly,

d) build up the applicant's confidence for the day of the interview with the investigating doctor.

We opened our office with little fanfare on a quiet sunny morning as the milkman whistled his way around the streets and the paperboys cycled like maniacs and chucked newspapers at doors. I looked at the cheap little alarm clock on Assumpta's desk. Half-past seven.

As it happened, Colum McGeough had his appointment with the doctor that very day at ten o'clock, so that added to the apprehension in the air. There was obviously a lot riding on Colum's application. Richard stressed that *its* success could mean *our* success. I wasn't convinced of that. I still felt the strong tide of the sceptics pushing against us. Regardless of how well we did, there were those who just wanted us out. You can never win over those people. Not in this country. Believe me; they're more than happy to recline in pastures old, if it means they can shun change.

Cathal still didn't fully realise that as an Englishman he would never be truly trusted by most, despite their genuine friendliness and acceptance. There were some who would never accept him, even if he brought prosperity to the area. He was beginning to tire of me telling him that.

We had devoted a considerable amount of time to Colum's application. It was vital that Colum appreciated how his ailment should affect his physical appearance. Although our first priority was of course to enable people to make a successful claim, we felt a moral obligation to help and advise in anyway we could. We wanted to make any suffering less painful.

We explained Colum's symptoms to one of our advisers, a doctor Williams: back pain, muscle spasms, weakness in one leg and a slight numbness in the other. The doctor at first thought it might be sciatica but disregarded that initial diagnosis on account of little, if any, pain running down the back of the leg. He suggested the pain was more of a sacroiliac nature. He added that if Colum had flat feet, that could contribute to his problem. He knew a clinic in Carlow which specialised in custom-made orthotics. He also recommended avoiding prolonged sitting and referred us to the "Alexander Technique", a system of posture adjustment.

Doctor Williams had found himself up in front of the General Medical Council the previous year and had been struck off. The DSS informed the GMC that he had been involved in illegally prescribing drugs. The GMC didn't see the need to investigate further; the word of the DSS was enough upon which to issue an expulsion.

As Cathal sat on the easy chair near the window with his legs crossed and twiddling his thumbs, I was pacing the room waiting for Colum to arrive. Assumpta was behind her desk, a new frilly white blouse nearly choking her. A packet of unopened chocolate digestives beside her Charles and Di mug. The computer flickered grumpily at its early start. Richard sat near the door and Pat stood looking out at the mountain view, which was sporting a hairline of mist.

'An oath,' Richard called out.

'An oath? What are you on about?' I asked him.

'We should, you know, take some sort of oath, a pledge. A pledge to, eh, I don't know. Eh, a pledge to bring down the DSS or something.'

Right, I could see what he meant. I could see the value in all of us pledging our loyalty, but what words could we use? I couldn't think of any off hand. I asked Cathal for an input.

He shook his head and merely raised his eyes.

'Okay, look, it's a good idea. We'll look at it in more detail later,' I said, hearing the downstairs door open.

Colum arrived. He greeted us all by handshake and a nod of the head. On my insistence, Cathal took his blood pressure. A little high, nothing to worry about, though.

'Any coughs, sniffles, other than your usual habit?' Richard asked, anxious to get his healing hands into action.

Colum shook his head. He looked fairly calm in his blue shirt, a tightly buttoned grey cardigan, leading on to a pair of black trousers, which strained to reach a size-ten off-white pair of trainers. He was looking less stooped.

'You look well, Colum,' I said.

'Well, I'm not sick, so…'

We heard a car coming to a halt outside.

'Cecil?' Pat called out.

I looked out. Cecil waved up, I waved back. We had, of course, told Cecil about our new premises. God! He really needed a new car, a bigger one. Either that or go back to not wearing those big boots on duty.

We had invested a good sum in a video system, a means by which we linked the inside of Colum's house to a TV we had installed in the office. The picture wasn't great, but it would allow us to watch Colum's progress, or otherwise, during his meeting with the doctor. If nothing else, the recording could well prove a useful training tool for future claims.

My mobile rang; it was Siobhan. She rang to blow me a kiss before going to school and to tell me, in a whispered voice, Roger was going to London for a few days.

That's my girl.

'Are you all set, Colum?' I asked.

'As I'll ever be,' came his less than encouraging response.

Colum left our premises at a quarter to nine, his mind full of positive advice: stay calm; listen to the questions; answer in a clear and concise tone and remember not to make any sudden moves. Oh aye, and get that frigging stoop back. Aye, and above all, don't make any sudden moves, Richard reiterated.

We all shook his hand, hoping we weren't seeing off our futures.

Pat made a pot of tea. We all had a look out of the window at various times. We chatted about nothing in particular. It was raining now, although the sky promised better. Time was dragging. It seemed to take forever before the clock approached ten. Pat flicked on the TV.

The screen was blank!

'What's happening?' I shouted, banging on the top of our TV set. I decided to panic now, not leave it to later.

Minutes passed.

'Has he not turned the frigging thing on?' asked Pat.

'Stupid bastard! I knew we couldn't trust him,' said Cathal, adding to our unanimous support for Colum. We all let out a sigh of relief when the screen sprang into action revealing the gobshite features of a nervous Colum McGeough. What had we let ourselves in for here?

'Take that cardigan off, for Jesus sake, Colum! Your face is on fire,' I said. But as the system didn't benefit Colum in the same way as us, he couldn't hear a word.

'Forgot to turn it on,' he said, looking at his watch, the sweat plainly visible on his brow.

'He's going to make a bollocks of it,' I said, looking over at Cathal, who shrugged his shoulders. Pat and Richard just shook their heads and returned their eyes to the TV. I suppose it was in Colum's interest he didn't hear my little pep talk.

Seconds seemed like hours as our faces were glued to the screen. Colum had indeed taken off his cardigan. He looked more comfortable now. He sat on the black leather sofa, looking all round the room. We hadn't told him where we had located the camera. If we had, he would have been looking into it all the time, alerting the doctor to its location and making him suspicious. You know what people are like when there's a camera about.

Just think, without cameras we could have been spared Julian Clary, Jeremy Beadle, Cliff Richard, Graham Norton… the list is endless.

Colum's doorknocker exploded. He jumped.

Make that the last jump of the day, Colum, for Christ's sake! We sat upright, holding our breath. It was time, time for the big picture. The camera was able to follow Colum as he made his way slowly out of the living room and into the hall. He looked back and smiled weakly. He then tripped over a mat.

Jesus!

'Who is it?' he called out

'WHO IS IT?' We shouted in disbelief, but it was left to me to provide identification.

'It's not the frigging pizza man. Jesus! Who is it? It's the frigging doctor. Now let him in.'

I looked at Cathal. I wondered was he thinking the same as me. Oh, to be back in the Royal Oak with all the sane misfits.

We heard the doctor's voice. 'Mr McGeough, it's Doctor Kennedy. I'm here for our ten o'clock appointment.'

I noticed something. 'Quick, Cathal, check in Colum's notes if it says anything about a head tremor?'

'Jesus! Look, his head is frigging shaking,' said Cathal, leafing through the notes. 'No, nothing here, nothing at all.'

Miraculously, the tremor stopped as he opened the door. Must have been nerves. The doctor offered Colum his hand as he came into the house, closing the door behind him. Colum slowly, and with pain etched on his face, shook hands with the doctor. Good, Colum, good.

Even better when Colum walked into the living room using the doctor's arm as a crutch. Pat thought it rather theatrical; I thought it a touch of genius. Colum eased himself into the sofa and, with a nod of his head, offered the doctor a seat opposite him. Two glasses of water sat on the glass coffee table.

Doctor Kennedy was a tall thin man who wore rimless glasses. He spoke with a posh North Down accent and carried a weather-beaten brown briefcase. For a moment or two he looked round the room, jingling loose change in his pocket. He then sat down.

'Right, Mr McGeough, I have here a copy of your claim sent to the DSS for the Incapacity Existence Allowance,' he said, opening up his briefcase. 'Now, I want you to take it easy. I can see you are a little nervous. There really is no need to be. I'm not like any of the other doctors, believe me.'

I was immediately reassured.

Without warning, the doctor scattered the contents of the briefcase on to the floor. Forms, all shapes, sizes and colours. In an instant, he was up and moving around the room like a misguided missile. Targeting cushions, moving furniture and opening drawers. He was evidently searching for something.

'I'm not sure what you're looking for, Doctor, but I would be grateful if you wouldn't search my home.'

Good, Colum, good.

Nice strong voice, head only slightly forward, no twisting and turning. The doctor stood behind Colum, holding out his hands like he was going to strangle him. Oh Christ! What should we do?

Was this a rogue doctor you sometimes read about? Should we rush to Colum's house and rescue him, or should we leave it a few minutes? We really didn't want to blow our cover. I for one, God forgive me, would have sacrificed Colum to the mad doctor. We had to think of our other future claimants.

'You're not wired up, are you?' the doctor asked, walking round to stand in front of Colum.

'Do you mean in a Belfast way, or do you mean do I have an electronic device about my person or premises?' replied Colum.

Coolness personified. I whistled in admiration.

'It was an electronic question. I'll soon find out if you're Belfast wired up,' said the doctor, who now lifted up a pink form from the array on the floor.

This was it. The pink form with the questions.

Gird your loins, McGeough, gird your loins.

With pen poised in hand, the doctor chucked his first question at Colum. 'Do you get anxious or panicky?'

Colum shook his head, ever so slowly.

'Feel that someone may harm you or that you may harm them?'

The questioning did not appear to be in any sequence. Colum gave this one some thought, scratching his head, licking his lips before answering.

'No, to the first part and, eh, to the second part, a no, also. No, all round, really.'

The doctor then asked was he ever aggressive; or did he feel he couldn't cope with any changes in daily routine; did he ever neglect his personal hygiene; or did he hear voices? Colum carefully nodded his head to some; he denied any experience of others. Roughly translated, and I'm no expert, but it appeared that on occasion Colum did hear voices telling him to be aggressive; also to be mindful that he didn't come to any harm.

Difficult to know what Doctor Kennedy would make of this. Me? Well, I would have ordered an ambulance for Purdysburn. For the both of them. The doctor sat down and stretched out his long legs. He took out a handkerchief and loudly blew his nose. Settling back in the chair, he then rubbed his nose with his hand and removed his glasses.

'He's not going to sleep, is he?' asked Cathal.

'No chance, he's up to something,' said Richard.

The doctor rummaged about in his briefcase and took out what looked like a rusty item.

'What's that?' I asked, peering at the TV.

'Well, to me, it looks like a gong,' said Cathal.

A gong?

Maybe Cathal remembered something from his days at medical college.

'A gong? What does he want that for?' asked Pat.

'Maybe it's instead of a hammer,' I suggested, to querying looks all round. 'You know, in the old days doctors used to use a hammer to test your reflexes. Whack you on the knees, remember?'

Pat was busy looking through the notes we had on Doctor Kennedy, supplied of course by Cecil.

'Anything there, Pat?' I asked, glancing over at him but keeping one eye on the screen. I was worried.

Pat shook his head. 'No mention of the use of a gong. There is, however, the merest mention of dressage activities in Ballymena.'

Maybe we could use that another time when Horseman of the Year is on telly. Colum was on his own now. We didn't brief him on this. On his own, he was. And believe me, if there was anyone you didn't want to be on your own with, it was Colum. If you see what I mean.

'Right, Mr McGeough, now for the main event, so to speak.' The doctor looked up and smiled. He put his glasses back on. Colum didn't smile; his face was registering a severe problem somewhere. The doctor busied himself with his notes again, occasionally nodding his head or raising his eyebrows, depending on his interpretation of events.

'What the hell is wrong with Colum?' I said, looking over at Cathal and Richard. We watched as Colum wriggled about in his seat, his eyes squeezed shut and his tongue beginning to protrude.

'Is he having a fit of some kind?' asked Pat.

Cathal and Richard nodded at each other. It was left to Cathal to pronounce the diagnosis. 'He's got cramp. Look, he's moving his right leg about and trying to slip his hand down to ease it.'

Colum's tongue came fully out, as an expression of his pain, just as the doctor looked up again. To be fair to him, Doctor Kennedy was either immune to insults, having seen it all before, or he was too tired for a fight. He merely stuck his own tongue out at Colum and got on with the next stage.

With an understanding tone, the doctor explained the procedure. 'Mr McGeough, I really need to be satisfied that you are mentally competent to have made this claim in the first place and are therefore able to understand what is being asked of you today. The first few questions I asked were a wee taster. This test is the definitive one.'

He then lifted up the frigging gong. He was a fly one, this doctor, no mistake. Fair play to him, I suppose. I grasped at the last thing I hoped could help us. Prayer. I said one for all of us.

'For Jesus sake, God, get your act together and save us.'

A direct quote, perhaps, from the *Book of Wisdom*.

Colum McGeough had the look of a condemned man.

'Right, now, do you watch TV?' the doctor asked.

The impact on Colum was immediate and encouraging. His eyes lit up as if to say, well, this is going to be easy. A few questions about *Eastenders* and possibly *Pingu* and he'd be away. He nodded slowly in the affirmative.

The doctor continued. 'You do? Good. Now, do you remember that old "YES" and "NO" lark they used to have on the TV programme *Take Your Pick?*'

'Eh, no, I don't,' said Colum.

Doctor Kennedy hit the gong.

'Oh, wait a minute,' said Colum. 'Of course, I do. Yes, yes, I do.'

The doctor sounded the gong again. 'So, you do remember the show?' came the follow-up question from the doctor.

'Aye, I do indeed. The one where if you said Yes or No…'

The gong sounded again. The doctor was not impressed. 'Jesus! You would have been a riot on the show. Hughie Green would have had you, no problem.'

Colum stirred in his seat, the leather creaking along with him. 'Ah, you see, that's where you're wrong. Hughie Green? It was Michael Miles. Common enough error though, Doctor.'

Doctor Kennedy made a note of this revelation. 'Right, so you've got the hang of it now. I ask you questions and you answer, avoiding the two words Yes and No, okay? This is for real now, Mr McGeough. Fun's over.'

Fun? Christ! He must be a riot at chucking-out time.

Colum nodded and sat up straight. He kept his head leaning slightly to the left.

Good lad, Colum, you're a star. It was agony watching, though. All four of us were edging further and further off our seats. At times, we jumped up, head in our hands. The stress was getting to us. A hipflask full of whiskey was passed around in silence, and by Braille. None of us needed reminding of the importance of a good performance from Colum.

A lot was riding on Colum's ability, as yet untested, to be neither verbally positive nor negative.

Doctor Kennedy rolled his shoulders, took a deep breath and began. 'Have you been watching any nasty videos recently?'

'Indeed and I have not, Doctor.' Colum's reply was slow and deliberate.

'You're a liar, are you not?' came the next accusation-laden question.

'Me a liar? Oh, I wouldn't have said so.' Colum actually looked indignant.

The doctor then peered menacingly at Colum through his glasses which were steadily slipping down his nose.

'Do you deserve the IEA?'

'Well, I think I do. What about you?'

'No.'

'Got you. Bang that gong for me, will you?' shouted Colum, smiling widely.

'Oh, very funny,' said the obviously miffed medical man. His bottom lip was beginning to curl in a huff. He turned a page. 'Do you know the answer to three multiplied by seventy-four, divided by sixty-two, add one thousand, three hundred and four, then take away seventy-three?'

Colum had no hesitation. 'N... eh, I wouldn't have thought so.'

Good recovery, Colum.

To the right of me, Pat spoke. 'One thousand, two hundred and thirty-four and a half.'

'Nice one, Pat,' I said.

'Now, if that was in Peruvian *soles*, you would have about three hundred and fifty-two US dollars,' he felt the need to add.

We all looked at him.

'Of course if you wanted to visit Peru you would have to learn either Aymara or the language of the Incas, Quechua. A word of warning, though, avoid the Upper Huallaga valley, home to drug barons and...'

'What are you on about?' Richard interrupted rather forcefully.

'Yeah, I thought you knew only about Russia,' I said.

'Yeah, but the thing about Peru…'

'Bollocks to Peru, Pat!' I almost screamed and immediately felt bad about shouting at him. He looked crestfallen, but there were more pressing things going on.

It was a battle of wills for the next fifteen minutes. The doctor had abandoned the "question and answer" routine, his gong now back in his briefcase. He tried a more convivial approach and chatted quite amiably with the applicant. Making the odd reference to his showjumping activities, he then talked in some detail about Colum's ailment. He was visibly impressed when Colum mentioned the Alexander Technique. Good old Doc Williams.

My neck was aching with tension, but I felt we could begin to relax a little. While we were not exactly home and dry, we could at least see the shoreline. Cathal, however, began to look a little anxious; didn't like that, although he later told me he was still trying to figure out the Peruvian thing with Pat.

Pat and Richard were nodding off. A sign of confidence? Or a result of last night's late rehearsals for Richard's turn at the GAA Club in two days' time? Earlier, he'd told me he had been putting the finishing touches to *Putting On The Ritz*. Enthusiastically, he said he was going to start with that one and finish with either *The Continental* or *A Pretty Girl Is Like A Melody*, Pat favouring the latter, apparently.

The previous night, on behalf of Richard, I had asked the doorman at the club what time Richard would be on. He said he wasn't sure but hoped it was about ten minutes after he went home.

Doctor Kennedy took off his jacket, then slowly undid his tie and rolled up his shirtsleeves. He complained of the heat.

'Just a couple more questions and we're done, Mr McGeough.'

He did, admittedly, look a bit flushed. The doctor then drank eagerly from the glass of water, his hand shaking a little as he wiped his mouth and returned the glass to the table. He was taking deep breaths and staring oddly at Colum, his eyebrows going up and down.

'I don't feel very well, Mr McGeough. I've got a crushing sensation in my chest.'

And with that, he slid down the chair, pulling some papers and his briefcase with him, and ended up on the floor, holding his chest. You could see Colum was battling with indecision. He moved as if to get up, then, wisely, slunk back into the sofa.

'Oh Jesus!' I jumped up and stared at the screen, which at that moment began to flicker. 'Cathal, Cathal, what do you think?' My anxiety wakening both my uncles.

'Oh, I don't know. Ask Richard,' he replied, reminding me he didn't want to get involved in any medical observations.

'CATHAL!' I was in no mood for such reticence.

'Okay, okay. Let me see.' Cathal moved closer to the screen, which fortunately stopped flickering. 'Heavy breathing, rapid chest movement... mentioned the crushing feeling in his chest. He looks to be sweating, doesn't he? Oh, I don't know, I really don't. Stay calm, Colum, stay calm.'

It seemed like hours, probably no more than a few seconds.

Cathal spoke, 'I know it looks like it, but I don't think, I can't be sure, but I don't think the doctor is having a heart attack at all.'

Richard nodded his head, seemingly in agreement.

'Are you sure, are you sure?' I nagged.

'In the absence of being able to do an electrocardiogram test, no.'

As if by telepathy, Colum seemed to pick up on Cathal's diagnosis. In the face of a man supposedly having a heart attack, he remained remarkably calm.

'I think I'm having a heart attack, Mr McGeough,' the heavy-breathing doctor said. 'You'd better call for an ambulance.'

This was it, Colum, your moment in time. Play it cool, play it cool.

If he got it wrong, the legacy was simply the demise of a GP. I mean, it's not as if we were in France with their "duty of care" policy.

Colum held his hands out in resignation. 'I think you would be best placed to ring for yourself. By the time I would get to the telephone, it might be too late. Once I get settled in, it's painful to get up, so it is. It's all there in my application.'

We watched the doctor. His breathing seemed to be returning to normal. Ours had almost stopped. Certainly, a resigned look was dawning on his face. He then gave Colum a dirty look and got to his feet. God, that was close! Had Colum been fooled by the charade, he would more than likely have jumped up to call an ambulance, thereby revealing his true agility.

Claim immediately dismissed.

Aye, many of the applicants were aware of the tactics used by the investigating doctor. This was a new one, though, and Colum dealt with it admirably. The doctor took a seat and, with the merest of glances at Colum, scribbled a few notes and then packed everything away in his briefcase. He got up, nodded at Colum, and made for the front door. Colum looked all round the room seemingly trying to find the camera, his face iced with a sugary smile.

'Oh, Doctor, mind you don't slam the door now. It might make me jump and, well, that wouldn't be good for me, now, would it?'

We heard the door slam shut.

I immediately switched off our screen and wrote in big lettering on our notice board: BEWARE OF BEING TOO COCKY.

It was advice I could well have used myself. I was sure we had Colum's allowance in the bag. There was no way Doctor Kennedy's report could be negative. Cecil told us that the DSS invariably followed the doctor's recommendations. The DSS had in the past managed to reject all claims on some technicality; this one was a dead cert.

We needed to celebrate. I sank more than a few with Cathal and then I caught a cab out to Saintfield. I needed to see my daughter. Roger, as Siobhan had told me, was in London, leaving my family at the mercy of me.

All in all it had been a good day.

The house was at the far end of a tree-lined avenue. That frigging gravel path again. Why can't Roger conform and have that block paving like the rest of the boring world? The shingles announced my stumbling arrival with a volume I couldn't really control. I had a limited command of my senses, you see.

Nicely drunk, in barroom speech.

No lights were on. I squinted at my watch. Half-past eleven.

Was that late?

'Mairead, Mairead,' I called out as quietly as I could.

Being pissed, you see, it alters one's knowledge and understanding of local custom. Like legal decibel limits.

'Mrs Dooley, Mrs Dooley.' I raised my voice, dispensing with any further need for noise regulation.

A thought, a troubling one. 'Here, I hope you haven't changed your name, Mrs Dooley.'

The top window opened. 'What the hell do you want at this time of night, ye frigging drunken get, ye?' In the dimness, descended both from the night and my alcohol intake, I couldn't actually make out who it was. Kinda recognised the voice, you know. I was fairly sure it was the woman who had once promised to honour and obey.

Now that she was angry, her Belfast accent was more pronounced.

Must have been her, for, let's face it, when you think about it, who else would have such a prepared speech to hand? You know, on the off chance that someone would call at your house and shout up at the window. Oh God! I suddenly thought, don't start calling me a useless bastard; a drunk; a lazy get; a loser... you know, like before. I was in no fit state to fill in the gaps.

I was an uncomplicated soul most of the time, or so I thought. I felt I could wrap this one up in a sentence. What the hell did I want?

'I want to come in,' I said. What a profound line full of hope and slur.

'Well, you can't come in here. Go away,' she hissed. 'Think of my neighbours, Thomas Dooley.'

That one threw me. Think of her neighbours. I couldn't. I hadn't a clue what any of them looked like. Dim light, dim brain, I hold my hands up.

'Go away before I call someone,' she said, looking up and down the street.

'Ye selfish bitch, ye.' I suddenly became annoyed. 'You'd call someone at this time of night, waken them out of their sleep, panic them into thinking something was wrong. I'm telling you, Mairead Dooley, you can be shocking thoughtless at times.'

She slammed the window shut.

The record was stuck. 'I want to come in,' I again challenged the dweller.

Window opened again. 'Well, you can't. There are lots of things I want to do, Thomas Dooley, you know. Like, like, see the back of you for the last time, have a life where you're not constantly in it. I'd like go to Barbados too.'

'Fair enough, fair enough,' I conceded. I moved forward, now directly underneath her window, hoping all the while she hadn't developed any unsavoury habits, like spitting. 'But all I want to do is come in. That could be achieved by you opening the door. While you... while you and your desire to travel halfway across the world would require planes, passports, injections...'

The window once again slammed shut, that silenced me. Then a downstairs light came on and when she eventually got the front door open, I was standing there to attention with a DIY tip. 'Tell Roger to get that door oiled.'

'Do you know what time it is?' she fumed.

I noticed she had let her hair grow again and there was a hint of a streak in it. It suited her but she always said she didn't like streaks.

'What do you want?' she said, hands on hips, her nose turned up like it did when she had a few and snored.

Did I know what time it was? What did I want? So many questions, so little time, so few brain cells still functioning. 'I want to see you and I want to see you now.'

She obviously hadn't been drinking, 'cause personally, I would have responded to that one with: "Well, you *can* see me. You're looking at me." Clever, eh?

I never get the good lines.

She half-dragged me into the house. 'Keep your voice down, I'm not having Siobhan woken.'

'I believe Roger is in London,' I said as the door eased shut like on a tube train. 'Looking at a few English molars, eh? Leaving my wife, that's you, to the mercy of someone who has definite designs on her. And that would be me.' Deep breath, expelling the brain-numbing alcohol. 'What a quirk of fate that your husband, again that's me, should be at your side at such a moment...'

Mairead was adamant as she tightened her hold on her pale blue dressing gown. 'Well you can't see me, so would you please go home. I'm asking you nicely. And it's nothing to do with you what Roger is doing.' Her voice was getting louder.

'Shush,' I slurred considerably. 'Think of the neighbours.'

'Look at the state of you!'

God, how I hated that face! It was so dismissive of me. I fought back, but not as ferociously as I would have liked. Not ferociously at all, really. Don't you just hate it when alcohol gets it so wrong sometimes and dilutes one's natural aggression?

'The state of me? The state of me? You want to have seen the state of Cathal the other night! You see, we hooked up with these two women. Well, when I say women, without access to birth certificates we were unable to positively identify…'

'Shut up!' she said. A short, but successful interruption statement.

She completed the dragging process when she again half-dragged me into the kitchen, although I offered less resistance this time. I wasn't exactly clear on the layout of the house. For all I knew, she could have been half-dragging me off somewhere else. More intimate, if you get my drift. I checked in my pocket to make sure I hadn't dropped the CD I had gone home for before journeying over there.

Wouldn't have been the first time in our relationship she had taken the initiative. Oh no siree, boy.

To be honest, she hadn't really the look of a lusty lover this time. I could have been misreading her; it had, after all, been a while since Mairead and I had read each other, so to speak. I did, however, wear the face of optimism that manifested itself in an inane grin plastered on the kitchen-wall mirror.

Mairead turned on the cold-water tap and poured me an unrequested glassful. I looked at it, then, solely out of politeness, sipped a little. I grimaced; it tasted foul as water always tends to when adrift of its natural partner.

Whiskey, woman, where's the whiskey?

'Sit down,' she ordered.

I complied, pulling a chair out from the table. It squeaked.

'Shush,' I said, nervously putting my fingers to my mouth. I could see her angry mood subsiding a little. As it usually did, thank God. She filled the coffee machine with water and switched it on.

'Well, I suppose we should all be grateful you managed to stay sober so long,' she remarked, standing by the sink, her arms folded.

Through the lager mist, I thought I could see signals. Was she sending me signals? I did my best to decipher them. Now, please, in my defence, at that moment in time, I did not have the benefit of a single, fully operational brain cell.

Do you want me to stay the night; are those the signals you're giving out? Need to check, don't want to make an arse of myself.

'So, what has gone wrong this time for you to have your face back in the bottle?' she asked.

No, I think. Mairead, we need to take things a day at a time. We'd regret it, my darling, sweet wife, if we rushed into it. No, no, don't get me wrong, angel, it's definitely, most definitely something for the future. You and me lounging around in HIM and HER dressing gowns in a mansion in Dalkey. I'm happy to leave things as they are for now. Oh, okay, okay, we'll renew our marriage vows in the morning.

I could tell by her face I had gotten it wrong. Signal failure in area surrounding Tom and Mairead's relationship.

She stood there looking all smart arsed. Stay cool, Thomas, stay cool. By all means look like an eejit, if it's part of the game plan, but stay cool, Tom. You have, after all, the trump card, although it was temporarily missing.

I tired to regroup enough brain cells to continue. 'I just wanted to tell you…' I searched for the words. I feared my search was in vain.

I needed help, I needed inspiration. I pulled the trump card from my pocket and showed it to my wife. She stared at it, then at me.

Glenn Campbell, do your stuff. I motioned with my hands for her to put it on. She looked at me as if I was mad. This was no time for acute observations, Mrs Dooley, I wanted to say, but I was limiting my word output, on account of a definite shortage.

'Go on, go on,' I urged, as if this could be the defining moment of her life. 'Put side one on, track two.'

A few words were required, I thought, as way of introduction. I cleared my throat and tried to stand up straight. I failed. Okay, no problemo, no problemo. I can do Quasimodo. 'I, Mrs Dooley, am your husband, although my name is, of course, Mr Dooley. As you know, or should know… are you with me so far?' I didn't hang around for a reply. 'And… I am a working-class hero. According… hic… to Cathal… he… hic… hic… told me tonight.'

She put the CD on. Go on, my son, give it some…

Like the first apartment that we had
That bumpy little couch that made into a bed
The shower down the hall
The footsteps overhead
She said it's just fine
Times were hard for us for quite a while
But through those hungry days
She faced it with a smile
Not wanting me to know she's carrying my child
She tried to ease my mind
If I am anything today
I owe it to the love I had along the way…

I've cracked it, I thought. How on earth could any woman resist those sentiments, eh? Response, Mairead, response, I think I remember my brain screaming instructions. She'd have to be quick.

I stood up and slowly slithered, in a less-than-orderly fashion, to the floor, miming along with Glenn. I just caught the beginnings of the next verse…

No matter what went wrong
No matter come what may
She stood by my side…

I have a very vague memory of that moment. I thought it went wonderfully well.

Siobhan had been standing at the bottom of the stairs watching and she was able to fill in the blanks a couple of days later when I took her to McDonald's. She told me, in a giggling fit, how she watched her mother trying to drag me into the living room before giving up and leaving me for the night in the kitchen with her suede coat over me.

'Do you want to know what she said, daddy?' Siobhan asked excitedly.

I wasn't sure I could tolerate hearing my daughter swear. 'Go on, then. What did she say?'

'Mammy said, so she did, mammy said, "Thomas Dooley, what are we going to do with you?"'

'Was she shouting, love?' I asked.

Siobhan shook her head and sucked deeply from her strawberry milkshake. 'No, no, she wasn't, daddy. She had a big smile on her face, so she did.' Siobhan gave me a big hug when she saw how pleased I was. 'And do you know what I said to her, daddy, 'cause I went into the kitchen to give you a goodnight kiss? I did, honest. I said, "Mammy, mammy, why don't we keep him?"'

While we waited for a decision on Colum's case, we dabbled in a few fresh applications, but it was difficult to concentrate. We wished we knew what the hell was going on at the DSS. It had now been seven weeks. Cecil was unable to enlighten us, said the file was still with the Englishman in the SECRET cabinet. God forgive me, but I was beginning to have my doubts about Cecil. There was, however, no evidence to suggest he was anything but straight with us.

It was a cold, wintry afternoon when we heard the grave news. Colum's application had been rejected. Cathal and I sat in the office stunned. We'd given Assumpta the day off; Pat and Richard were elsewhere. We stared out the window in silence, a mist completely covering the mountains. Everything seemed to be closing in on us. We had been banking on Colum, staking our reputation on him.

Cathal maintained often that the people knew us well enough by now, knew we were doing our best. I was quick to point out he didn't really know these people. Aye, they might well consider us to be a couple of well-meaning, even, to a degree, competent duo, but in the end we hadn't been successful.

We had failed.

We had followed the previously well-travelled road of those who had gone less-than-enthusiastically before us. They had failed the people; we had merely followed suit. Whether our intentions were more honourable than those before us could well be a topic of heated debate, but, when it came to it, we all reached the same end product.

Failure.

Breathing in the air of despondency that now greedily held onto the area was both unpleasant and demoralising for all of us.

Cecil was on the phone. He, too, was amazed that the application had been rejected; it fitted all the criteria. He told us to appeal. Cecil promised to do all he could to find out how the Englishman managed to block Colum McGeough's application.

I felt doubly sorry for Cathal; after all, it was his inheritance that had financed our deeper involvement. He said he wasn't at all bothered about the money, stressing he wouldn't have missed the last number of months for the world. Typical Cathal.

We talked about how we might have improved the application but couldn't see any real gaps. We chatted for hours about what we might do now.

Would we appeal? A pointless exercise, really.

We had made half-hearted appeals in a couple of cases; but with no luck. We doubted whether anyone at the DSS actually took the trouble to read our appeals, for a standard letter, confirming the original verdict, was usually back within days. I sensed that Cathal and I were on the verge of jacking it all in. It was hard to lift ourselves. Not only had we to contend with our failure, but the very real image of whether we could remain in Belfast surfaced with a hard-to-deny vividness.

Our project had kept us alive, gave us a purpose for getting out of our pit in the morning. I couldn't see either of us settling for an ordinary job just to bring in a few bob. To survive. We might as well be back in London. Later that evening, we called into the club. Pleasingly, we got nothing but sympathetic comments, even, surprisingly, from previously hard-bitten sceptics.

I did feel, though, that the locals thought we had tried our best.

But what had we really done?

We'd gone, well, actually, *I'd* gone, heart first into the building up of hope. And the basis for that hope? The hope that we would come in, with no experience whatsoever, and take on and defeat the might of a corrupt government department which had the full backing of its Whitehall masters.

Did we really think that we, a couple of gobshites, could make a difference? Where did our arrogance come from? Did someone paint over the signposts pointing towards reality? We threw out a lifeline to these people; everyone else had deserted them. The governments of Britain and Ireland; the Republican Movement, who, over the years, took what they wanted and then scurried away; the Americans and their money; the Europeans and their ideas for investment.

All gone.

We had lit the litmus paper that had gone a nice shade of hopeful blue.

Still, if someone had said to me this time last year, "Dooley boy, you will be in Belfast going hell for leather at something," I would have laughed in their face. I would have thought it too ridiculous for words had it been suggested that

Cathal and I would put so much effort into something other than drinking. So at the end of the day, did it really matter that we would once again return to nothing, to the nobodies with flimsy unobtainable aspirations, which we were, for a long time, happy to be identified with?

At least we had given it a go, had been there, ready and willing at the kick-off. Heard the bell go and came out guns blazing. We had encountered controversy and circumstance and met them head on. And by Jesus, did we enjoy it! Hey, let's look at the positive side of failure, what harm had we done?

Why, then, did I feel so bloody awful?

Why could I not accept we had given it a go and leave it at that? Pack our bags, move on, upwards and onwards. The problem was I didn't really believe there *was* an upwards and onwards out there. Not for us. Best we could hope for was a sideways move.

This had been it. This had been the big one. And now it was over. And once again I felt I had let my mother down.

I called Siobhan the next day. She was really settling into school. I was happy that she was at a church school. She was developing into a kind, considerate wee girl. I liked to think my presence in Belfast helped her. So, for that, as good, God-fearing Christians like to say, I should be thankful to God.

I suppose I had grown up a little. Didn't get so angry, finally accepted that maybe life's twists and turns were mapped out for me. More importantly, I reached a conclusion which most of us do, or should do at some stage, if we're truly honest with ourselves.

At the end of the day, the choices we make are what really shape our lives. Either way, I had nobody to blame anymore.

Cathal and I seemed to be dodging the main issue: to stay or not to stay, that was the question. I got the feeling that whatever I decided, Cathal would fall in with it. That annoyed me a bit. He had to make his own mind up. I couldn't be responsible for his future. I could see Cathal resting quite easily on some bar stool somewhere; he would revert to his old ways.

He said as much. He had given it a go, it hadn't worked out. Simple as that.

I, on the other hand, realised I needed more. I couldn't just leave it at that. My report on my time in Belfast had to offer more than "Could do better". These people were *my* people. Yeah, those same people I had kept at a safe distance for all those years. Their working-class hero had let them down. At the end of the day, Thomas Dooley had amounted to little. According to Richard and Pat, my mother didn't get despondent. The thing is, you see, my mother was a realist; I was still firmly wedged to the state of dreaming. I wanted to be the person these people wanted me to be. I wanted to show Mairead that I could be something. Someone.

I knew I now had her respect, and not grudgingly. When I had woken that day in her house, I explained what Cathal and I had achieved, or thought we had. She was genuinely impressed by my knowledge and I knew my enthusiasm touched her. As she good-naturedly said, I no longer seemed to be the angry young man, still ranting at thirty, unable to shift it approaching forty years of age.

I truly didn't want to return to the old me, not here in Belfast. And certainly not in front of Mairead and Siobhan.

God! I never wanted to be scalded with that anger ever again. I wanted to be normal. I wanted not to immediately see the bad in everything, in everyone. Those feelings had become second nature to me. All the while I could do little about it, I accepted I was a prisoner to all the negativity. Coming back to Belfast allowed me to bury a few ghosts, confront the past.

Bully it, even.

I hadn't what you might call a strong faith, and my thoughts on the "afterlife" were, like many, riddled with doubts. I did, however, fervently believe that even though my mother was no longer with us in a recognisable form, then her spirit, whatever that may be, was undoubtedly driving me on. The spirit of her life, the spirit of what she had instilled in me. The person she was, the person she had made me.

Cathal and I moped around for a few days. He with his head stuck in crosswords, me ranting and raving about the inadequacy of daytime TV. I told him to away on out and see Maureen. He told me he didn't know where that relationship was going. Recently, and he didn't like it, she had been trying quite forcefully to convert him to the ways of the vegan. I told him it served him right, that he had in the past waylaid people in his attempts to increase gates at Tranmere. You're both extremists, I told him, you belong together.

We stayed away from the local clubs, preferring instead to go into town if we did venture out for a few jars. Emmett would call round, and both he and Sammy were great in trying to lift our spirits. As Emmett said, even if we never got another successful claim, the craic had been powerful.

Sammy told him to speak for himself; he needed his claim.

We left him and Emmett arguing on our doorstep one evening as we jumped into a taxi. That evening when we got back and Pat and Richard joined us for a nightcap, Cathal produced a couple of holiday brochures.

'Let's get the hell out of here for a few days,' he said and immediately cast aside my protestations that while I could accept him financing the project, there was no way he was going to pay for my holidays. Richard said if I didn't go, he would. I noticed Cathal's face crumbling. I knew he was very fond of Richard, but when you go on holiday with a spiritualist, you never know who might be coming with you and putting pressure on your baggage allowance.

The following evening we were at the airport. Just about got there, the taxi struggled with heavy snow and strong winds. Maybe this time we would actually get away. We were off to Malaga, not a place I would actually pick out and get excited about, but the deal was good, and, sod it, it wasn't Belfast. I suppose it wasn't much of a surprise to find the flight delayed.

The airport was crowded and many wore the uniform of the holidaymaker. Even in the depths of winter. Bright clothing, baseball caps, artificial suntan and a desire to shout for Ireland. All souls escaping the elements.

'Couple of drinks, my young Irish friend?' Cathal suggested.

'Oh indeed, my good man, Oh indeed,' I nodded.

Pre-med for Malaga.

I was determined I was going to give it some. Really let go. And give it some we did. Not, however, at the airport. No, nothing as straightforward for us. We attacked the beer barrels at the local GAA Club.

If that flight hadn't been delayed, we would have missed the call from Cecil. The man was a hero. I was just about to switch off my mobile when he called to tell me Fortesque-Smith had altered his decision on Colum's application. The bastard had granted it.

Apparently, rumour had it, Cecil explained, that the change of heart was brought about by Miss Webster catching the Englishman *in flagrante delicto* with his secretary in the main conference room at DSS HQ. Miss Webster had been incensed that Colum's application had been rejected. Cecil's voice on the phone was priceless; he took on the tone of a haughty Englishman telling me Miss Webster, the wily old Civil Servant, had blackmailed Fortesque-Smith. He then warned us that he heard rumours about a possible imminent raid and told us to keep our wits about us.

We invited Cecil to the celebrations in the GAA Club. I asked him did he think now was a good time to maybe enquire as to whether we could *turn* Miss Webster? He shook his head as he did when I asked did he think she might have suspicions about his involvement with us.

It was a treat to see Cecil up on stage later in the evening. Noddy would have been proud of him.

'Slade live on!' he roared before falling off the stage, a traditional enough means of exit for many at the club. It was good to see Cecil fitting in.

Cathal and I were back on form; the jokes were flying. It was a second chance for us. He admitted that he really dreaded the thought of going back to London. I, too, admitted that the thought of having to pick up the pieces somewhere else and start again filled me full of dread.

'We could be in Malaga now, Tom, soaking up the sun,' Cathal said without the slightest hint of yearning.

'Aye,' I said as I looked around the club, watching Emmett trying to carry six pints without the aid of a tray; catching a glimpse of Richard doing the foxtrot with Joey Donnelly's mother; smiling warmly as Assumpta Daly blushed in conversation with the handsome bingo caller. You could stick Malaga where the sun don't shine.

Pat stood at the bar, smiling over at us; he had taken an evening off from the trials and tribulations of mathematics. I smiled inwardly on noticing he still kept a distance from the main event.

Colum was in seventh heaven, cigarette in hand, bottle of stout in mouth. He was almost in tears as the back slappers formed an endless queue to congratulate him and to remind him not to forget his friends.

He came over to us. 'I really don't know how to thank you boys. I have my official letter here. Look,' he said, offering us the government-issue brown envelope. There it was, in black and white. Also inside the envelope, the bright blue card that would enable Colum to choose from Joey Donnelly's range of cars.

Colum McGeough was now the proud owner of the IEA to be paid monthly. I would resist the call, if it came, to accompany Colum to the showroom; sometimes in life when you see something like the dancing queens, it prolongs mental wellbeing never, ever, to witness such events again.

I got the feeling Emmett was a bit peeved that he was no longer the kingpin among claimants. I hope I reassured him when I told him he had been the trailblazer; he had set the standards. As he admitted later, where the hell else would he have had an opportunity to be a trailblazer?

'Aye, and I wouldn't have done it without your ma, Tom,' he said, shaking my hand.

'Aye, and I wouldn't have done it without her son,' said Colum, grabbing my other hand.

Could it get any better?

I told Colum to take a seat, for his back was still playing him up a bit, a legacy of having to sit for so long that day of the interview. Richard offered some healing there and then. Colum said he didn't have time for it. He said there was too much fun to be had. He spotted Miriam, the behavioural specialist, seemingly teaching a couple of old dears to tap dance at the side of the stage. I handed Colum a leaflet on lumbar exercises. Christ! We wanted him to be in proper shape to enjoy his good fortune.

Before he left to join the tap-dancing trio, he threw twenty pounds on the table, 'Get yourselves a drink on me. I took a hundred pounds out of the Credit Union this morning.'

As the evening progressed, Cathal and I were way ahead of ourselves. We tried to discuss a future business plan. We wondered might we apply for lottery funding. Perhaps look for donations. For two pounds a month, you can help firm up the infirm, that kind of thing.

Exciting times. I rang Siobhan, told her she was the best wee daughter in the world, then blew her a kiss goodnight. I hope she heard me over the sound of the band on stage, busy rehearsing for their out-of-tune Beatles tribute gig later on. I spoke to Mairead, told her I was sorry for everything. She just sighed, saying she had heard it all before. So had I, but not with this amount of conviction. I felt content for the first time in ages.

No, fuck it! I felt happy.

'Long may it reign,' said Cathal, before being dragged up onto the floor by three middle-aged women, who proceeded to dance around him in a style which went some way to proving we really are descended from apes.

And then, suddenly, the lights went out.

'Fuck! It's the raid!' someone screamed. Strangely, apart from one or two people who knocked their glasses over, there was little physical panic. We all seemed rooted to the spot with fear.

Nobody spoke as the main door into the club slowly creaked open. Our breathing like loud, melodic drumbeats in the cloying silence.

Footsteps.

Our eyes adjusting to the dark. Misty rays of light from the street lamps sneaking through the dirty windows illuminated the figures now wholly inside the club. There were four of them.

It was difficult to see, but, yes, yes, they appeared to be in uniform.

Someone, I think it was the barman, switched on a torch to give us all a better view of the raid. The swirling motion of the light flashed into the faces of the four as they lined up before us.

We soon had the measure of them.

I think we all showed remarkable restraint in not grabbing their copies of *The War Cry* and secreting it about their person so firmly that even an experienced surgeon would have difficulty removing them completely.

'Salvation-bloody-Army,' someone shouted just as one of them tapped out an unrecognisable, but in the circumstances, brave, little ditty on her tambourine. I think a trombone accompanied her.

'Stupid bastards must have hit the trip wire on the way in,' shouted the barman as he moved to repair the damage.

It was dark, we were heaving simultaneously with both anger and then obvious relief. The members of the Salvation Army must have sensed it too, for in moments, they tentatively struck up a rendition of *Onward Christian Soldiers* that seemed to lack their traditional *Oompah* until the lights came up and many of us stood up, pints in hands, and joined in with strong, Christian voices.

We were so relieved it wasn't the DSS Enforcement Unit that we forgave the four of them. We didn't give them a penny, though.

Have you ever wondered whether a hangover would be as bad if you woke up knowing you had won the lottery?

I thought we had won our own jackpot. My head was splitting. I popped round to see Siobhan. My knock was answered by a sullen Mairead. She invited me in. She was wearing a dark blue tracksuit and had on rubber gloves that were dripping with suds. I had expected Siobhan to appear once she had heard my voice. Mairead told me she was feeling a bit under the weather, so I went upstairs to see her. Fortunately, Roger the Codger was not at home. Invariably I missed him; I tried to make sure he wasn't there when I called.

I knocked on my daughter's door. 'Siobhan?' I called out gently.

'Is that you, daddy?' Her voice was definitely weak.

I walked into the room. It was in semidarkness, the blinds still down, a *Barbie* bedside lamp was on. The duvet was up at her chin and a half-drunk bottle of Lucozade sat by the lamp. I was pleased to see she was hugging the teddy bear I had bought her.

'Are you not well, love?' I asked, stroking her brow. It was warm.

She shook her head.

'Is Danny not well either?' I asked.

She hugged the teddy bear and again shook her head. 'Would you like some of my Lucozade?' she asked weakly.

'No, thank you, love.'

'Granny used to tell me that when someone is sick, it's okay for them to have all the Lucozade to themselves. It's the only time, ever, ever, they don't have to share. Isn't that right, daddy?'

'Yes, it is, love,' I laughed, pleased that she remembered.

'Is granny looking over me, daddy?' Her eyes began to moisten a little.

I hugged her tight and told her, yes, granny was looking over her and mammy and daddy.

'Do you think she's looking over Roger the Codger?'

'Siobhan!' I tried to stifle a laugh.

'What?' she said, mischievousness creeping into her watery eyes.

'Now, you know you mustn't call Roger that.'

She put on a very good Belfast accent. 'Okay, sorry,' she said, moving the duvet a little from her face. 'Can I call him Roger the Lodger, then?'

We both burst out laughing.

'You're a shocking wee girl, so you are.' I knew I should have chastised her again, but this was my wee girl and me united again. I realised that no matter how close she got to Roger, and she would, for she was that type of child, my relationship with her was unique and for keeps.

'Roger says I should drink plenty of fluids and not to forget, to, eh, not to forget to…' she looked up at me. She was hoping for a duet, I think.

I didn't disappoint. We sang loudly in unison, *'DON'T FORGET TO BRUSH YOUR TEETH.'*

I checked my watch. I had things to sort out. Leaning over, I kissed Siobhan and she gave me a big hug back and wouldn't let go. I eased her arms from me.

'I have to have a wee word with your mammy before I go. I'll see you soon.' I blew her four kisses. 'Those are for when I'm not here.'

She blew me four back.

'Daddy?'

'Yes, love.'

'Try not to argue with mammy,' she said before turning over in the bed. 'It does my head in, so it does.'

I found Mairead in the kitchen drying a few dishes. Terry Wogan was just finishing his stint on Radio 2. The washing machine was spinning, the smell of coffee inviting. She offered me a cup. A poetry book lay opened on the table. Walter de la Mare's *The Listeners* stared up at me.

It was Mairead's favourite from school. I remember she used to bore the arse off me reciting it. She thought she was doing me a favour. I considered that now was maybe as good a time as any to return that dubious treat. I launched into a poetic ramble. '"Is there anybody there?" said the traveller, knocking on the moonlit door…'

Mairead turned round, her face betraying a half-smile.

I continued, this time reading from the book. 'And his horse in the silence champed the grasses…'

She took the book from me and closed it. It was her turn. 'Of the forest's ferny floor…' she recited from memory, an impish look on her face. 'And a bird flew up out of the turret above the traveller's head…'

'Okay, okay,' I said, holding my hand up to silence her. 'So, you still remember it?'

She nodded.

'So do I.'

'You bloody don't, don't lie.'

'I do, I do. I learned it off by heart, I swear. Cross my heart and hope to die,' I said, making a sign of the cross on my chest.

'You always moaned at me for reciting it. You said you hated it.'

'Aye, but you loved it.'

'Yeah, but…'

The realisation of why I had learned the poem suddenly hit her. She blushed.

I hoped to God she didn't ask me to recite it. I had only ever learned the first line.

She filled up my coffee cup. I changed the subject. 'So, how are you managing with yer man out all day?' I asked, leaning against the breakfast bar. Jesus! That coffee was strong.

'Fine, thank you,' she replied tersely, busying herself dragging some towels out of the washing machine. 'Siobhan doesn't look too bad, does she?'

'No, she's fine. After a bit of TLC,' I said, and before I realised it, I was off the stool and moving slowly but purposely towards my estranged wife. God knows what I was going to do, but I was drawn into the intimacy of being there with her, talking about our daughter; remembering my wife blushing.

Cathal, Cathal, where the hell were you when I needed reining in?

She raised her head and gave me a look that would have sunk a ship. I felt foolish and managed to re-route myself and walk over to the sink where I emptied the remnants of the coffee. As I looked out the window, feeling my face going bright red, I hoped to Jesus she hadn't really noticed what my approach was all about. Well, she couldn't have, for sure as hell, I didn't know. Did I expect to sweep her up in my arms like a romantic hero from some crap Hugh Grant movie? Did I expect the theme from Dr Zhivago to pump into the room like some logic-numbing nerve gas?

'So, who would have thought it, eh?' she said, finally ending her ownership tussle with the washing machine. She rested her back against the sink. 'Thomas Dooley, working-class hero?'

'Is that what Roger is calling me?' I asked angrily.

'No, no, not at all. You said that was what Cathal was calling you. Don't be so defensive. I think what you are doing is admirable. Molly would have been so proud of you. You know she thought the world of you.'

I hoped the pain I felt wasn't evident. The words spilled out though. 'Aye, so did you once.'

She shrugged her shoulders. 'I never thought you had it in you. You proved me wrong.'

'Maybe it just needed bringing out,' I countered, instantly regretting the words.

'Are you saying I didn't bring it out in you?'

'No.'

'Let me tell you something, Thomas Dooley, I was too busy bringing up my daughter to pander to your...'

I stopped her tirade with a raised hand. 'Look, I'm not saying anything. I've found my niche in life, that's all. I always knew I would. You didn't, that's the only difference. And I know I didn't exactly bust a gut finding it. I expected it to find me. I'm not blaming you. Certainly never expected this, though. Look, I'm happy. I don't drink so much. Haven't given it up, thank God. I enjoy it now. I don't need it to bury things anymore. I know my mother would have been so proud, people keep telling me. You don't know how that feels.'

I looked at her face, she smiled at me. Of course she knew. 'Of course you do,' I said softly. Her whole demeanour melted to softness as she gently touched my arm.

'I am really pleased for you, Tom, honest to God, I am. I only ever wanted what was best for you. I just didn't ever know what that was.' Her eyes never fell from my face.

I was sober; there was definite warmth to her. Should I take the risk, tell her how I still felt?

How did I feel?

I was inches from what could well be my best, even my last, chance to convince Mairead that we should try again.

Worst case scenario, merely the usual rejection?

I'd been there often enough before. But not sober. Rejection could never really penetrate excessive alcohol, so it imposed only a rather small dent on one's ego. Go on, my son, go for it. Easy, Tom, easy. OK, Cathal, thanks for the input, but it's my life.

Bollocks! Go for it!

Words, thoughts, that's all. Go for it? You must be mad! If ever I was not prepared for rejection, that day in her kitchen was it. When, and if, I made another move on Mairead, it would be my final one. The other night I promised myself that.

One more move, all guns blazing and that would be it. I did, I'm sure I did, notice a slight, a very slight, wavering of her usual resistance. I think.

Chapter Eight

Someone in the movies, probably Woody Allen, once said, 'Love is a mere distraction from the fun things in life.' Well, the fun things in life for me once were supping ale and chasing women. Now, I was getting my kicks from taking on the DSS.

We all needed to sit down and really discuss the way forward. It was time to take stock. Richard was still on about us taking an oath. Yeah, later, Richard. The hard work was just beginning. From now on, we needed to be able to put the time and effort we invested in Colum into every single application. We couldn't rest on our laurels even though we had built up a level of expertise and had a good network of contacts.

I took a call from Cecil. He said he needed to meet with me. On the phone he told me the DSS were revamping the IEA form. Usual reason – baffle the claimant so much that they just give up. Completing the new form was, according to Cecil, going to be a much more time-consuming and laborious exercise. Despite his best efforts, Cecil was unable to get us a copy of the first draft. I found myself wondering why. He said he wanted to discuss something other than the new form.

I met Cecil downtown in a side-street bar.

'Why do you keep getting your hair cut so short?' I asked him, unable to ignore the severity of his recent trim.

He ignored me. 'Tom, you know I've been going on and on about this Enforcement Unit, the one Fortesque-Smith is trying to get up and running?'

I nodded.

'Well, last night at the Civil Service Table Tennis League, I was speaking to this guy from the Inland Revenue…'

'Table tennis, you play table tennis?' I interrupted.

'Aye, every Tuesday evening.'

'But last night was Wednesday.'

'Oh aye, we had to swap this week with them'n's from the Manic Depressive Society.'

'Manic Depressive Society! Jesus! What's the Civil Service coming to!' I laughed at the idea that the big club that was the Civil Service had now seemingly a club for damn near everything.

'Oh, you don't argue with that lot. It gets them down, you know.'

Yeah, I could see the reasoning behind that.

Cecil explained that a County Kerry-based recruitment agency, which had been brought in to set up the Unit, was having major problems in recruiting local people. I reminded him that he told us he thought the Unit was going to be manned by retired police and misbehaving constables who had once dozed away their careers in South Armagh. He said that was what was first envisaged.

'So, how come some guy from the Tax Office knew this and you didn't?' I asked.

'Oh, apparently they're offering some major tax concessions to get people to join. Rumour has it they'll be looking to bring people in from abroad. You see, people from here are refusing to even consider joining such an organisation.'

Many said it was immoral, unethical; indeed such action could well polarise communities.

And, of course, many more thought the pay was crap.

Things were moving on at a pace we didn't envisage; we had no real plans for that. I told Cecil to inform us of even the slightest rumour of any developments.

Make a video, make a video, that's all the ever-imaginative Cathal could offer as a first move when I told him what Cecil had said. We need an oath, we need an oath was all Richard could offer. Oh, so no need to worry about the Enforcement Unit, then?

Emmett was up for the video; maybe he thought it was his next career move. Cathal suggested we make a video in which we should try to instruct people on the correct bearing when suffering from a particular ailment.

A sort of lack-of-fitness video.

It would enable applicants to study poses and postures in the comfort and safety of their own homes. Initially, I was reluctant, but soon I could see the sense in it. So, next step: enthusiasm for it. I felt a degree of levity would help; we were becoming too damn serious about everything.

A real obstacle remained, so maybe the video would help. We were still up against it when the interviewing doctor put the applicant through his paces. We were only too well aware that many people needed to exaggerate their lack of wellbeing to secure the allowance.

We had no fitness instructors to advise us at the coalface; all our contacts were made on the phone and then we passed the advice on. If we were able to get something on film, we could streamline our approach and offer standard but sound advice. We also looked to provide a series of exercises to help the sufferer.

We bought a second-hand video recorder, not this time from Mr McGiver, but from a cousin of Assumpta's who used to take wedding videos until one day he accidentally caught on film the bride and the best man at the back of the chapel prior to the ceremony. In a bit of a clinch, so to speak. For health reasons, he decided that the dual role of being best man and videoing weddings didn't mix. The bridegroom had some right hook.

As God is my judge, I swear if I'd known how our 'training' video was going to turn out, I wouldn't have bothered. Cathal laughed all the way through filming. I know the locals did their best, but for Jesus sake…

I'm sure somebody put them up to it. Cecil? Or Father Rice, who, despite promising to attend, was conspicuous by his absence?

It was our intention to create an instructional film, but one with a bit of humour to keep the interest alive. We put the word out we wanted volunteers; people who would feel at ease in front of the camera, people who *wanted* to be in front of the camera. I soon understood how *Big Brother* featured so many prats. We booked the school hall one Friday night. We didn't get as many positive responses as I thought we might.

Mary Duggan, a seventy-three-year-old dinner lady; Jimmy, the local postman who bore a striking resemblance to nobody I had ever seen before; and then there was Alice and Bertie, a married couple from Dublin who were in the area for a spell. We met with them all a few days prior to the actual recording to discuss what we really wanted the video to say and what we wanted from them.

Simple enough. Aye, for Simon, maybe.

My two uncles got to the hall early and laid out a few mats and towels for the poses and exercises we had in mind. It was chilly that night, both in and out of the building.

Is it good or bad things that are supposed to come in threes? Let me tell you, bad things must also come in fours. Cathal and I were going through our notes in the hall when the door opened and in walked Mary, looking less than resplendent in her tiger-skin leotard, the lower part nicely rounded off with the help of purple bobby socks. She had her long, dyed-blonde hair tied up in a bun fit for a Big Mac. Jimmy was just behind, still in his Post Office uniform, which looked as if it could have done with an iron; in fact, Jimmy looked as if he would benefit from a bit of crease control himself too. He was about five foot four, thin as a whippet with a craggy face and little remaining of his once-full head of ginger hair. Over his shoulder rested his letter-free postal sack.

Also eager to make their entrance were Alice and Bertie, who were jostling with Jimmy. They both appeared to be sweating and, in their cowboy outfits, looked slightly more out of place than the other two. What we hadn't known was that the pair were up North to compete in some Line Dancing contest in a club off the Falls Road.

Bertie was bow-legged, boasted quite a beer gut and was quite tall, with a constant strained look on a face framed by flapping, flimsy black hair. Alice, well, apart from the auburn colour of her hair, Alice could have been Bertie's twin.

We discovered, much to their still-active displeasure, they had come only third in the contest. That explained their less-than-convivial approach to each other. Until you have seen two enraged cowpokes threatening each other, and following through with sly trip-ups, you haven't lived. Or have been to Line Dancing where, seemingly, the competition is fierce. Cathal was impressed by the dress mode; well, they were in there with that old Country and Western crap he liked. I looked at him when the two cowfolk nearly came to real blows.

It was like a student production of *Calamity Jane.*

'Never a sheriff about when you need one,' Cathal said, turning his head away before adding another smart-arse comment. 'They're your people, Dooley, not mine. You wouldn't get the likes of that in Birkenhead.'

Background music. What would we use?

We all knew what Cathal wanted, but I didn't think the musical antics of Conway Twitty or Kenny Rogers was quite what we were after. Same with Richard pushing some crap from *Oklahoma.* I decided on my favourite music. Andrea Bocelli.

I particularly liked *Con Te Partiro.* Roughly translated: *Time To Say Goodbye.* Which in time could be our anthem. When we explained my choice of music to Alice and Bertie, they asked us to play a bit first, which I did. They agreed, shaking their heads in unison. No, that wouldn't do, they said, explaining that they moved to the delights of the Oak Ridge Boys or Emmylou Harris. Anything else could result in Bertie's knees locking. They did, however, state they sometimes used more modern music when practising at home. I was hopeful of something I could work with. Alice took out a tape from her handbag.

Okay, I wasn't expecting Eminem…

I don't know whether you recall Brotherhood of Man, but when Alice and Bertie started to limber up to *Kisses for me, Save all your kisses for me,* I felt, as Private Frazer from Dad's Army used to say, that we were doomed.

Jimmy with his wrinkled face and uniform took a shine to Alice, which she found rather pleasing if her increasingly red face was any clue. She got what I assumed was her preferred reaction from Bertie. He responded by becoming jealous, tramping round the room throwing dark, menacing glances at the local postman. Someone draw first, for Christ's sake! I thought.

Richard looked in no way perturbed as he watched the antics, hardly flinching at all. He probably could *see* some of his "other world" contacts who, in this life, might well have been ballet dancers.

I swear Bertie would have taken Jimmy, GPO bag trailing from his shoulder or not.

I sensed Mary felt left out, but she did get on with her postures, which, after all, was the main reason why we got that bunch of eejits together in the first place. To her eternal credit, Mary kept going, even when the elastic on the top half of her leotard twanged.

In my mind's eye, I could see Mairead laughing her head off. Joined arm in arm with my mother. I should have stopped filming there and then.

We advised our *actors* to limber up a bit more. We didn't want them injuring themselves. Jesus! We had troubles enough without locking swords with the DSS over that crew. Jimmy quite jauntily made his way to the middle of the floor, followed closely behind by Alice, who giggled girlishly when catching his backward admiring glances. Bertie was doing stretching exercises and Mary decided a bit more lipstick was required. Bertie called Alice over and, surprisingly, she went willingly and stood beside her husband. They limbered up together and did look quite elegant, compared to the others, in a slow motion, doctor-is-there-any-hope-for-them sort of way?

The pair slithered rather than glided across the floor, their line-dancing experience serving them well. They then suddenly, but definitely grudgingly, grabbed hands; they would both have been arse-over-proverbial if they stuck to being stubborn, for they hit a slippery bit of the floor. Watching Bertie's overall movements, which I can only describe as flamboyant, I don't know whether he was trying to impress Jimmy or his knees had gone completely, with possibly his back accompanying them. I took a quick glance through some books I had already looked at a couple of weeks before. I was now fairly well versed in exercises for the lumbar region. This would enable applicants to be more supple, and therefore more pliable, when it came to maintaining accurate poses for long periods during the investigation by the DSS doctor.

We eventually got them on their hands and knees. Bertie took a while but eventually made it, accompanied by the sound of creaking knee joints after a thump in the solar plexus from his caring spouse. As Cathal was shaking his cowardly head, it was left to me to issue instructions. 'Now, keep breathing normally,' I said as I began to throw advice at them, little, if any of it, sticking. 'Right, knees – hip-distance apart – back slightly hollowed, let stomach relax and sag down,' I continued.

'Is this video really necessary?' asked Pat, who was standing in the corner, arms folded and looking a tad disinterested. With a yawn, he announced he was counting eejits. He got to four.

Ah, at last. A flaw in Pat's mathematical genius.

Five, Pat. Five eejits.

I included myself for agreeing to this in the first place.

'I think a video will really help, Pat,' I said, trying to appear optimistic in the face of traffic lights all showing pessimism. I waved our participants over. Out of the corner of my mouth, I tossed a question in Cathal's direction. 'Tell me again. Why are we doing this?'

His whispered reply slithered out. 'Because, Tom Dooley, we have yet to discover a sense of the ridiculous.'

Well, if that truly was the case, we had the Discovery Channel on at full volume. Their exhaustion, coupled with my now lack of mental strength, brought proceedings to a halt. Jimmy lay flat on his back, legs spread-eagled and inches away from Mary Duggan's heaving chest. I've known the banns read for less intimate acts. Alice, too, was lying stretched out, her head resting on her hand. She looked none too pleased at Jimmy's apparent desertion for she mouthed a few insults in his direction, most relating, with a weary unoriginality, to the married status of Jimmy's parents. She then grabbed Bertie's hand in a loving grip, that brought tears to his eyes and weakness to his knees, for he fell to the floor and knelt, panting into her ear. Sweet nothings, it wasn't.

In a club a few weeks later, we were sitting over a couple of pints when Cecil unexpectedly called in. Wearing his trademark duffel coat, hood pulled down, he walked through the bar, feeling his way, walking into a few tables and chairs.

'It's Cecil, Tom,' the barman called out a warning.

Cathal went up to the bar to get him a pint. Cecil was still a novice at this undercover lark.

'Come over here, big man, and take the weight off those big boots of yours,' I said.

Cathal placed a pint in front of him when Cecil took a seat, spreading his duffel coat around him.

'Well, Cecil, how's things in the world of the DSS?' I asked.

Cecil drank deeply. 'Oh, don't get me started. See, in the old days, you just got on with your job. Now, now there's fucking mission statements, focus groups, management meetings where nobody knows what's going on. Training courses telling you how to behave at training courses. It's up the left, Tom, up the fucking left.'

He gulped again from his pint. Cecil was plainly troubled. The world of conformity was closing in on him. I patted him on the shoulder. 'Stick with us, Cecil, and who knows?'

'Yer man is on to you, Tom.'

'WHAT!'

'Aye, Fortesque-Smith has been made aware of your advisory role within the community. Hey, don't be looking at me like that. He never heard a word from me. Believe it or not, we have a copy of your video. It was mailed in the other day. It's quare craic, that. One of the dancers is the spit of my Aunt Jean, God rest her. It's in a file now alongside that photo of the lot of you at the car showrooms. The Englishman is fair pleased with himself, so he is. Reckons he'll have you in a matter of weeks.'

'What does he mean "have me"?' I asked.

'Well, the thing is, Tom, I know you think you know what is going on in this country, but believe me, you don't. The DSS have far-reaching powers. They can put you out of the country. Why do you think a lot of the doctors who used to work for them are now in the Republic? He's also in the process of getting Miss Webster moved out to the back of beyond somewhere. Always swore he'd get her for blackmailing him over the Colum McGeough application. The Union got on to it, kicked up a stink. The Union guy has now been transferred to a small country office facing closure. There will be no redundancy payments there. I'm telling you, they're wild. You just don't speak out against them. We need to bring this bastard to his knees, so we do. Miss Webster has only less than a year to go before retirement; she doesn't want to move now. She's putting on a brave face, but she is frightened of change.'

We really had to get our thinking caps on. Despite our unfettered optimism, if we were to face reality, then we knew only too well we were no match for the cunning strength of the DSS. Undoubtedly, we could strike a few successful blows, Colum being the prime example, but sustained success was truly, truly out of our reach. If the DSS, and the Englishman in particular, put their minds to it, they could crush us.

'They're actually planning a raid, so they are. For real,' announced Cecil.

'A raid?'

'Aye, Tom. You've heard the rumours and what I've told you about the new Enforcement Unit envisaged for areas like this. Well, they're nearly there. It's still very hush-hush. As I mentioned, it's thought they're bringing in foreigners. The DSS are keen to get the Unit up and running.'

Cecil said he had no idea when the raid might be and said it would be difficult to forewarn us. Only Fortesque-Smith and Miss Webster would know in advance. There was, apparently, no chance that Miss Webster would tell Cecil about the raid. Misplaced loyalty again.

'They are genuinely scared of you, though, Tom,' said Cecil, delivering some better news. 'I mean, your mother was a shrewd wee woman and did her best. They know you're better. By the way, Cathal, the Englishman knows about you as well. Feels you're a traitor, you being English and all. I told him you were a Scouser; didn't seem to see the difference.'

'Bastard's from Sussex, bleeding Southerner; he wouldn't understand,' Cathal said, looking quite pleased that he was being named as well. I, too, felt a surge of pride.

Cathal must have noticed. 'Watch out, Tom. You know what they say about pride: it comes before a fall.'

'No, modernise it and it means twenty pints come before a fall. I don't drink that much now.'

I was worried, though. It was obvious the authorities didn't give a damn about places like this; I think that was well documented. Despite the addendum to the Good Friday Agreement containing financial provisions for the deprived, ghetto-style areas, governments could not be trusted. What was to stop them reneging? Nothing.

As we were witnessing, The North was thriving: money-sucking restaurants; nightclubs and bars were springing up everywhere. There was money around but we weren't getting it. But still I asked myself the same questions: were we being immoral in trying to obtain a State benefit, one which hard-working taxpayers contributed to? Were we being dishonest in the means by which we strove to get this allowance? Were we dole scroungers?

Yeah, probably.

But, hey, sometimes, just sometimes, morality turns a blind eye to the needy. Sometimes you're left with having to take things into your own hands. Sometimes that's all that's left. For the likes of us. Were we becoming the underclasses?

Not if I could help it. I'd seen its creation in London, read about it in Leeds, Manchester and Glasgow.

Once there had been mills in this area. Locals followed a well-worn path: born; school; factory; die. It was all mapped out back then, but at least there was a map. I can remember, as a child, the screeching, screaming, attention-demanding factory hooters methodically toying with the workforce. Commanding their presence in the morning, freeing them for an hour at lunchtime. And at the end of another day, releasing tired, disinterested people on to the streets.

Masses of human robots shuffling to and from work.

Then, Fridays.

Fridays were offered up as some solace. Fridays bringing pay day. Battalions of men striding down the streets into the pubs. Rent men, bakers, milkmen, coalmen, all forming snatch squads infiltrating the area, all looking for their cut of the pay packet. Women struggling to make ends meet. Street fighting, puking, family rows. Saturday, rest day leading on to Sunday. Then Monday, and the bastarding hooter again.

But could anyone honestly say we were better off today, in our present predicament?

There was more bad news from Cecil. 'There is no way the department are going to clear Samuel Devine's application. The Englishman is still seething at having been forced into allowing Colum's through.'

'There is not one flaw in that application. There is just no way they can turn it down,' I protested.

Cecil shook his head and exhaled loudly. 'Maybe not, but Fortesque-Smith's promotion is riding on this. Basically, if he can get areas like this to buckle, he'll be the government's blue-eyed boy. And if he does get promoted, then there will be no end to his powers. Many, if indeed not all, benefits will be in line for the chop. And not just here, Tom. Belfast is the test case for the rest of the UK. Believe me, boys, it's not just the Irish you're fighting for.'

'Hallion,' I said.

'English hallion,' shouted the now integrated Scouser.

This was a whole lot worse than any of us could have possibly imagined. It brought a new and worrying intensity to the need to be more circumspect about everything we did from now on.

We were really up against it and we were being threatened with a raid.

I recalled some of the older people at my mother's funeral talking about life in Belfast in the 1930s. Someone mentioned queuing for stale bread, holding on to a white bolster slip or pillowcase to get a shilling's worth. At Hughes' or Kennedy's bakery. Sometimes Kennedy would hand out fresh bread. I heard a woman laughing as she talked about getting eggs from Gracey's in York Street. Sixpence for a bowl of cracked eggs. Apparently, if they liked you, you might get upwards of fourteen eggs.

We were not, I repeat, *not*, returning to those days.

I felt pangs of doubt again gnawing at me. The responsibility that appeared to be solely on our shoulders, to secure a better way of life for people, to stop them slipping back into an era we had all thought was firmly embedded in the past, was one that I, at that moment, wished had other ownership.

I couldn't shift the feeling we were now out of our depth. Cathal and I agreed there would be nothing to gain from divulging this latest information, not even to Pat and Richard.

In a way, we felt responsible for this latest DSS hard-line approach. Had we not taken on the mantle of advisors, and had we not scored some success, then the future of existing benefits might not be under such a threat.

Casualties of our war against the DSS?

The Royal Oak, with all its trappings of failure, was becoming more and more enticing. It was all very well being a working-class hero, but what if the working classes were sacrificed in the process?

My thoughts were interrupted when two men in their late twenties came into the bar. They wore long, dirty-grey overcoats and each sported a red woolly hat. They glanced around noting our presence before taking a seat near the door.

Would you just look at them, I thought, the remnants of a past tyranny.

While successive Republican splinter groups had been formed and then whittled away, succeeding in bleeding the area of anything worthwhile, they departed, leaving only the likes of these two, who didn't have the gumption to move on. One of them, the short fat one with an over-long attachment to acne, shouted over to us, 'Up the 'RA!'

Original!

Up the 'RA. Hearing it did, however, bring a chill to my bones. A reminder of how it was. 'Fuck the 'RA! Up the IEA!' I shouted back. 'Fuck you bastards! You've had your time!'

I glanced over at them. The taller guy, a ruddy-faced misfit, whose sneer revealed a row of misshapen teeth, seemed less than happy with my comment and stood up. I noticed him making a fist with both his hands.

'Dooley, you see in our day, we wouldn't have put up with you, so we wouldn't. We'd have fucking had you.' He turned and grinned at his mate and then looked over at us. 'Anyhow, if it wasn't for the Republican Movement, half the wee shites round here wouldn't have been able to claim the IEA.' His mate laughed and himself arrogantly looked round the bar like a two-bit comedian doing his turn on "Losers Night" in a back-street boozer. He sat down again.

No way was I going to let this bastard away with it. I felt the anger – not just with him, but with the past – rising, but managed, somehow, to keep it under control. 'Aye, right enough, thanks, boys. The Movement did its best to cripple a brave few. But sure now we can break our *own* legs.'

Genuine laughter from the rest of the bar nailed the two boys to their insecurities.

It was a defining moment for me, and one I could have bathed in for ages. I looked at the two of them and that terrible night came back with its usual scarring vividness.

For the first time though, the very first time, I didn't dwell on it. I realised that it had for too long impeded my desire to live. To live normally. To live unshackled by the past. I felt I now deserved that freedom of mind. As I looked at those two, it helped immeasurably to realise that whatever I was, or whatever I might become, it was still a hell of a lot better than what those two had to offer.

I promised myself there and then I would no longer relive that night. Well, I couldn't be so sure of that, but I was sure of one thing: I would no longer allow it to torture me.

Those misfits had hurt Mairead. Not me. Oh aye, they came after me, but I tried to save her. I tried to make it up to her and in doing so I had destroyed what we had. I would never ever again take the blame. Not for that night.

I celebrated this beautiful relief, not by getting blathered, but by merely breathing life in deeply, looking up from my usual stance of seeing the bad in so much. Hallelujah! I was reborn! Oh aye, I soon dispensed with that new-found, albeit momentary, thought that perhaps alcohol should take a back seat in my sense of renewed freedom. As the evening wore on, I downed a brave few.

Cecil left, promising to keep us informed of any developments. We knew he was taking a risk coming here, putting his job in jeopardy. We also knew how disgruntled he was with the DSS and that that was his real reason for helping us.

Would we have sacrificed him?

If need be.

If we thought it would have benefited us to inform the DSS of his activities. If I had been asked that question a week ago, I would have said no. Now, though, things were much more serious. The very living structure of the area was under threat. When all was said and done, Cecil wasn't one of us; oh aye, he might well have been an active rebel within the establishment camp, but he still had the words "Civil Servant" on his CV.

With those thoughts in mind, I was glad we didn't see him for a while.

If there was going to be a raid, I decided it was too risky to have Siobhan staying over at the house with Cathal and me. Despite Mairead's occasional protestations, I still insisted she came to stay. Sometimes she also stayed a couple of nights with Richard and Pat, who was teaching her how to play chess, but it wasn't safe there either. In the surreal world we found ourselves in, and despite Cecil's claim of foreign recruitment, I couldn't be sure that the new Unit would not be staffed by people from the area who disagreed with what we were doing and would see this as an opportunity to put us out of business.

Imagine sharing the same aim as the DSS? And imagine it, a frigging County Kerry recruitment agency helping them. Southerners, hah!

The way we proceeded with our latest claim would be vital. We needed to do some damage to the DSS, if nothing else. To at least ensure we fired one last piece of heavy artillery in their direction. If we were about to be eradicated as an advisory service, then by Jesus, they were going to know they had been in a battle. It might be hard for most people to know what it was like living in an area like this. We never saw a policeman; the rule of normal society did not apply here. We were left to our own devices. Strangely, there was little, if any, crime and seldom did real violence occur. A recognition of how we were being treated seemed to have begun, over the past few months, to inject a new sort of pride in the area. I noticed a cleaner, prouder locality. Perhaps it was that old thing called *HOPE* again.

God! It worried me though.

One evening as we sat in the office finishing off a Chinese, me and the Scouser decided some old haunts needed revisiting. Old mental haunts, that is. So we went out and got blootered. We took ourselves off to a club in town and sampled some of the agreeable atmosphere and pricey booze while attempting to charm some members of the opposite sex. We chatted most of the night with a couple of nurses from the City Hospital. I don't know why, but we always seemed to be surrounded by nurses.

They complained about the lack of suitable males in their lives and moaned, in a good-natured way, about their chosen careers. I told them how lucky they were not to have to drink with Wee Hughie from Govan.

They were off to Spain the next day. I don't know whether it was the drink talking or what, but they invited us. And again, I don't know whether it was the drink replying, but we said yes.

So, we were off to Spain in the morning. No tickets, nowhere to stay, not sure where our passports were. We were ready. It was comforting, in a way, to be back in the land of the carefree, where only the consumption of large amounts of alcohol takes you.

Next morning, we were indeed at the airport, but we were heading, not for Spain, but for London. Through the night, Cathal and I had talked about our present predicament. He, too, felt a great burden of responsibility. It all seemed to be coming in on us: the raid; the Englishman's determination; the hassle I was getting from Mairead about Siobhan staying with us. It all pointed in one direction. For the umpteenth time, I reiterated that I didn't once again want to be classed as a failure; he said it wasn't that that bothered him so much, it was the potential end of a dream. Yet in the past, he had said it didn't bother him; we had given it a go. It obviously did bother him.

It was a dream, he said, a dream that he had hoped for all his life.

Look, we hadn't signed any contracts. We could leave when we wanted. We didn't owe anything to anyone.

Yeah, maybe we were running away.

So…

With a glass in his hand and a surprising weariness to his voice, Cathal spoke in depth about his past. He told me how much he hated studying medicine, but felt that it was something his family really wanted him to do; they were going to be so proud of him. Lucky he wasn't Irish; he could have ended up a priest.

He said he always felt that one day he would find a sort of peace in helping people. He thanked me for giving him the opportunity to do something worthwhile. I said we couldn't have done it without him or his money. He said we couldn't have done it without me; without my drive, my enthusiasm, my desire to help. My vision.

I said that if he was still single by the time he had reached sixty-four, I'd marry him. I felt obliged to, seeing as how he was uttering such sweet nothings!

Like me, and we had talked about this many times, mainly when drunk, he, too, had been searching for something, anything to give a true meaning to his life. We both kept the search well hidden, though. It all sounded rather simplistic, but then life can be. It's really only us who complicate it. As we sat in the airport lounge, Cathal said he had a feeling he would remain in London. No, he said, he wouldn't go back to Liverpool.

So, what was there here for me?

I was genuinely frightened. The thought that I might once again become that angry, frustrated man surfaced again. And I didn't want Siobhan to be dragged into that way of life again. If we weren't actively and positively engaged in the IEA work, then what could I do for the people here, what was the point? Ah, bollocks to it all!

I was becoming so tired of all the indecision. Mine, in particular. One day I was up for it; all was well. The next day… I just wish we would make up our minds and stick with it.

'Do you think we've bitten off more than we can chew?' Cathal asked, draining his pint and downing half a packet of dry roasted.

'I think you shouldn't talk in clichés.'

'No sooner said than done.'

'A bird in the hand…'

'Frees up the other hand to hold your pint…'

'Now you're talking.'

'Sixteen to the dozen.'

We decided that a few days in London would serve us better than going to Spain. I wanted to make sure we didn't spend the next day, well, not the entire day, pissing it up against the wall in our favourite boozer in Camden. And as it turned out, it was a needless concern.

The Royal Oak in Camden High Street was no longer. The windows were boarded up, the echoes of our past buried somewhere in the rubble that lay outside the pub.

Jesus! Where was Wee Hughie?

There wasn't a pub in sight in which the wee Govan man would have felt comfortable. They were all new, all the same, all geared to the needs of the young. These bars had no place for Ronnie Corbett lookalikes.

For Cathal and me, it was somewhat disconcerting to discover that one's bolthole was no longer. We had a few pints in a couple of bars that we had purposefully avoided in the past. I yearned for a past in which I felt safe and where nothing was asked of me. At that moment, I certainly didn't yearn for Belfast, but I was lost here too. Faced with the realisation that a return to Belfast was really not on the cards, I was left once again in no-man's land. I cheered myself up slightly by thinking if I did stay in London, I could always pop over and see Siobhan whenever I wanted.

My eyes strayed over in Cathal's direction and I thought, Jesus! Don't let me end up with him in some grotty flat moaning about the cost of baked beans and arguing about whose turn it is to go to the chiropodist. Oh Jesus! Even worse, discussing the merits of *Grecian 2000*.

Where do you go to when the signposts are no longer clearly marked?

The next evening, I spoke on the phone to Richard and he told me that Sammy Devine was really despondent that we were not around. Said he really needed us to help with his latest attempt to secure the allowance.

Sammy had been on Prozac for years; his nerves were shot. He lived a hand-to-mouth existence. Time meant nothing to Sammy; life even less. Sammy deserved better, Richard kept saying to me.

Sammy had lost his two children; one, a girl, aged four; the other, his son, aged six. Car bomb in the centre of Belfast. His wife left him; he drank, you see. The doctor told him he drank too much.

Too much for what? was apparently Sammy's response.

I chatted to Cathal about Sammy Devine. God forgive me, but my initial thought was to let Sammy get on with it himself. But eventually, with Cathal's more sympathetic stance, I began to think in a more charitable way. Should we at least try and help him, have one last go?

I finally allowed myself to realise that Sammy was one of those people who make you detest yourself for moaning about life's little inconveniences. He seldom, if ever, complained about the cards life had dealt him.

I can't recall exactly who made the decision to catch a flight back to Belfast, but after a few days imbibing in London, we were back. I think it might have had something to do with Cathal's love of Paris buns. I reckoned it was more to do with the lovely vegan woman, but I didn't mention it.

Once again, I didn't know whether we were doing the right thing or not. I rang Siobhan, she was out playing. Mairead thought we would have stayed in London once we had returned.

Christ! Does that frigging woman have no faith in me at all?

Next day, we opened up the office and Sammy came to see us. Understandably, Sammy suffered from long-term depression, yet he was entitled to nothing over and above the State benefits of mere existence. Samuel couldn't work. Christ! He had trouble getting out of bed in the morning! And he drank! Samuel's neck problems were getting worse. He was now permanently hunched over. His black hair, slightly greying at the sides, was, however, always neatly trimmed. Today, he wore black tracksuit bottoms and a bomber jacket. His eyesight was poor, but he seldom wore glasses, preferring to squint instead. He always fiddled with a pair of rosary beads in his pocket.

Blind faith?

We had recently noticed that more and more people were coming to us for all sorts of reasons unrelated to the IEA. They asked us to sort out rent problems; talk to any local kids who were causing any bother; intervene in any neighbour disputes. We drew the line, however, at organising coach trips to Daniel O'Donnell concerts, maintaining that without certain principles, you really are nobody.

Our return seemed to be a catalyst for the people. They started picking up leaflets from places like Age Concern, solicitors' offices, doctors' surgeries and indeed from the DSS itself, and dropping them off with us. That was what we needed – a co-operative of effort.

We went through Sammy's application with a fine toothcomb. It was fine, he was ready. Later in the day, I tried to get Cecil on his mobile phone. Voicemail.

At about five o'clock, when we were packing up, Cecil appeared at our office. He was out of uniform. No duffel coat.

Cecil had been suspended!

Assumpta made him a cup of tea with three stress-busting sugars.

'Afraid so, Tom. Some bastard's been tailing me, tailing you. The allegation is that my relationship with you is not entirely appropriate. That's all they said. But you know what really got to me – it was Miss Webster who told me I was suspended.'

That was a blow, no mistake.

Through Cecil, we were able to keep at least one step ahead of the game. Leaked memos were a godsend for us. And Jesus! This was not a good time for us; we had Sammy's application up for consideration.

I could see Cecil was distressed. 'But sure you were pissed off with the place anyhow, weren't you?' I said.

'Aye, I was. But I've done ten years there, so I'm entitled to an extra four days leave in a month's time, also a pay increase for having done the ten years. And you get one of those big blue desk diaries rather than the wee one I have now.'

Spoken like a true Civil Servant, which he wasn't. Another of the establishment's tentacles had begun to suck him in, platform shoes or not, rebellious tendencies or not. It was not a pleasant sight. I truly hoped, for his sanity, that he got the boot before it was too late. But for our sake, we needed him back in there.

Sammy's application had, of course, focused on his neck problems, which were causing him frequent painful spasms, and, on occasion, numbness in his upper back and shoulders. Sammy suggested we make another video; Pat and Richard nodded in agreement, saying it should perhaps be an even more light-hearted one than the last, but with a stronger message. What was it with this lot and videos? I thought.

I think it fair to say that most people watched the other one after a night out. Good for a laugh. I didn't think we were breaking any Equity rules when we decided not to use the previous crew again. Myself and Cathal were to be the *stars*.

We called it "Limp Along with Tom and Friends".

The opening bit appealed to me, with Cathal looking all serious and staring intently into the camera. 'Remember, the IEA is not just for Christmas, it's for life.' Then, totally unscripted, he added: 'This video may contain scenes upsetting to DSS staff.'

Sammy was relying too heavily on the video; he would watch it three or four times a day. On the eve of his meeting with the investigating doctor, the rewind button on our video was on fire.

'Calm down, Sammy,' I said. 'You can sometimes fill your mind with too much information. Just remember to keep your head leaning to the left a little and all will be well.'

He was unconvinced. 'Here, Richard, you can see into the future. Do I get the allowance?'

As ever, Richard played his calming role and managed not to look superior. 'Samuel, I'm a spiritualist, not a psychic.'

Sammy was not deterred. 'Well, then, do you know anyone dead who knows the outcome?'

Richard didn't even bother replying, merely raised his eyes to the heavens with a superior look.

There was a knock at the door. It was Father Rice, dressed in his working clothes. He was a site labourer. The priest was well over six feet tall, wore a baseball hat that struggled to contain his unruly, wiry ginger hair. The fingers of his left hand were heavily stained with nicotine. He wiped his boots on the mat before coming in.

'Morning, all,' he said with a smile creasing his whole face.

'Morning, Father,' we replied almost in unison.

He rested his hod against the door. Father Rice was, thank God, a maverick. Very few priests managed to go the distance in this part of Belfast. Now that the Catholic Church had sold off the chapel to developers, they had no further interest in maintaining a presence. Therefore, no money got through. Hence, the good priest had to work on building sites. Diversity being the name of the Roman Catholic priest game.

For someone like me, it was rather strange to see a priest carrying a hod. From my school days, I was more used to them carrying a rod and the threat of violence. The priest had something to look forward to, though.

It wasn't all doom and gloom for him. In two weeks' time he was off to London to appear on the show *A Question of Doctrine?* hosted by one Lily Savage. Don't you just love the impudence of the average TV producer!

'Let's all kneel,' the priest said, joining his hands together. 'All except you, Samuel, of course. I'm just going to say a wee prayer. No harm in asking for a bit of help. Dear Lord, we ask you to look kindly on Samuel Devine's application for the IEA. Samuel is a good man and deserves a break. He's not a greedy man, Lord. Samuel would welcome the low rate, but would obviously be eternally grateful for a wee car and the top rate.'

'Amen,' said Sammy, getting in before the priest. Now that Sammy had Father Rice's blessing, how could he fail? Before the priest left to mix cement, he apologised for his absence the night of the meeting in the school hall. He explained he had been one of the judges at the Falls Road Line Dancing contest. Told me he had been really reluctant to put Bertie and Alice in third place, but was left with little option, such was their performance. As only three couples had taken part, it was impossible to put them fourth. The priest thought his presence at the meeting might inflame Bertie's knee joints and Alice's temper.

Next day in the office, I took a call from someone calling himself Big Frankie. When I told Richard, he became a tad annoyed, to say the least. 'What the hell did he want? You don't want to be mixing with the likes of him, I'm telling you.'

'He was just enquiring about our service.'

'You have no idea who Big Frankie is, do you?' Richard asked.

I shook my head. 'No, should I?'

'Well, you would if you lived round here.'

Big Frankie was a Loyalist from a nearby area and was not exactly liked round about these parts. It wasn't that he had been involved in violence or anything like that. Or that he had a sectarian hatred of Catholics.

Oh no, nothing as traditional or normal as that.

A while back, for a year or so, Frankie, although not actually a tailor by trade, ran a draper's shop just off the Shankill. A local wedding party from our area had been let down at the last moment and were in desperate need of suits etc for the big day. They really had no alternative but to use Frankie's services. He promised good quality clothing at a reasonable price. No problem, he'd said.

Frankie was late delivering; that pissed the people off for a start. No time for adjustments. Richard said it was fair to say that no wedding photo should ever contain snaps of adults wearing shin-length trousers, held up, if you looked closely, by cord braces. No bride should stagger up the aisle in what appeared to have been hastily cleaned butchers' aprons – ill-fitting ones at that. A bride should remember her wedding day for more than that, and black was not the new white in wedding circles. As Richard did concede, there perhaps was some artistic merit in the photograph; it would be hard to imagine being able to find another wedding group photo where the entire cast were bawling their eyes out. Not one tailor-made anyhow.

Frankie wanted to meet me.

'If you meet up with Frankie, they'll lynch you round here,' advised my uncle. 'He has bodyguards, you know. We call them "The Draper Twins".'

Richard thought Frankie could well be trying to muscle in on our efforts with the IEA. He stressed that many Protestant areas were also feeling the chill of desertion.

I arranged for Cathal and me to meet Frankie the following Friday. Little did we know at that stage that I would be having high-level meetings the week after.

With the enemy.

Chapter Nine

I was that excited. My hands shook, yet not a drop had touched my lips. I hadn't felt such a buzz since all those years ago when I was in Stranraer waiting for Mairead to join me. Ah, shouldn't look back.

My mind was running away with itself. The potential here for all things as yet unrealised in my country was there for the taking. If the two communities could unite in this common cause, I was convinced the DSS wouldn't stand a chance against us.

And hey, I could see it all. The fame, the fortune, and possibly the greatest accolade of all, they might just consider removing a Pope, or even Martin O'Neill, and putting me up there. Modesty would, of course, prevent me from having too smug a look on my face.

And then, Mrs Mairead... Theresa... Dooley, where will you be then, eh? Not with the working-class super hero. And you about to divorce him.

So, be honest, which would look better on her CV?

a) shacked up with an English dentist bloke who had a charisma bypass; or

b) rekindling relationship with unbelievably talented and handsome working class hero, still available for negotiation on marital status.

Hurry while offer lasts.

I had difficulty sleeping that night; Cathal taking part in a snore-a-thon in the other room didn't help. God! Who would have thought it! Me and the Scouser going down in Irish history? We were going to be at the kick-off, when the bell went, crashing headlong into controversy. The Belfast boy and the Scouser, no-hopers, full of hope. We'll write a book about it; it will be made into a film. We could take our pick of TV shows, producers would be queuing up. We would, of course, avoid the lower end of the market: the likes of *Pop Idol*; anything to do with gardening; anything in the vicinity of a continent near Dale Winton; and as for anything to do with Soaps...

In the morning, I vented my enthusiasm on Cathal. He made one comment, almost choking on his cornflakes. 'Stay the hell away from Max Clifford.'

It was worrying to know that he would consider participating in a gardening programme. But only one with Alan Titchmarsh in it. He did suggest my uncle Pat becoming our agent. He would get us double the money.

A film? Who would play me? We'd have to include a Cecil-type character. Least we could do. No film worth its salt could possibly attain box-office success by excluding a gigantic, low-ranking Civil Servant taking on the persona of Noddy Holder and banging out *Merry Christmas, Everybody.*

It would be up there with Wee Hughie's *Jumping Jack Flash*. We would get Ronnie Corbett to play Wee Hughie,

I was so tempted to lift the phone and tell Mairead, tell her the good times were at last beginning to roll, but Cathal stuck a precautionary foot into my plan.

'Wait until everything is settled,' he said between mouthfuls of toast. 'You've been made to look an arse on so many occasions before. Success of this magnitude will be new to you, so you must get it right.'

As usual, he was right.

I heard the morning post hit the mat. A single white envelope with my name scrawled on it with a red biro. I quickly opened the door to catch a glimpse of a man pedalling away on a bicycle. It wasn't Postman Pat. I looked at the envelope. Red biro, Civil Service issue, Big Cecil?

I often wondered why Fortesque-Smith, a fairly high-ranking Civil Servant, should take such a keen interest in IEA claims. Even when you took into consideration his promotional aspirations. The leaked memo I now had in my hand explained a few things.

It showed quite clearly what was being recommended and, seemingly, seriously considered for areas such as ours. A type of benefit genocide. No other way to describe it. According to the memo, it was to be staggered and staged. Some Whitehall mandarin had advised a government minister that the burden placed on the taxpayer by such areas as ours was just too great and was ever increasing. So much for the Good Friday Agreement! The recommendation that families basically look after each other and that benefit payment should be scaled down, before being withdrawn, had been discussed at some steering-committee meeting.

Jesus! Things were hotting up.

Families looking after each other? As most of the families were in the same boat and had little in the way of money or prospects, I couldn't see many people holding out a paddle and hauling their neighbours aboard.

Let's face it, the emergence of malnutrition and associated ailments, even the demise of people from certain areas of Belfast, wouldn't keep many awake at night. Then, leading on to Chapeltown in Leeds; Moss Side in Manchester; Hackney in London. Would hardly prick the nation's consciousness, would it? I mean, can you see people taking to the streets in protest?

Yeah, right!

A worrying aspect was the recent closure of our Medical Centre. A mysterious fire had completely gutted it. The authorities refused to even consider rebuilding, citing insurance problems. The last remaining dentist suddenly upped and went. To another part of town, a much more affluent one. Rumour had it he was offered a rent-free surgery. The powers that be were becoming sinisterly more powerful. Our supermarket closed last month, couldn't get delivery lorries to come into the area. Whatever we needed, we now had to leave the area to get it. There was a creeping erosion of normal everyday life.

Jesus! What was all this leading to?

'It's looking pretty grim,' said Cathal. 'I mean, we've always known we'd be no match for the power of government, but I didn't ever think it would get this bad.'

He was right. What had effectively been a game for us, elevated at times by a sense of duty and mischief, was now something altogether different.

'Do you think if we could get a meeting with this Fortesque-Smith bloke that it might help?' I asked Cathal.

'No,' he replied.

'No? That's it? You're not even going to consider the possibility?'

'No.'

'But what if we all sit round a table and try to hammer out some compromise, eh? After all, we are in the right, these people are entitled to what they are claiming.' And as I said those words and looked at Cathal who just stared at me, I realised how naive I could be sometimes.

Since when did right ever win over power?

We were up against the might of a government department, seemingly with the full support of its Government, hell bent on making us the displaced. Aye, and not a squawk from the Southerners. We were to be sacrificed. And this DSS Enforcement Unit apparently up and running. Aye, running towards us.

However, logic raised a hand, asking for a moment's consideration. Cecil had so consistently warned us about a proposed raid that in the end we started to become immune to its possibility and, with only just a little reticence, thought it a load of bullshit. All that crap about uniforms and so on.

But then, another anonymous bulletin arrived...

A large organisation, as Cecil had mentioned, had recently discarded a set of relatively new uniforms and this new Unit had reluctantly accepted them. On an interim basis only. Sounds fanciful? Remember, this was Belfast.

The day we were due to meet Big Frankie arrived and I have to confess, my feelings of euphoria — that we were going to conquer the universe — were fast receding. If indeed Frankie wanted our help, or some inside information on the IEA, then I really wasn't sure I could help, or indeed wanted to. However, by the tone of his voice, when Big Frankie called, you came. Unless, of course, he was after your inside-leg measurement.

It was a pleasant enough day when Cathal and I, accompanied by squealing kids, barking dogs and a longing for the Royal Oak, made our way to a neutral bar on the Glenpark Road. The desire to bring the DSS to their knees, or at least to their senses, was still as strong as ever, but the reality of the situation was an awesome opponent. Myself and the big Scouser, we had little experience of reality. For years, purposely shying away from it had been our career path. Despite Richard's warning that we would be lynched, we received only a few dirty looks along the way. Had the wedding party still been living in the area, I suppose things may well have been different.

We were, however, now out there, the bell had gone, and the final whistle was a long way off.

The pub where we were to meet, The Glenpark Bar and Grill, was still predominantly a Protestant domain, although some Catholics did frequent it. We were told Big Frankie was big.

Dictionary: Big – of considerable size, amount, intensity etc.

No reference whatsoever to – Jesus! Would you look at the size of him!

Frankie was in his early forties and was standing at the bar when Cathal and I opened the creaking, paint-peeling door of the Glenpark. Stale beer fumes, a heady welcome. Somebody in the corner was smoking a pipe. We stood still for a moment, our eyes getting accustomed to the unfamiliar surroundings. Despite my warning, Cathal had insisted on being considered less than the full shilling and wore his Tranmere Rovers lapel badge.

Frankie almost filled the whole bar area. We glanced round as the occupants, sitting in groups of two or three, slowly became aware of our presence and shifted about in their seats, mean-looking eyes narrowing even further. The odd nod, not exactly brimming with *bonhomie,* was, however, chucked in our direction. We moved a few paces forward. I noticed the bright red carpet fell short of its target and covered only half the floor, revealing wooden tiles.

Frankie wore faded blue jeans that hung on his hips round about his lower back. Complementing this made-to-measure denim was a slightly scratched, tan leather jacket and a pair of Reeboks. Frankie's dyed blond hair reached his collar. The bar was devoid of any tribal sectarian symbols, the only genuflection to football rivalries were a couple of Man U posters featuring the Madrid sub, Beckham, still in his red jersey, and a photo of Michael Owen in full flight. Amazingly, there were also a couple of yellowing photos of Ian St John, Tommy Lawrence and Roger Hunt – Liverpool legends of another era. None of Bestie. Morons!

I could hear Cathal's increasingly heavy breathing. It was drowning out my own thumping heartbeat.

Standing either side of the big man, facing us, were two guys. Two half-full pints in their hands. One was fat, barrel-chested, with straggly hair and wore a neat, dark blue suit. Obviously tailor-made, against Frankie-made. He twiddled with a ring on his left hand. The other, less formal one was tall and thin, had closely cropped black hair, and wore black jeans topped with a red shirt marked by white sweat stains under the arms. An ample belly asked a lot of the elasticity of his trousers. He tried to look hard, but twinkling blue eyes let him down. We could but assume a drum roll would have announced we were now in the presence of The Draper Twins.

The big man turned round. 'Tom,' he called out with a voice as big as his frame, but reassuringly warm, a big grin filling his handsome but slightly pockmarked face. I suddenly felt nervous, though.

'Frankie,' I said. 'How are you?'

We moved forward to greet the open hand he was offering us. I hoped my hands weren't sweating too much. Hey, things had changed in Belfast; most people were weary of past antagonisms but…

My eyes glanced over to the corner of the bar; two old men were playing draughts and drinking bottles of light ale. Very English, I thought. Frankie shook my hand warmly and nodded at Cathal who was behaving like a two-year-old; he was standing behind me, grabbing on to the back of my jacket for all he was worth. I half-expected him to tell me he had wet himself.

The jukebox coughed into life, one of Frankie Valli and The Four Seasons' old hits puncturing the air. Frankie began to mouth a few words of *My Eyes Adored You* and rolled his head as if his shoulders were sore. He was a little in tune with something, but it definitely wasn't his vinyl namesake.

He then pointed to the corner of the bar, where the table by the window was empty apart from a couple of dead pint pots. 'Come on, lads, let's sit down.' For such a big man, he moved easily. He sighed loudly when he saw a bit of cigarette ash on the carpet and bent down and brushed it up with his hands. He returned to the bar and disposed of the residue in an ashtray. He asked us what we wanted to drink and shouted our order to the barman. The four of us followed him. The Twins were rather close for comfort. Cathal's peeved look revealing a degree of discomfort. When we sat down, The Draper Twins closed in on Cathal. The barman soon brought us over a tray of pints.

'What's with all this?' Cathal asked, nudging the two lads with his elbows.

'They don't trust you, son,' said Frankie with a sudden seriousness.

'Why?' asked Cathal. 'Oh Jesus! It's not this old stereotypical crap, is it? I thought that applied only to Dooley's lot. You Irish and your much-documented problems with the English, eh? Whether you lot like it or not, I'm an Englishman, a Scouser, yes, but when push comes to shove…'

And indeed push was coming to shove as Cathal and The Twins tussled for seating supremacy, faces blushing with the exertion. Not a word was spoken. Don't you just love the intensity of silent warfare?

'Take it easy, Cathal,' I said, not used to, and definitely surprised by, this display of patriotism.

Frankie drank deeply from his pint. 'Oh, it's not because you're English, son. We've moved on here, haven't we, Tom?'

I nodded.

'It's more serious than that, lad. It's that frigging badge. You don't support Tranmere Rovers, do you? Is your head all right?'

Cathal looked at me; I tried to keep a straight face. Frankie must have done this before, for he looked all innocent, but suddenly burst out laughing, as did I. Then, slowly, Cathal was drawn in. The Draper Twins, however, remained steadfast.

'Tranmere?' said the fat one. 'You support Tranmere, that bunch of no-hopers! When you've got Liverpool and Everton! Michael Owen, the wee boy, Rooney! Christ! Even that carthorse Heskey! Tranmere? I thought you were wearing that badge for a gag. All you lot ever had was John Aldridge; and he was finished by the time he got to you.'

'Finished, was he?' spluttered Cathal. 'Let me tell you, Belfast boy. In his first season he equalled the club scoring record by hitting forty goals. Forty goals!'

I nudged Cathal. 'Jesus! Let's not get into the finer points of John Aldridge's play.'

The Scouser was incensed. 'He was Irish, wasn't he? Didn't he play in the World Cup in America? Remember him swearing all over the place trying to get on to the field?' Cathal's face was flushed.

'He wasn't the right type of Irish, Cathal,' I said.

'Well, he could manage your frigging country. He got Tranmere to a Worthington Cup final. At Wembley too; before things went all Welsh. Look what McIlroy did for you!'

'Ah,' said Frankie, looking at me and The Twins. 'Now, Sammy Mac was the right kind of Irishman.'

'Jesus!' said Cathal, raising his eyes to the heavens. 'You people!'

'Last of the Busby Babes, Sammy was,' I said. 'You keep your English thoughts to yourself, Cathal.'

'But you lot never scored a frigging goal under him...'

'Last of the Busby Babes,' said Frankie. 'Enough said.'

The sunlight tore through the grubby windows spotlighting Frankie. 'Like being on stage,' he laughed, blinking in the presence of the rays. Old barrel-chest played with a couple of bar mats, the other twin chewed frantically on gum.

'You two can piss off now. Leave me and Tom and the Englishman,' said Frankie. The Draper Twins reacted with surprise. 'Go on, now, go get yourself some sweets. No sherbets, they'll rot your teeth.' As they reluctantly stood up, Frankie opened his wallet and offered them a fiver. The fat one took it and walked to the door.

'See those two?' said Frankie, cracking his fingers. 'Harmless enough, like, but miserable as sin. They're our Kathy's two lads. I give them a bit of work when I can, keeps them out of mischief, for they'd be in it full time if you didn't keep an eye on them.'

I wanted to ask Frankie what line of work he was in at the moment, but thought better of it. I wanted to ask him what he wanted with us; I also wanted to ask him about a new suit for Cathal, but thought better of that too.

Frankie told us he had also been out of the country for many years. He ended up in Iceland, of all places, driving a bus at Keflavik airport. Had met an Icelandic student in a bar in Belfast, had married her, and laughingly told us he had fulfilled a lifelong ambition to be an Icelandic bus driver, before the fish diet and his lazy wife made him long for his native city. A few years as a sheep farmer in Wales exhausted his desire to remain free from the shackles Belfast imposed. I wondered was it in Wales that he picked up his less-than-tailor-made skills.

We chatted in general. Frankie kept getting the pints in, wouldn't let us pay for a thing. I was beginning to like the bloke, not just for his generosity, I felt that he, too, had his reasons for leaving Belfast, and they weren't all of a Nordic flavour, and now that he was back, uneasiness was a constant companion.

I was still wondering and worrying about when he was going to get to the nitty-gritty.

'Good drop of beer in here, eh?' he said. 'You should come here more often.'

'We will,' I said. 'The thing is, Frankie, you didn't ask us up here to sample the beer, nice and all that it is.'

He laughed. 'No, no, of course not.'

The Draper Twins returned and took their place again at the bar. Naughty fat one, he was sucking sherbet through a liquorice pipe. Their stare again focussed on us. Cathal was on his feet. Uncharacteristically brave, I thought. The Twins tensed, making fists as I grabbed Cathal.

'Take it easy, ignore them,' I advised.

'Hey, you two,' Cathal shouted, immediately dispensing with my advice. The bar went quiet; a pin dropping would have burst your eardrums. 'Were you born dickheads or did you work at it, eh? For let me tell you, if it was the latter, well done.'

'Cathal, for Jesus sake!' my voice barely squeezed the words out.

He appeared to be on a roll. 'Eh, well, lads, I'll take the answer from either of you.'

The two men stood open-mouthed at the bar, seemingly in a quandary as to whether etiquette required a verbal response before they beat the hell out of the quizmaster. They looked at each for guidance.

Frankie jumped in, 'Calm down everyone, for Jesus sake! Sit down, Cathal. You two at the bar, turn round, you're getting on my nerves as well.'

Cathal sat down, never taking his eyes of The Draper Twins.

'You're some boy, Scouser, I'll give you that,' Frankie laughed, then he placed his glass on the table. The sun had gone in and the inadequate pub lighting struggled with the sudden dimness.

Frankie rubbed his face with his hand. 'Look, Tom, I am aware of what you are attempting to do in your community and, basically, I want the same for the people here. Get them a bit of what they deserve. I'm only too aware of the money that places like Londonderry and South Armagh are getting. It's frigging flooding the place. But I've heard your neck of the woods is like ours, not a lot is getting through. I could do with your advice, your help. I want to set up something in my community similar to what I've been hearing you're doing.'

What had he been hearing and from whom, that was the question running through my mind.

I should've only brushed my teeth with a little enthusiasm that morning; then maybe my tongue wouldn't have felt the need to run off at the mouth. 'I was hoping you were going to say this, Frankie. I was saying to Cathal here, you know, Jesus! If we took on the DSS together, the two communities, like, Christ! They wouldn't stand a chance. I've always felt that if only our people could unite over a common cause. You know, like the night... Oh Jesus! When was it? Oh aye, the night before Bobby Sands died, do you recall, the people from both sides protesting? Eh, do you remember?'

'Aye,' Frankie said languidly. 'It was about housing, wasn't it?'

'Yes, yes, it was. If we can get our two communities...'

Frankie held up his hand and stopped me. His eyes narrowed, then widened in what appeared to be in amazement. 'Hang on a wee minute, Tom. You're getting a bit ahead of yourself. I want your help to, eh, kick-start my community's onslaught on what we are entitled to. I don't think I even mentioned, even hinted at, all of us being one big happy family, like,' he added crushingly.

Frankie stared at me, awaiting a response. I hadn't one. I felt deflated. My air of optimism leaking like an overfilled balloon. 'Do you not think we could unite?' I asked a little hopelessly.

Frankie shook his head. 'For God's sake, man! I'm trying to get this community a fair deal, that's all. Where have you been? Yeah, maybe we would all stand a better chance if the two communities joined forces, but I'm not prepared to risk losing out just to satisfy you and what is probably a fanciful desire to make a difference. Make a difference, Jesus! Some chance! Better to have tried and failed miserably.'

'Well, is that it, then?' said Cathal.

'Is it, Frankie?' I said, suddenly feeling angry, slightly duped, but aware that at no time did Frankie or anyone else even hint at such a stance.

Frankie got up. 'I'm off to the bog. Tom, I want your help, I need it, I'll admit that. I can assure you, however, that you might well need my help more than you think. Let me just say one thing: the future of your endeavours is not as secure as you might like to think.'

From his inside pocket he withdrew a brown envelope and handed it to me.

I watched the big man walk away. Strangely, a number of people looked over at us with definite grins on their faces. Whatever was going on here, I didn't like it. I didn't like it one bit. There was a sudden chill in the air, the grey clouds just about visible through the murky windows adding their unfriendliness to proceedings.

'Let's get out of here,' I said, rising from my seat.

Cathal grabbed my arm. 'Sit down. Look, we came here to listen to what he has to say. Don't just abandon what you had hoped for. Just take it a step at a time. Have a look in the envelope.'

'It's well seen you know nothing about this country. Can't you hear alarm bells? We're in a Protestant pub, surrounded by Protestants, and that Frankie bastard has made it clear he wants nothing to do with us. He's using us. I'm telling you we're off back to London tomorrow.'

'Just open the envelope; we've nothing to lose by doing that.'

I slowly tore it open. Inside were forms, DSS forms; the pink IEA580, sections 1 and 2, and accompanying guidance notes.

'These are the frigging new DSS forms. How the hell did he get hold of them? We couldn't.' Cathal was in first with the questions.

Frankie returned with a big grin on his face. 'Let's get you boys a drink. I think you need it,' he said, raising three fingers to the barman ordering more pacifying alcohol.

'How?' I asked.

'Who?' Cathal asked.

'Who, how?' said Frankie. 'You sound like that frigging Fred Dineage.'

I stared at Frankie. I wasn't going to speak, but my eyes questioned him. He held my glare. 'These are the new DSS forms; where did you get them?' I had to ask, glancing at the two boys at the bar. They were making faces at us. I turned to Cathal. He had joined in and had his tongue out. Jesus! Here was I in a state of confusion and the big Scouse bastard was miming insults with those two.

'You see that's the trouble with you boys: you think you know it all. Do you really think that this community has been sitting on its arse and letting whatever benefits that are going to slip down your way, eh? You must take us for some buck eejits.'

'Okay, fine,' I said, trying not to let my voice reflect the mixture of anger and fear I was feeling. 'Answer my question then. Where did you get the forms?'

'In a minute. Do you mind if I put on a bit of music?'

'What! What are you playing at?' I was becoming more and more agitated. Music! This guy was really taking the piss. I nudged Cathal; I needed his help. His mind was seemingly elsewhere, though. He had his thumbs in his ears, his palms open wide, a sophisticated kindergarten insult, if my memory serves me right. Its authenticity only slightly sullied by Cathal's failure to keep his tongue out. He was letting the side down. I looked up at The Twins; no such discrepancy was evident on the Protestant side. Tongues to the fore.

Frankie nodded at a bloke now standing by the jukebox. He gave Frankie the thumbs up and then inserted money in the machine. A click announced a record had been selected. Was this some kind of ritual for these people, a legacy of too keen an interest in *Jukebox Jury*?

I got up, accompanied slowly by Cathal, who was now back in the land of the adult. 'Look, Frankie, we're off. I'm not putting up with this bullshit. Fuck knows what you're up to. Come on, Cathal.'

Frankie's big frame moved from his seat and strode, cowboy fashion, towards the music. One or two men who had been seated quietly in the corner also rose. The Draper Twins joined them, a kind of line formed as if we were going to take a free kick against them.

Just as the record kicked in, they started. They started to dance and sing as Slade's *Mama, Wor All Krazy Now* reverberated round the bar. They all started to laugh at us as Frankie began to play an imaginary guitar and his accomplices performed exaggerated Slade dance routines.

It clicked. 'Cecil? You know Cecil?' I asked, my question just about audible above the din.

Frankie was now clapping his hands and motioning us to join in. 'Aye, Cecil's my nephew, lads. Our Angela's eldest.'

I didn't know whether to laugh or cry. Cathal, with his foot tapping, looked as if he wanted to join in. It was as if my vocal needle was stuck. 'Cecil?' I again asked.

'Aye, Tom. Cecil,' Frankie shouted over, before taking a couple of steps, affording his next sentence greater profundity. 'Aye, Tom lad. Cecil was *our* mole in *your* organisation.'

Cecil a mole?

He was *our* mole, *their* mole and a *DSS* mole. With his earth-moving abilities, I must remember never to let him near my lawn.

It transpired that Cecil had been relaying to Frankie most of what we had been doing in terms of success and failure. And there was us thinking Cecil was a true friend to us, when all the time he was a three-legged mole burrowing us as and where he felt the need. Come to think of it, my Uncle Richard never really trusted him. At times, neither did I.

Ye bastard ye, Cecil.

Then it got me thinking who else might be swinging both ways, so to speak. That vegan girl, I never trusted her; my Uncle Richard, nah; Emmet, I don't think so. But who knows? After all, Emmett had the allowance; he had nothing more to gain. Cathal, even. Could Cathal…

I shook my head to rid myself of these rather unlikely culprits.

Still, as the afternoon wore on and the pints flowed, I had to admit a grudging admiration for Frankie's operation. Even when he told us that on Cecil's advice, we should be left to get on with it, soften up the DSS, if that was possible, and then the Protestant community would descend and take the rich pickings.

Let us do all the donkey-work. Remind me never again to trust a bloody Slade fan in big boots. And they say people from South Armagh are sly, what with their smuggling antics over the years. Jesus! They had nothing on those Belfast bastards.

'Do you trust the Englishman, Tom?' Frankie asked.

'No way, no bloody way. Did Cecil not tell you about Fortesque-Smith?'

'Oh, I don't mean him. I mean yer man here, Cathal?'

'What?' was all Cathal could manage to slur. The Twins noticed a fairly inebriated Cathal struggling to his feet. They watched closely. It seemed that anything untoward directed at Frankie set them in motion. Fists clenched, glasses placed on bar with a menacing thud. Frankie nodded at them and winked. They relaxed.

'You really must learn that in this country it's part and parcel of our survival kit to vet people. We make no bones about it,' said Frankie.

'So, it's once again because I'm an Englishman,' said Cathal, his slur lessening, his indignation again rising. 'Well, you, Tom, you're a Fenian. Are you okay with that, Frankie boy?'

I jumped in. 'Ah, but I'm an *Irish* Fenian. Might not like me, but they know where they are with me. Whereas you, you're English, and an atheist to boot. There's no way of figuring you out. No way at all.'

I could see Cathal was having difficulty figuring all this out, and as he didn't have access to an Irish logic handbook, he remained somewhat baffled. And would be ever thus, thank God. I have always believed that it is essential for the wellbeing of we Irish that we keep certain things from others, particularly the English.

Imagine if the day came when they actually *understood* us. And us battling to try and understand ourselves. Couldn't have them getting there first now, could we?

Setting aside national differences, we all then embarked on a discussion, which masqueraded as an intelligent conversation if, like us, you had spent most of the afternoon in a bar. Oh, bullshit and alcohol, a potent mixture, each constantly vying for prominence. Despite his pleas that he was in fact a Scouser and was, by nature of his birthplace, different, Cathal failed to convince us that he wasn't tied to the State of England. We told him we couldn't see any difference. Indeed, Frankie went further and said no Englishman ever did our country any good. I was quick to add that there hadn't been many Irish who had done much for us either.

We all nodded, seemingly bathing in the wondrous idea that *we* were going to be the ones who would do so much for Ireland.

Despite his best efforts, which gave him a pained expression, I think at that stage Cathal lost the thread of the general conversation. Either that, or suddenly, and for no particular reason, he had developed a wonderful sense of recalling minute, uninteresting, details of recent conversations. He declared, his words peppered with a burp or two, that if he was ever called upon to fight in a battle to free a land, he would have to choose Iceland. Poor deranged Cathal.

He was further perturbed, certainly more than I was, by Frankie's sudden and intense disclosure that he hated the Republic of Ireland, didn't see why we should have anything to do with them at all. Wanted us to swear, cross our hearts and hope to die, that no matter what happened, we were not to involve anyone from there. He knew we had used some doctors now living there, but he was able to reconcile this by stating they were born in the North.

It was a little worrying. Were we witnessing Frankie's true Loyalist colours?

Unlike Cathal, when Frankie explained himself, I could see the sense in it all. His tale also reinforced Frankie's attitude to religion, one not dissimilar to my own.

'Now, I want you to state categorically here and now,' he began, 'that we will have nothing, absolutely nothing, to do with them Southerners.' When we looked a little puzzled, he merely stared more intently at us. Cathal looked at me. I shrugged my shoulders, kind of agreeing with his proposal.

'It's the Virgin Mary, you see…' he stressed.

We were all ears. He went on to inform us that it was something that had troubled him for years, niggling away there like a persistent flea.

'Why, tell me why, does the Virgin Mary only ever seem to appear in the South, eh? Tell me that. All those frigging times over the years, eh? Has she ever been spotted in Portrush, at the fair in Ballycastle, or boating on the Lakes of Fermanagh? No, she frigging well hasn't. You know why we in the North are in such a state? Nothing to do with that aul' shite about opposite religions. I'll tell you: we in the North were doomed from the frigging start. This total and seemingly contrived lack of mystical visitation.'

It certainly got me thinking; it got Cathal away from making faces.

Frankie supped deeply from his pint. 'I have a theory, you see. All I can think of, and nobody has offered me a more believable explanation, is that when Jesus allegedly walked this earth, he must have got annoyed with someone here in the North. Eh, maybe on the Antrim coast, eh? Did somebody cut him up on a donkey while he rode like a bat out of hell to cram in all the touristy spots? And him late for the ferry, maybe? Even if all that happened, why tell his mother to avoid us in the North? I mean, to hold a grudge for all those thousand of years, eh? Some boy, that!'

I nodded, seeing the complete sense in it all. He began to ramble on about how he sincerely doubted at times the validity of these sighting claims in the Republic.

Really? I thought. Surely not?

'So, what is it you want with us?' I asked, eager to change the subject, hoping that I could shut him up. There was only so much Virgin Mary bashing one can take on a full stomach.

'Oh, not a lot, really. Not at this juncture. Just wanted to meet you face to face.' Frankie's voice was now calmer, but he was giving little away. Ah well, I suppose I should have thought it fortunate he wasn't giving away fabric samples.

Chapter Ten

Maybe if we hadn't sunk so many pints that day I would have had my wits about me more. I would challenge anyone not to be gobsmacked, no matter what state they were in, when they rolled into the area that night; well, two-thirty in the morning, to be exact.

The previous week, the threatened raid, the one Cecil had kept on about, took on an air of credibility, grudging inevitability, even, when someone in a nearby street had sworn they had seen what appeared to be a Unit of sorts. All that was actually seen was the smoke from some old, rusty, backfiring blue and white Ulsterbuses and some accompanying swear words from within.

Voices, most definitely, not from the locality.

A heavy, chuntering sound approaching our house woke me from my deep, content slumber. In my misty thought process, I could identify the sound of backfiring vehicles.

'Cathal?' I called out in a weak voice, my tongue sticking to the roof of my mouth. No response from the next bedroom. I roused myself and went to the window, drawing back the curtains to be greeted by a convoy coming down the street, not in any particular order, of decrepit buses bound at one time for Portrush, Newry, Aldergrove Airport and the seaside town of Bangor.

It seemed a lacklustre momentum of an ageing transport system was edging towards us. Then, the screech of dodgy gearboxes, a prelude to the condemned vehicles grinding to a hiccoughing stop.

Lights popped on in houses.

Soon, people stood in doorways in their nightclothes, rubbing sleep from their eyes, trying to focus on the rather surreal events unfolding before them. It appeared at first glance we were witnessing the stuttering arrival of the DSS Enforcement Unit.

The *raid* had begun.

This was for real; there was no Sally Army and their tambourine jingles.

Cathal had awoken and was now in my room. I turned to catch his wide-eyed look, his hair standing on end. He looked less like John Lennon and more like Marty Feldman. He was in no fit state for a raid.

Neither was I.

Come to think of it, when you looked out the window, neither were they.

Maybe they were just doing a trial run; nothing for us to worry about.

'Where are our safe houses?' Cathal asked, showing more alertness than I would have given him credit for.

'Safe houses?'

'Yeah, we discussed the need for safe houses, remember? We knew if things got heavy, we needed to be able to flee to places the DSS wouldn't think to look.'

Oh, I remembered, the discussion that is. Only thing was that was all we did – discuss it. We never actually identified any. I tried to think on my feet. Where could we go, where would be safe for us? Was there anywhere we could flee to that the occupants of those trusty, rusty old vehicles couldn't follow?

We watched, spellbound, as the vehicles' inhabitants struggled with the creaking doors to free themselves and then jump on to the darkened street. Some of them seemed to be stretching themselves, possibly easing stiffening joints. They then took up positions in doorways, behind hedges, and one or two lay flat on their stomachs in the middle of the road. It made you wonder what training manual they had studied. It was good to notice they weren't armed, for all the evidence so far suggested they were a right shower.

And a right shower should never have access to guns.

Suddenly a bus, no longer on its way to Portrush via Cushendun and Cushendall, and whose horn could only croak, sprang into life and nearly ran over the couple of blokes who had taken up their positions in the middle of the road. As it trundled along the street towards our house, it also banged into a couple of dustbins, knocking off their lids.

They rolled nostalgically down the street. A number of older people couldn't help themselves. 'The Brits, the Brits, it's a raid…' they shouted. Old habits…

'We'd better get dressed,' I said to Cathal, suddenly awakening to the actual peril we might be in. In a few minutes we were downstairs, glancing quickly out the window. There was no way I was going to open the door; they would have to kick it in. If they had come for us, by Jesus! They would have a fight on their hands.

Well, at the very least a Chubb lock or two with which to contend.

Funny, the things you think about at times like that. I thought if I ended up being imprisoned, I didn't want Siobhan coming to see me. And I would get Uncle Richard to bring me some of his stew.

First things, first, though, the pressing need to deal with the present.

A sudden wave of bravery completely eluded me as I contemplated putting the whole blame on Cathal, claiming I was an unwilling participant in the Scouser's attempt to overthrow a government department. Tell them it had all been a Trotsky-influenced campaign. They'd go for that.

But then as I looked at Cathal standing beside me, scratching his armpits and yawning extravagantly enough to catch flies, I realised that any mug shot of him would never truly reflect a determined reactionary.

A degree of sense prevailed and I made the decision to open the front door a little. Couldn't have them kicking in my mother's front door. Oh, she would have hated that. A blast of icy air slapped me in the face as I peered into the shrouding darkness, just about making out the figures of what clearly must have been the DSS Enforcement Unit. Either that, or a touring circus had taken a wrong turning. The first thing that struck me was that, as unprofessional as they looked, both in military stance and bearing, immeasurable improvement, and a degree of credibility, could have been easily obtained had there been even the smallest alteration to their uniforms. I could see now why the Unit had reluctantly accepted the new uniforms.

Outside our house stood four members of this new Unit, shivering slightly in the cold. They appeared not to have any headgear on and had their backs to us. They stood in a row. Was I the only one to notice?

Suddenly, there was a terrible racket coming from one of the buses. It seemed the foursome outside our house were waiting for a colleague to disembark from a bus that, in a previous life, had clattered its way to Ballycastle. The colleague must have been in charge, for he kept shouting warnings from behind the malfunctioning automatic doors that they were to do nothing until he got out. It was hard to identify the birthplace of the voice in question.

A female neighbour came out from one of the houses, struggling to retain her dignity as the wind grabbed at her blue dressing gown. She shone a torch on the guy as he finally struggled free from his bus.

He was black.

Ah, so they had to recruit from abroad.

The woman then turned her torch on the four outside our house and, although we couldn't see their faces, we were now treated to their illuminated backs. We could now clearly see their uniforms. In full view was its large lettering.

Fairly distinctive, quite polite, and universally recognised as something which has irritated all of us at one time.

WOULD YOU LIKE FRIES WITH THAT?

McDonald's' loss was Ireland's gain.

A number of people started to laugh.

We all seemed stunned into immobility until the black guy held up his megaphone.

'Mr Dooley, Mr Thomas Dooley. Hello, can you hear me?' He blew into the communication piece like he was dying on stage in some dodgy club and then cleared his throat. 'Is this frigging thing working? Anyhow. Mr Dooley, would you please come out? We wish to speak with you. If you can hear me, that is.'

Oh, I could hear him all right.

The accent? I couldn't pinpoint it. Not immediately.

Then it came to me. Think West Midlands, think Dudley. Think Lenny Henry.

So, this was the DSS Enforcement Unit calling for me and not once offering me a free milkshake or, as it was early morning, soggy hash browns. My neighbour, torch still in hand, walked over to my pursuer. 'Do you not know where Tom lives, then, love? Are you just hoping he'll come out in the hope of getting a Big Mac?'

To give him his due, by the tone of his reply, the guy seemed to be an agreeable sort. 'Oh aye, well, we have a fair idea where he lives, if not the exact location. But we didn't want to be waking up the whole street by knocking on doors. Thought this would be a better idea.'

He once again lifted up the megaphone. 'Mr Dooley, could you please make yourself known?'

The woman finally switched the torch off, throwing us all into semidarkness. 'God! Wouldn't it be great if the staff at McDonald's were as polite and considerate!' she said.

One or two people enquired whether they had come just for me, or did they intend a more general, sweeping raid?

Oh please, no trouble, I thought. It's not worth it. I'll be okay, don't get yourselves lifted on account of me. There have been enough frigging martyrs in this country. Keep quiet.

'Just Mr Dooley,' said the black guy. With that, most of my neighbours tossed a collective yawn on the proceedings and withdrew indoors, but not before mentioning that a nice cup of tea and a bit of toast would go down well. Somebody mentioned hot whiskey and a hand or two of poker was also suggested.

So much for solidarity, community support. Bunch of bastards.

'Mr Dooley, Mr Dooley, could you please identify yourself for us?' Lenny Henry was on the megaphone again.

I opened the door fully. 'Aye, I'm over here.'

With that, the four members of the Unit nearest to me sprang into action and approached me, grabbing my arms.

'You have no authority to arrest me,' I said

The guy in charge came over, his black shiny face suddenly lit up by the flickering street light. 'Oh, we're not here to arrest you, Mr Dooley, merely to ask you to come with us. We have been asked to take you to someone who wishes to speak to you.'

'And what if I don't want to go, what if I refuse?'

One of the others spoke. Another Black Country accent. 'The thing is, Mr Dooley, before we came over here, we read a bit of this country's recent history. God! You've had the time of it, no mistake! Personally, I couldn't have coped. Anyhow, if you don't come with us, we'll raid every house in the area.'

The black guy nodded.

'Okay,' I said.

Cathal, too, had gone back to bed when he heard that they were here for me only. I really must speak to him about this. His ready and willing support brought a lump to my throat that would soon be in his, the frigging get.

The four guys led me to the Newry bus that the driver was busy revving up. A voice from a couple of doors up, one I couldn't identify, asked would we drop off a birthday present to his sister who lived just outside Newry. He was told to piss off. By me.

'Any chance of going in the Bangor bus?' I asked. 'Nice crisp morning for a walk by the sea?'

They didn't respond. Maybe it's a Brummie thing, chucking people into buses rather than responding negatively. A cavalcade of vehicles departed the area, backfiring and screeching once again in vogue.

As we journeyed, they started to chat among themselves. To a man, they all had Birmingham accents, or ones from some area of The Black Country. I was curious as to how they managed to be here in the first place.

'Oh, that's simple,' said the black guy, unwrapping a piece of chewing gum and stuffing it in his mouth. I declined a piece. 'You see, we answered an advertisement in the *Birmingham Post Herald* asking for men to join a specialist unit here in Belfast. The ad was run by the DSS.' He went on to tell me that there was now little work in the West Midlands for the likes of them ever since Maggie Thatcher allowed the manufacturing industry to die. 'Oh aye, in Walsall, we used to make all the washing machines, fridges, cars, for God's sake! But all that went to Italy and places like that. Our factories became big warehouses, and when the stuff used to come over from Italy, we stored it and then delivered it. Now, they deliver direct from Italy. So, when we saw the advert, we thought, why not?'

'Money's good; we pay no tax, like. People are very friendly,' added another. 'Only wish I could get home at weekends. I miss watching the Villa, although I have my doubts about O'Leary as manager. Good with the kids but useless with money.'

Another was glad he was spared the anguish of Walsall's slide down the league table.

Jesus Christ! A bunch of out-of-work Englishmen had been gathered up by the DSS, with the help of a frigging County Kerry recruitment agency, to police a bunch of out-of-work Irishmen.

I settled back in the bus as I peered out the window, not having a clue where we were going. After about ten minutes, I turned round to see most of the vehicles take a left turn. I also saw Father Rice pedalling off to work; he's early, I thought at the time. Jesus! Was he in on it?

There was now only the Newry bus accompanied by one for Portrush. I have to admit to having had feelings of unease, but the Unit that we had feared for so long now showed a friendliness which made me feel a little calmer as we took a left, then a right, ignoring the red traffic lights, and pulled into the driveway of a large detached house, the gravel path spitting out our arrival.

All the lights in the house were on and I could make out the muffled sound of music, and indeed laughter.

Jesus! They've brought me to a party!

'We're here,' one of the guys said as the bus came to a halt facing a garage. 'Would you like to get out?' He opened the doors of the bus and as he did so, the electronic double doors of the garage, which I could now see were blue, slowly opened.

'We've been told to take you in there,' said the black guy.

He gently took my arm as we both got off the bus and walked towards the garage. I felt rain on my face. As we moved inside, somebody switched a light on. The first thing I saw was the presence of a massive train set in the middle of the floor. It had the lot, a rural railway station and small village shops and houses. It even had rubbish and leaves on the track at the station. The trains sat dormant.

Whoever lived in this house, Mr Lloyd Grossman, had a keen interest in rail networks.

'We'll be off then, Mr Dooley,' said the black guy, holding his hand out. Instinctively, I shook it. 'It was nice to meet you, Mr Dooley. And, by the way, thanks for listening to us about our jobs, you know, in the manufacturing industry. I could see you cared. You stay here. Oh, by the way, if you're ever over in Birmingham, call into the Bit and Bridle in New Street. We're there sometimes at weekends.'

I was in no mood for making dates. 'Have you brought me here to play with a frigging train set?'

He shrugged his shoulders, and as I walked further into the garage, he moved outside. The electronic doors closed. I looked around for an exit. There was a brown door in the corner probably leading into the house.

I tried it.

Locked.

I heard the spluttering sounds of the Enforcement Unit as the Newry and Portrush buses departed. Then, a sudden screech of tyres and a shrill Brummie voice.

'Christ, Cyril! Take it easy, you're not in frigging Solihull now.'

Apart from the train set, it was a fairly standard garage. My mind went into overdrive as I scanned the shelves and floor seeking out instruments of torture. My breathing became a little laboured and my sweat glands were having a clearance. At first glance, there appeared to be nothing to unduly worry me.

Although I really couldn't rule out being forced into the bucket seat of a child's bicycle, or made to spend hours in a standing position ironing the rows of sheets that were drying off.

It made me realise that torture was all about imagination.

What the hell was going on?

Suddenly, the trains started up.

I pulled my hands away. I hadn't touched anything, had I? Four trains sped round the tracks. I watched the network come alive.

The brown door opened and in came a tall man, his face readily lit up with a smile. He was wearing a light blue Ralph Lauren shirt, the sleeves rolled up, and his hands were carelessly wedged in black trousers. He brushed his hand through his floppy black hair. I noticed his left eye flickered, no, winked; no, it was a definite flicker only.

Had to be sure, no point in returning a wink if it hadn't been offered, if you see what I mean.

'Mr Dooley, thank you for coming.'

'Well, I really had little alternative seeing as how it would have been rude, not to say negligent, to refuse such an early fleet of buses and a horde of Brummies.'

He smiled, a smile, I had to say, not lacking warmth. 'Do you like trains?'

'As against buses?'

'Yes, quite,' It was an English accent, quite refined.

'I take it you are Mr Fortesque-Smith?' I said. The details of my preferred mode of transport could wait.

'Indeed, Mr Dooley. Might I call you Tom?'

'Only if I can call you in the morning and tell you that whatever you have in mind, it is not going to work. There is nothing you can say that is going to make me alter my course. I know you know about me.'

Funny, he wasn't at all how I imagined him to be. He seemed quite an affable character, not the strict, terrorising bloke Cecil had described.

Cecil, that get. The more I think of him…

'I often come out here and spend an hour or so with the trains,' he said. 'Especially if, like tonight, my wife is holding one of her ghastly dinner parties.'

'You have quite a collection there,' I said, relaxing a little, for I was genuinely impressed.

He went on to tell me that his father had driven locomotives on the Settle-Carlisle line, and while his stories had bred a deep interest in the old rail network, he had little time for the modern system.

'As you can see, I have collected a number of locomotives. There you see the Midland Compound 40555 used in the early twentieth century,' he said, pointing to a terrific looking old engine. 'There's a Class 47 and the more modern Virgin Voyager.' He stressed that he liked to return to Sussex at weekends and travel on the Bluebell Railway. 'Although very recently, I have been unable to do so because of intense work pressure,' he added, giving me a dirty look.

'In other circumstances, Mr Fortesque-Smith, who knows? We may well have enjoyed a pint or two together. But really, I am at a loss as to why I am here, and particularly when you went to such trouble, if not expense, to bring me here.'

'Ah, the old Volvo-engined Leyland Tiger. Ulsterbus at its best, don't you think? Don't make them like that, anymore. Look, would you rather I spent taxpayers' money wisely, on paying out benefits, or on smart new vehicles for this Unit?'

'But you don't pay out on benefits: that's the problem.'

He moved closer to the table holding his pride and joy and moved a signalman out of his box and placed him on the platform. 'Always be aware, Mr Dooley, that I and my department know a lot more about you than you realise.'

Aye, and you be aware, Mr Fancy Dan, that I and my people know a lot more about you than you realise. Aye, and that Frankie knows a lot more about me than I realised and that Cecil, that get. Cecil, he's a frigging know-all.

The Englishman moved the railway figure nearer to the end of the platform and then glanced up at me. 'Shall we call this signalman Roger?' he asked.

Call him what you like, I thought. He then moved what I assumed was the Station Master and placed him on the platform, but further back from the edge.

'Now, shall we call the Station Master Thomas?' he said, looking up at me, a grin, not exactly filled with benevolence, pinching his features. His flickering eye became more intense.

Whatever, I again thought. 'Thomas, Roger, what the hell?' I stumbled for words as an express train sprang into action and approached the station.

What was this eejit up to?

The train came slowly to a halt just outside the station with the Englishman's hand firmly on the controls. 'Tell me, Tom, would it be opportunistic, I think that's the word, for you if Mr Roger Burnside met with some unfortunate accident and was no longer in the picture, so to speak? I mean it would allow anyone with a vested interest in his partner and, there is a child, I believe, to, well, rekindle what once was?'

Jesus!

What was this guy saying? I decided to play it cool. I mean, I knew he was only a Civil Servant, and I knew from my own experiences in London that many of them were a bunch of arses, but to suggest this type of violence could well mean that he was in a position to arrange something sinister. I could hear the rain pounding on the roof.

Play it cool, Dooley, play it cool.

'Let me out of here. Help! Help!' I shouted, banging on the electronic door.

'Rather pointless, Mr Dooley. The garage is, for security reasons, soundproofed. You understand.'

'Soundproofing for security reasons? Aye, and you this big-time government minister. Not.' I recovered a droplet of my sanity. Not to mention self-respect.

He was quick to concede. 'Okay then, not for security reasons, but that locomotive there is so loud, the neighbours complained so I soundproofed the place myself.'

I had perhaps found a slight flaw in his make-up; he had a degree of honesty about him. Maybe I could use that to my advantage.

Or, or maybe this guy was just bluffing. Maybe that little slip has merely revealed a desire to be something or someone he wasn't.

'Shall I call you Walter or Mr Mitty?' I asked, feeling a bit calmer.

He pushed the controls and the train sailed through the station. The signalman remained on the platform.

Unharmed.

'Look, Tom, I think we can do business. I can make things happen for you. I can have Mr Burnside removed. You could have your family back. Worth more than all this IEA work, don't you think?' I stared at him. 'No, no, don't panic. That bit with the trains, just my idea of a joke. Mr Burnside would not be removed by violence. A very close friend of mine works in the Secretary of State for Health's office in London. He owes me a favour. I could get Burnside transferred back to the mainland.

'To the mainland?' I said, suddenly interested.

Roger the Codger back in the mainland. It had a certain ring to it.

'Yep, to the mainland,' he confirmed with a sly grin.

I had been so engrossed in the project recently that my thoughts about getting my family back had fallen and submerged themselves somewhere in the dark recesses of my memory bank, there to be dusted off now and again, but with no real intent. I knew that things had gone too far now for there to be any real chance of a reconciliation with Mairead, even though I occasionally fantasised on a different outcome.

But if Roger the Codger was transferred back to the mainland, there was no way Mairead would disturb Siobhan's schooling and return with him. So, who knows…?

My face must have reflected my interest.

'You would, of course, have to do something for me in return.'

'Like what?' I asked, eager to test the waters but recognising the need to be vigilant. I kept my eyes peeled on the railway track.

He sniffed deeply and drew a hand across his face. He didn't mince his words. 'I suppose what I'm really asking is that you desert your people.'

Oh, that's fine, then, no problem. Nothing major, anyhow.

I drew back from him as if hit in the face. I couldn't hide a sneer and looked him up and down like you would a Daniel O'Donnell fan. At that moment, the train came round again and it slowed down. He stared at me, a wild look creeping into his eyes, the flickering now almost hysterical. His hand, steady as she goes, clasped the controls.

Should I make a grab for them? Could I in one fell swoop save the lives of the signalman and the Station Master? Their fate in my hands. Could I live with myself if I didn't at least try?

Jesus! And there's me always so critical of people getting carried away on Playstations. Catch yourself on, Dooley boy.

My eyes fell to the track as the Englishman pushed the controls to make the train pick up speed. It was over in a second. I would have been too late anyhow. The plastic figure of the Station Master lay on the track, in among the rubbish and debris.

'Now, that, Mr Dooley, I can arrange, believe me.'

Good God, no! Surely not!

The Station Master was called Thomas; Jesus! It was supposed to represent me, wasn't it? Christ! I had been so slow. The Station Master was me, although a couple of pounds heavier than I was. And I would never have my hair cut like that. And as for the hat…

Surely this one man's influence and contacts didn't stretch to such an extent that he could, with no questions asked, get you a fairly well-paid job on Northern Ireland Railways and then belittle you by making you pick up the rubbish from the tracks? That was what he was hinting at, wasn't it?

This man was fiendish. Perhaps cuts in the Civil Service threatening budget meant he had to play both parts; the good cop *and* the bad cop.

There was no warmth in his face, no affable chat now. This was the hard-faced bastard Cecil described. I gulped deeply. There really was no way out for me, was there?

'Go on, what is it you want?'

Chapter Eleven

I arrived back at the house at around six-thirty in the morning; the rain had eased a little. I found lights on in most houses. I was feeling cold, wet and felt miserable. And frightened.

But to be back in among my own helped a little.

Some of my neighbours had felt the need to get dressed; others felt their nightwear was the proper attire for a good gossip. Some were standing outside their houses. I looked around me and immediately felt a bit peeved that there were no WELCOME HOME banners stretching from one side of the street to the other, no bunting, nor indeed any sign of relief that I had returned safely.

'So, did you go to the seaside?' a man in a torn green dressing gown asked. 'Or did you get them to take you up Slieve Gullion? I didn't see which bus you caught.'

Somebody commented on how beautiful the mountains were at that time of year and an old woman, with a dead roll-up glued to her toothless mouth, remarked how her courting days began on the seafront at Bangor. Jesus, woman! What about me?

Not a bit of wonder, Kathleen O'Halloran, I thought looking at her, that your husband ran off with that woman from the home bakery. I didn't say anything to her, though. I looked at her again, charitably this time. To have such a strong, but understandable, dislike of all things flour-based, yet to be plagued with gum disease, responding only to lightly soaked biscuits, was punishment enough.

'I'm so happy my incarceration and terror have prompted reminiscences among you,' I moaned as I walked past them and up to the door of our house.

Their ears pricked up. 'Oh go on, then. Tell us, were you tortured?'

'Look, I'm not going to exaggerate...' I said.

'If you haven't been tortured, you won't get into the history books. Not in this country,' the man in the green gown said.

I decided to make my way into the house, telling them I was tired. I would reveal all later, I told them. One voice, that of a man, asked if I'd been to see the Englishman.

Assumpta was inside. She looked up at me, worry etched on her face. She was all over me like a mother hen, checking my head, my arms and legs, asking had they hurt me. I've had gentler frisks from Security at the airport. But none as well meaning. I suppose I was pleased with her concern, but would it have been such an onerous task for the rest of them to put out a few flags? They were forever flying flags here, why not for me?

My uncles were also in the house waiting. You could tell by the softening of their tired eyes they were so relieved to see me alive and well. Sammy Devine looked concerned as well. Jesus! There was a full house. I felt a sudden desire to hug him.

'It's okay, Sammy, I'll be fine,' I reassured him while resisting a more intimate greeting. Thankfully, though, I was once again warming to my people.

'Sure that's grand. Now, was my case mentioned, eh? Did anyone make any mention of my claim?' he asked, almost dropping a number of holiday brochures he had tucked under his arm.

How could they have known where I had been? Did someone tell them? Who? Probably only guesswork on their part.

I just shook my head while Sammy took up a conversation with Pat in which he asked my uncle how long would it take him to save up for a couple of weeks in Costa Rica. In a flash, Pat advised him that if he knocked ten quid off his weekly shopping bill, drank a cheaper brand of lager and stayed out of the Bookies on weekdays, then four months should do it. Five, if he wanted to bring someone with him.

God! If they only knew what I knew! But then, if I had known what Cecil had known, and indeed what Frankie had known!

Need to know. That, seemingly, was the name of the game.

I just told them all that the Englishman wanted to meet with me to discuss my involvement with the IEA, to tell me in a friendly way that what I was doing was not going to work.

The request from the Englishman that I betray my people would have to be kept under wraps. For now, at any rate. In fact, I tried not to dwell on it myself.

I was understandably tired. Once I got my bearings, having left the Englishman's house, I was able to walk most of the way; I mean, you'd be hard pushed to get a bus at that time of the morning. Well, not one going in my direction, at any rate.

I hoped I would never again hear a Black Country accent.

I was less than pleased to discover Cathal still asleep, but I realised I needed to talk to him. I swiftly complained to him about his obvious lack of concern about my wellbeing, indeed about my whereabouts, even. He cast aside my criticisms by telling me that if he had to be in a position to help me, he would need a good night's sleep first.

Cathal and I took stock of the situation. The DSS had at last shown their hand. I had been introduced to both the Englishman and the Enforcement Unit. We now could put a face to the enemy and they to us – well, to me, anyhow. I knew I was betraying Cathal by not telling him the full story, but how could I?

God forgive me, but I had yet to make up my mind. I knew that whatever route I chose I would be letting somebody down; my people, my family, myself, but I had a sneaking feeling, one probably bolstered by optimism, that my mother would approve, no matter what I decided. I felt she would have understood the crossroads I had now reached. Go with your heart, son, I could almost hear her saying.

I rang Siobhan to speak to her before she went to school and to confirm arrangements for our visit to the Odyssey later that day. Roger answered the phone. He didn't seem to notice I wasn't my usual off-hand, sarcastic self. If only he knew what I knew; if only the Englishman knew what I knew; if only Frankie knew what I knew; if only I knew what he knew. There was a lot of knowledge around.

Yeah, but who knew about it?

Siobhan was in good spirits; she had drama class that morning and was looking forward to our evening out. She asked was Cathal coming, and when I said he wouldn't be, she then wanted her uncles to come. I said I would see if they could make it. My uncles, Pat and Richard, and indeed Cathal, were supposed to come, but how could I face them, knowing what I knew and them not knowing?

Knowing them, however, they would soon figure out what I knew and hadn't told them.

Where was that frigger Cecil, the know-all?

Cathal decided to go into town to meet Maureen, the love of his life; or, a mere friend, as he sometimes referred to her. She was up in arms about the raid; not out of sympathy for either me or our project, but because she didn't get the chance to rant and rave about the McDonald's-led destruction of the rain forests in their quest to feed us carnivores.

I was pleased that the Scouser seemed to have found someone, someone with whom he could be close. Okay, he and I were great mates; he had shown his true loyalty to me in recent times, if not exactly the most recent time, like that morning. He had propped up my ambitions with both money and, more importantly, enthusiasm. He, however, needed a woman in his life.

Cathal had mentioned to me recently that maybe it was time for him to settle down. To most, that might indicate a desire to tie the knot, set up a secure home with a loved one, even think about a family. In Cathal's case, it was more likely to mean he was now at a stage in his life where it didn't really matter all that much if people actually thought Elvis was indeed better than Willie Nelson. Progress of a sort, I suppose.

I was more than happy to be left on my own with my thoughts and decided to go back to bed for a while. Although I was tired, I didn't feel my mind would ditch its restlessness long enough for me to fall asleep. Lying fully clothed on top of the bed, I soon felt my eyelids becoming heavy and before I knew it, I was interrupted by my mobile phone ringing.

I didn't recognise the number.

'Tom, it's Big Frankie here,' said the voice on the other end.

'Oh yeah? Hiya,' I slurred, trying to regain my thought process.

'Just heard what happened last night.'

'How come?' I asked, sitting up. I looked at my watch; it was eleven-thirty.

'How you do think?'

'Eh, well, have you a new mole? Who could it be? Let's see. What about Cathal, he's not here…?' My voice trailed off, the unthinkable again entered my head.

'That English bugger? Don't be daft. It was Cecil.'

'But Cecil has been suspended,' I countered suspiciously.

'Yeah, right. I'll explain that to you later. We need to meet. I know what Fortesque-Smith is proposing. Have you told anyone?'

I thought for a few moments. Should I tell this guy that I hadn't told my people about something so important? 'No, I haven't. No, I've told nobody,' I volunteered.

'Good. I need to see you. I'll call you later. Tell nobody, remember, tell nobody.'

'But, Frankie, I…'

He switched off.

I was with Siobhan at the Odyssey that afternoon when my mobile rang. Again, it was Big Frankie. He said he needed to meet me immediately. I told him where I was and that I was with my daughter and basically couldn't get away. He laughed, and then I spotted him out of the corner of my eye.

He walked over to us. He had a young lad hanging onto his arm.

'Tom, this must be Siobhan. Hello, love. How are you?' Frankie's big frame slightly worried Siobhan as she clung onto my jacket, but she then smiled shyly and said she was fine.

'This is my nephew Colin. I take him down here most Saturdays.'

'But this is Friday,' I said, smiling at the child.

'Must be a coincidence that we met, then, eh? Look, would you two like an ice cream? Here, Siobhan, take this money and go and get yourselves an ice cream over there.'

I nodded to Siobhan, telling her to say thank you and to get the ice creams.

'What's this about Cecil?' I asked. 'He hasn't been suspended?'

Big Frankie nodded at a couple of people he must have recognised, then chided me for raising my voice. 'Cecil is out of the country. No, he hasn't been suspended. But don't worry about it. We have Miss Webster on our side.'

Miss Webster?

'No way, Frankie. You're having me on, here. There is no way Miss Webster would turn.'

'Aye, that's what I thought. But all I know is that she told Cecil to take a couple of weeks off work, as she didn't want him caught up in things. Didn't divulge much else, but Cecil said he had a feeling she's gunning for the Englishman again. Said she only had a short while to go before retirement, so she had little to lose.'

This was more than I could handle at the moment. Where were you, Cathal, when I needed you? And to keep you in the dark about things!

'So, what is it Miss Webster intends to do that is so dangerous that Cecil has had to absent himself?' I asked, keeping my eye on Siobhan. I was glad she wasn't first in the queue, as I needed time on my own with Frankie.

'That's the strange thing, Tom; she wouldn't tell Cecil a thing, not a thing. Cecil said if Miss Webster is really up to something then somebody better look out. He said that when she wears her tweed suit and green beret with the pin in it, there is usually trouble in store.'

Oh, the Miss Marples of the Civil Service!

At that moment, my feelings on first coming back to Belfast once again surfaced; I felt we were way in over our heads. Now, however, it was a singular soul drowning.

Me.

Just as the kids came back, Frankie said we couldn't talk anymore and told me to come to the bar that evening. Alone. Clandestine, the name of the game again. Once more I would have to keep things from people I trusted, people I cared about. People who cared about me.

It had been our intention to bow out with a real body blow to the DSS. I did not, however, expect to be left in this quandary. If I were honest with myself, I would have to say that if it were simply a case of getting my family back or continuing with our IEA campaign, there would be no contest.

I'd sell my neighbours down the river tomorrow. That may well have been a graphic way of describing it; it was, however, the reality of the situation.

I had to get my facts right, though, to enable me to make the right decision.

It had been a while back when it dawned on me that I had cautiously been accepted back into the community, to a degree only, simply because I could offer them something. Was of some use to them. I wasn't that naïve to think I would be welcomed back with open arms; sure, I would have liked it, but I had changed too much for the rekindling of a relationship to be perfect. Pity was, they seemed not to have changed at all. I couldn't make up my mind whether that was something warming or something I resented. At times a bit of both, I suppose. I had to be clear in my mind exactly how I felt about the people and how they felt towards me.

If there was selling down the river to be done, I wasn't going to use guilt as a paddle.

I often wondered what my chances with them would have been had I returned to Belfast and simply tried to fit back in again. It was something I tried not to dwell on for too long. I felt uncomfortable with the creeping realisation that once you left this bloody country, you had a frigging job fitting back in. No matter how willing or otherwise you actually were.

But would my mother have deserted these people as easily as I was contemplating it? I had my doubts, grave doubts. To pacify my indecision, I remembered that it was she who really wanted Mairead and me to get together again. It was she who'd told me, I remember it clearly, that I would return one day. And hadn't she said it would be the making of me?

Well, I suppose in many ways it has.

But what of the immediate future? Would my eventual decision unravel all the good things I think Cathal and I achieved here, both for the people and, in a way, more importantly, for us both?

I honestly believed the Englishman when he said he could get Roger shifted. Some of these Civil Servants had power beyond their means and seldom used it to benefit anyone. Except, currently, me, perhaps.

And all I had to do was relinquish the reins on the campaign. That's what he said. Fortesque-Smith required nothing more from me than an assurance I would cease to be involved in the campaign to promote the Incapacity Existence Allowance among my people. Hey, Cathal and my uncles could continue, couldn't they? Nobody need know anything about the arrangement. Apart from Frankie, who said it was up to me to make my decision. I was the one who had to live with it. He said he certainly wouldn't think any less of me, whatever route I chose.

Family's important, he'd said. I asked him had he regretted not staying in Iceland and trying to make the relationship work. He shook his head and, with a wide grin, edged with a definite degree of regret, but more mischievousness, explained it wasn't half as much as he had regretted kitting out that wedding party.

I laughed as he slapped me on the back and asked was he any more popular in the area than before. I told him the DSS doctor was more popular. That shocked him.

I decided I would simply tell everyone that I had reached the conclusion that there really was no more I could do to help, adding, maybe, that I considered somebody, possibly Cathal, aye, Cathal, should take over the reins. Cathal would love that. He was moving on here; hey, the lovely Maureen was becoming more and more a major part of his life. Cathal was fitting in quite nicely.

People would understand, wouldn't they?

Big Frankie was on his own in the bar. Thankfully, the jukebox was silent. It was a warm evening, so the barman left the door open. The traffic outside hardly infiltrated my thoughts.

'No Twins today, Frankie?' I asked, sipping from a pint of lager.

Frankie was on Coke. 'No, I've given them the year off. It will take them that long to figure out how to pass the time,' he laughed.

I asked him about Cecil. 'Tell me,' I said, 'how long has the bugger been working for you?'

Without a trace of embarrassment, Frankie told me that from the day and hour he met me down the DSS office, Cecil knew I was up to something. But I never even mentioned the IEA to him that day, I protested. No need, said Frankie. Cecil said he saw me taking a detailed look at the IEA forms in the outer office and taking a few away with me.

Reminded me never to be seen visiting the chemist and perusing the info on haemorrhoids.

'Jesus! You can't trust anyone!' I said.

'Well, at least you've learned something,' Frankie threw back at me.

'So, Cecil had let us do all the donkey-work. All our efforts to break down the DSS barriers were actually for the benefit of his... your... community?'

'Not totally,' Frankie began to explain. 'Look, Tom, the thing is, well, it all began as a bit of a joke. Cecil told me about Fortesque-Smith and how badly he had been treated by him, with promotions and that. He was all for resigning until he told me about meeting you and Cathal, and to be honest, I saw an opening for him.'

'Why didn't he just feed the information to you? I take it you have some claims from your community?'

'Oh yes, of course we do. Airtight ones, thanks to you. No, I didn't want to do this just for my community. Believe it or not, I saw this as a chance to unite our communities. Yes, just like you. There was no way, however, that we could just have jumped in. I needed to be able to tell these people round here that it was your efforts in your community that would help us in getting our claims accepted. Yeah, you were going to be the big working-class hero, in my community as well. Make you more acceptable to them. There's no way, of course, that you will ever be acceptable to all; neither will I for having dealings with you. But hey, I reckon you and I can dream, eh?'

Dream? Oh aye, Frankie me boy. I can dream for Ireland, so I can.

'And I do know from Cecil that Miss Webster, until her retirement, will grant all claims if she can dispose of the Englishman. Cecil reckons that's what she's up to; she must have some plan to get rid of him,' Frankie continued. 'All genuine claims, that is. She will always have that Civil Service training niggling at her. This is to be her retirement blast. One thing she did say to Cecil was that both our communities should consider having a march into town on Saturday week. You know, highlighting what we're doing on the IEA. Into town and then up to Stormont.'

At that moment my phone rang. Damn it, Fortesque-Smith. I couldn't believe what I was hearing. He was demanding more and told me he had a plan in case I got cold feet. He said when we all arrived at Stormont he wanted me to publicly denounce my work. He cackled menacingly, telling me that if I didn't play ball, my uncles and everyone else involved would be arrested there and then and held indefinitely. Would my uncles be able to endure such hardship, he sneered? My mind went blank as he ranted on, something about smoking and asylum seekers. I really wasn't taking it in. The line went dead. Cold feet? Jesus, the penalty for chilblains seemed to be hellish severe hereabouts!

Frankie asked me was I okay? I said I was. *Why would Miss Webster suggest we go up to Stormont?* I wondered, my mind numb with panic. *How the hell did the Englishman know about the march?* As Frankie didn't mention that Fortesque-Smith wanted me to go to Stormont, I reckoned he didn't know about that. Should I tell him that that was what the Englishman wanted me to organise? Did Frankie know something I didn't? I thought I knew something he didn't, but in this world of information, who knows?

'I'd like to meet Cecil; can you arrange it? I really need to hear all this from the horse's mouth, so to speak.'

Frankie shook his head. 'I'm telling you, he's gone out of the country. Rang me last night from the airport. And anyway, you weren't going to see him again. His work with you, as they say, is done.'

So, I couldn't speak to Cecil; I knew what the Englishman wanted; I wasn't sure about Miss Webster, though. And I sure as hell wasn't at all sure about Frankie. Or myself. I told him there could well be problems when he met up, face to face, with the locals on the march, reminding him of his popularity stakes. The fact that we hadn't been lynched because of our dealings with him didn't mean everything was rosy in the garden. He sighed and said he would think of something to try and smooth things over. I wished him luck.

I just sat there dumbfounded. All along it had been a ploy. I genuinely believed Cecil was on our side, but in fact, he was working flat out for his own. No harm in that, I suppose. Getting up to leave, I told Big Frankie I would think about the suggestion of a march. I didn't exactly stress it was Miss Webster's suggestion, for I didn't know whether it was hers or whether she was acting on behalf of the Englishman.

I didn't know anything anymore. Anything apart from the fact that Fortesque-Smith had given me forty-eight hours to make my mind up. But hey, at the end of the day, what really was there to decide on? I had the chance, possibly the last chance, to at least try and get my family back again. No matter how hard I tried, or indeed whatever I did, it would come to nought all the while Roger the Codger was around.

Don't lose the dream, Tom Doolcy, don't ever lose the dream. Perhaps it would be best to always keep that in mind. It would help to douse down reality. And there was a bit too much of that around at the moment for my liking. Everything would be a piece of cake if Roger the Codger was out of the way.

Yeah, right.

Jesus! Would I ever learn? I had already reasoned that if Roger was transferred back to the mainland, then there was no way Mairead would disrupt Siobhan's schooling in Belfast. I also sensed that Mairead was quite happy that our daughter was being brought up in Belfast, the new Belfast. She knew I had changed; I was constantly in Siobhan's life. She would never sacrifice all that; I was quite sure of that. Wasn't I?

Of course, Roger could return to Belfast at weekends. Lots of people live like that these days, but that sort of lifestyle can cause problems. Even if the strain of living with this type of separation did break them up, what actual chance was there that Mairead and I would get back together again? Would Mairead ever really agree to us trying again?

If I made the wrong decision by taking up the Englishman's offer, I could well be left with nothing.

It wasn't easy being around Cathal or my two uncles. Fortunately, Cathal was so caught up with Maureen that he didn't seem to notice anything wrong. For once, Cathal's world was bright; no dark clouds. He couldn't see what I could, though.

My Uncle Richard did, however, seem to notice that I wasn't myself and asked me if I was feeling all right. My response that I was just very concerned about getting Sammy's claim through seemed to placate him.

Next day I decided to take Siobhan to McDonald's where I noticed she was now drinking chocolate milkshakes rather than her once-preferred strawberry. Roger's favourite, it seemed.

As I watched her playing in the park, I remembered something she had said a while back. She had nervously asked me was it alright for her to like Roger? I was momentarily stumped, and stuttered for a second. The idea that my daughter felt the need to ask me could she like someone in case it upset me, left me wondering what sort of a father I had become? What sort of a man? A child should never need permission to care. Was my daughter moving away from me, that she had to ask me this? I told her it was fine for her to like Roger, just fine. She smiled with relief and told me that she liked Roger but loved me and her mammy.

I realised it was time to do the right thing. For once.

With the time ticking and the Englishman's threats of arrest ringing in my ear, I sat in our office, the view of the mountains my only companion. I wondered was the Englishman thinking about me. I was but a phone call away from possibly making the biggest mistake of my life. I was about to lose everything or put myself in a position to have at least the chance to retrieve what was the most important thing in my life. No guarantees, though.

Could I be responsible for once again unsettling my daughter's life with an outside chance of us all getting together again? Would it perhaps be better just to leave things as they are, be my daughter's father, care for her, as I should, regardless of how I felt? Who knows? Maybe my mother was sitting at the right hand of God and she might put a good word in for me and he would sort out my relationship with Mairead?

Yeah, always pays to go with logic.

'Seeing Maureen tonight?' I casually asked Cathal later that evening as we sat down to a pot of stew Richard brought over. He made it every bit as good as when I was a child and my sister and I used to rush over every Tuesday after school to sample it. Piping-hot mutton stew with big dollops of treacle-thick Titbits brown sauce coursing through it.

'No, had a bit of a row,' he said, not lifting his eyes from the plate.

'Nothing serious, I hope,' I said.

'No, it's just that she's really a man.'

'What?'

'Only joking. Lighten up.'

'Oh, right. So, what is it, then, between you and Maureen?'

'She wants to be a nun.'

'Yeah, right.'

'Do you think I would joke about something like that, eh?'

I looked at Cathal's face as he ploughed through his food. There was no emerging grin. 'When the hell did all this kick off?' I asked.

'Oh, about the same time as you started to go all strange.' He placed his spoon on the plate and looked up at me. 'Are you going to tell me what's going on?'

I wanted to, I *so* wanted to. But what could I say?

Cathal just stared at me. I knew he must be going through his own hell, knowing how fond he was of Maureen. I didn't want to add to his woes, although inwardly I was screeching out for some guidance. I felt for him. Once your loved one takes the old vows of poverty, chastity and obedience, there's really no going back. Unless the Vatican has decreed otherwise, intimate dinners for two are still frowned upon in most convents.

'Do you want me to have a word with Father Rice?' I asked, only too willing to try and help the big Scouser. I must say, he seemed to be taking it all quite well, though. I would be absolutely devastated. Still, that was Cathal.

'Father Rice?' he said.

'Yeah, you know. I could have a word with him, ask him to have a word with Maureen.'

'Father Rice, you say.'

'Aye.'

'Father Rice? Tom, I don't want her becoming a brickie.'

'A brickie? Why would she be a brickie if she wants to be a nun.'

Cathal suddenly grabbed the remote control and turned up the volume on the TV. 'What's Aldo doing on the local news?' he asked, pulling his chair closer to the screen and nearly spilling his stew.

A picture of John Aldridge, the Liverpool legend and the Tranmere Rovers deity, according to Cathal, was on the screen. We listened as the reporter announced that following Sammy McIlroy's resignation, John Aldridge, the Scouser, was to be the new manager of Northern Ireland.

'I'll tell you something, Dooley boy, you lot better get prepared for success.' Cathal was beside himself, his face squashed with the widest smile I had ever seen on him.

So Aldridge, the Ian Rush look-alike, was the next poor sap to have to draw something out of our mediocre squad of players. Bring back Bertie Peacock, I felt like shouting. He'd play Bestie; in a holding role at the back. Allowances would, of course, have to be made for the great man's advancing years. Ah, nostalgia. A dreadful thing for those of us who witnessed the genius in a green shirt.

I didn't say anything to Cathal. This was truly an Irish thing.

The TV reporter then asked Aldridge how he felt about being fifth choice for the position. Recent media speculation had thrown up a number of names, and the Liverpool and Tranmere goal machine dismissed the other four candidates who, rumour had it, had been officially approached: Brian Clough, now too sober, said Aldridge; Michel Platini, too intelligent and gifted; Eamon Dunphy, too tactful; and the Bishop of Down and Dromore, too busy. Aldridge said he was proud to take up the post and saw no conflict in him having been a Republic of Ireland international.

It was with tongue in cheek, I think, that Aldridge said he refused to undertake a psychiatric appraisal before signing on the dotted line. Before the interview finished, he mentioned that he was looking forward to his official welcome to the post, which would be at a ceremony in Stormont Castle on Saturday week.

Saturday week! Stormont!

'That's the day of our march,' I said.

'Aye, so it is,' said the grinning Cathal, unable to take his eyes from the screen. He then turned to me wide-eyed. 'Hey, I might get to meet Aldo.'

Cathal's concerns about his Maureen devoting the rest of her life to God, and not to him, seemed to fade rather rapidly now that it appeared he would have something else to fill that gap in his life. Such is that fickle thing called love.

I made the call.

Chapter Twelve

That next week was stress on legs. In the many meetings we had with Big Frankie, which only me and Cathal attended on account of the fear we felt at being lynched if we made it too well known we had been seeing the tailor from the Shankill, we tried our best to plan the march and to drum up enthusiasm for it within both our communities.

'A thing of the past, marching. That's what people keep telling me,' said Frankie. 'So, it might be a bit of a problem getting them out on Saturday.'

'Aye, same with us,' I told him. 'People just keep saying things like, "Marching? Oh Jesus! We don't get up to that sort of carry on now."'

Just like the taxi driver, that day we arrived in Belfast for my mother's funeral, who felt that going into Corsta Street was digging a hole into the past, it seemed that the people from both our communities found certain things too firmly rooted in another time.

'No bad thing, really,' Frankie said. 'Sure marching was a scourge in this wee island of ours. But we need this march to be well supported.'

I nodded weakly. Oh God! If he only knew what I knew!

'But I saw on the telly the other night mention of a march in, where was it, Bally-somewhere?' said Cathal, looking rather mystified.

'Oh aye, but sure that's a regular one, every year,' said Frankie.

'What about the one in the paper the other day in Newry? That was a march, wasn't it?'

'Yeah,' Frankie answered. 'But that one is every two years.'

Jesus! I wish they would change the subject!

'Thinking of making it every three years, so I heard. Aye, and making it in the summer when it's warmer. So, the marching is dwindling,' said Frankie.

'I'm not having this,' said Cathal. 'You sit there and talk about marching being a thing of the past. A month ago, there was a march into the city centre. I can't remember what it was about, though.'

'Oh, aye, you know about that one, Tom?' laughed Frankie.

'I do indeed, Frankie,' I answered, trying to appear interested.

'Well?' asked the insistent Scouser.

'Sure that's a regular one. Takes place every two weeks, so it does,' I said.

'Don't ever see that one stopping,' Frankie said.

'What was it about?' asked Cathal.

'Don't you ever read the papers? That will be the asylum seekers from the South. We're inundated with them ever since their government announced they were introducing a no-smoking rule in bars and restaurants. They're getting out now before the ruling is in place,' I explained.

'And, even worse, they've reintroduced the Holy Hour,' Frankie said.

'I hadn't heard about that. That frigging Holy Hour used to get on my nerves.'

I explained to Cathal that each and every day between the hours of one and two o'clock in the afternoon, the pubs in the South close. Jesus, who in their right mind would have anything to do with that country?

The night before the march, we were down the club having a few nerve-easing pints. All of us had agreed that any banners being carried would be of a non-sectarian nature and would not contain any foul language.

'Our moment has arrived,' I said to Cathal as he brought drinks to our table. A couple of pints for Richard and Pat; a half 'un for Colum and a double for Samuel; Emmett was on rum and coke and Assumpta was on her third dry sherry. And, there's me thinking she didn't drink.

I had been unable to cajole my sister to come; that saddened me. I could live without my sister's approval, but I knew that as I got older, my desire – no, my need – to talk about the past, about my parents, my brother, indeed my uncles, God bless them, would overwhelm me. When I had nobody left, nobody from back then, from my first steps in life. I had, on occasion, tried to make things better with her, but had been rebuffed out of hand. Once, but only once, did I ever feel that she, too, wanted to at least explore the possibility of getting a degree closer. Unfortunately, it had been the day after Mairead and me had an argument and I was in no mood to be conciliatory. My sister never again tried to end the hostilities.

Who would be left to join me on that lonely journey down the road to where memories lie?

Tomorrow could well be the last time we were all together. I looked round at these people and felt a genuine sadness creeping into my ever-surer mindset.

I wanted my family back. I knew, as I looked round the club and saw the many smiling, happy faces that had meant so much to me in recent times, that I would be losing a hell of a lot.

Cathal, the big Scouse bastard. That first time he came into the Royal Oak, dressed in a denim jacket and jeans, his hair longer than any fashion code ever subscribed to. He had asked the barman what was on the menu. When told soup, he just cracked up. He told me later he had been sacked from his job as kitchen porter in a hotel in Bournemouth for throwing soup over the owner and his wife. He couldn't understand what the fuss was all about; it had been gazpacho. Oh, the craic we had in London! A constant image of him sitting on that torn stool in the Royal Oak would be one picture I would always keep of him. That and his steadying influence on me when my problems with Mairead cropped up.

My mother's brothers, Pat and Richard. The mathematical genius and the singer of old-time musical songs. I hadn't realised how much they had both missed me when I fled Belfast all those years ago. Pat told me I was only weeks away from grasping the intricacies of chess. Their words of comfort and welcome over my first few months back were heart warming. Aye, and I got to hear things about my mother I sure as hell didn't know about. It was good to know she was as rebellious as I thought I was. My uncles brought her closer to me.

Emmett, the warm, ever-happy first-time IEA guy.

Samuel. Samuel and his own personal agonies.

Colum. God! Did we have a time with his claim!

Assumpta, that willing, so polite, but unassuming, lady.

Siobhan, my beautiful daughter, who was life itself to me.

Mairead, my wife. I wanted nobody else, despite all my carrying on with other women. I had to try and get them back. I realised that if I didn't, the potential for me, in later life, to become that angry man again was a very real threat. An angry young man is a pain in the arse. A moaning OAP gets nobody's sympathy.

It was all making sense to me now. The real reason why I had been doing what I had for the past number of months was so evident now. Oh sure, part of me had been doing it for the people; for my mother; for myself, even.

Most certainly, I had been doing it to try and deal with that terrible evening all those years ago.

But more importantly, I realised, no – I finally admitted it – I was doing it, consciously or subconsciously, for one simple reason: to get my wife and daughter back. I suppose I had mentally suppressed this to a degree; to actually lay it bare and openly admit it to myself would have put undue pressure on me and I would have failed. Failed at everything. This way, I like to think I achieved something akin to my mother's belief – that coming back to Belfast would be the making of me.

Cathal came over and sat down beside be, kindly unleashing an explosion of alcohol breath and a stupid grin. Familiar elements of the big get. 'We've had the time of it, eh, Tom?'

'We have, Cathal, we have.'

'You should have got Mairead and Siobhan here tonight.'

I nodded. Yes, I suppose I should have. I had no time to lose.

'Cathal, will you do me a favour?' I was up on my feet.

'Name it, buddy.'

I reached for my coat. 'Come on with me.'

'Where are we going?'

'To Mairead's. I've got to tell her something. Come on, it can't wait.'

With that, we were away, Cathal quickly grabbing a kiss from his soon-to-be nun friend. In the cab, Cathal asked me what was so important. I said I couldn't tell him, not yet. I said I wasn't even sure I could tell Mairead. I stressed the need to get there quickly.

'Now, don't be going making a fool of yourself, Tom,' he warned me. This was not the time; this was definitely not the time.

Their house was in darkness.

'What time is it, Cathal?'

He peered at his watch. 'I think it's about half-twelve.'

I rang the bell. Nothing. I tried again. A light came on upstairs. Curtains then drawn. Mairead opened the window. 'What the hell do you want, Tom? And, you, Cathal, I'm surprised at you.'

'No more than I am at myself,' replied the grovelling Scouser.

'Is Roger here?' I asked.

She hesitated for a moment. 'No.' Her voice was weak but became stronger. 'And that doesn't mean you're coming in.'

'Mairead, please, I need to talk to you.'

All three of us sat at the kitchen table sipping coffee. Mairead looked tired, and not just because I had wakened her.

'So, Roger went to London yesterday,' I said cautiously, for I didn't know if the Englishman had gone ahead and put the plan into action, accepting my word that I would keep my part of the bargain. That phone call to Fortesque-Smith had been one of the most difficult, mind-wrestling things I had ever done.

'Yeah. He said something came up, caught the last flight,' Mairead answered, her tired green eyes darting nervously round the room. I watched suspiciously as they seemed to momentarily, but quizzically, land on Cathal, who responded with an exaggerated clearing of his throat.

'He will be back?' I asked.

'Yeah. What is it to you?' She reacted rather too angrily.

I inhaled deeply. Go for it, Dooley boy, go for it. Do the right thing. 'Mairead, Roger is about to be demoted and sent back to England.'

'What are you on about, demoted?' Mairead asked, her eyes narrowing. I could see she thought I was once again up to something.

'Trust me, Mairead, I know. I know because…'

At this point, Mr Dooley, you might like to take a moment or two before giving me your final answer. You might like to phone a friend, consult a solicitor, get someone to read your tea leaves? No? Perhaps apply for "I'm a dead man, get me out of here"? No, again. Okay, Mr Dooley, you have been warned.

'Mairead, I know because it is because of me…'

'Because of you…' Cathal asked, suddenly looking rather concerned.

I began to explain as best I could, my words tinged with both regret and embarrassment. I told them Fortesque-Smith had told me that if I relinquished my role as IEA advisor in the area then he would, with the help of some colleague in the Department of Health, get Roger demoted and sent back to England.

In disgrace. Not in a coffin, as I had first envisaged. I decided not to reveal that detail.

Cathal looked at me agog. I don't think Mairead believed me at first.

'Mairead, can you get in touch with Roger? Now. Please, you've got to warn him.'

Mairead and Cathal looked at each other, then at me.

'What?' I asked.

Mairead stood up, tightening her dressing gown. 'Tom, Roger and I parted company a month ago.'

'But you said he caught the last flight last night.'

'I lied.'

'Tom, Mairead didn't want you knowing...' Cathal's voice becoming dream-like to me.

'You knew? You knew about this and didn't tell me. Jesus! Everybody in this country knows everybody else's business. Even if they're not moles. Everybody except me. But I have...' I began to speak, but shame, I suppose, silenced me.

I have never, ever, in my life seen Cathal look at me the way he did that day. 'You have what, Tom? What have you done, Tom? Don't tell me, don't fucking tell me you've offered the Englishman something in return? You were going to allow him to do this to Roger, and in return...'

It was too late for cover-ups. 'I'm here, aren't I? I came here to warn Roger. I said I would take the march further than the City Hall. I said I would take it to Stormont Castle.'

'And?' asked Mairead, sharpening the guillotine.

'The Enforcement Unit is going to be there. To arrest all of us.'

'To arrest us? For what?' asked Cathal.

Good God! How did I get myself into this mess! 'We are going to be arrested for assisting the asylum seekers.' I could hardly look at them.

'What, those Southerners? And how are we supposed to have been assisting them?' asked Cathal.

'We are going to be found in possession of NO SMOKING signs which have been stolen from some Government warehouses in Dublin. They've been stored there in readiness for the introduction of the ban. Rumour has it, the thieves distracted the guard by asking him for a light.'

I grabbed Mairead's arm, a little too forcefully, it seemed, for she winced and shrugged me off. 'Why did you not tell me about Roger?'

'I couldn't,' she said, standing up and going over to the sink. 'If you had known, you would have been round here all the time. I know you, Tom Dooley.

You would have pressurised me. You being here would have confused Siobhan. I had to make her swear, God forgive me, not to tell you about Roger leaving.'

You know me, do you, Mairead Dooley? Do you not think I would have played a more tactical game, bearing in mind what's at stake, other than pleading with you to have me back? You've got a right opinion of yourself, that's for sure. Hey, take a look, Mrs Dooley, this is the new Thomas Dooley. Old tricks don't work with this new dog. Why hadn't that bastard Cathal told me what was going on? All that time wasted.

Chapter Thirteen

The day of the march.

It was cold and the drizzle was going to be a constant irritant, but a hell of a crowd turned up that Saturday. There were a few who must have feared bronchial problems, for a strong scent of *Vick* was in the air. It was comical to watch so many battling against the cold as foot-tapping dances mingled with frozen breaths and multicoloured umbrellas struggled with the wind. Reminded me of childhood games, wrestling with home-made kites and giggling at their rapid fall from the sky.

All through it, like writing through seaside rock, were the definite and encouraging mumblings of a determined crowd.

'I hope this is worth it,' said Big Frankie, as The Twins stood close to him, shivering in unison. They were wearing long brown coats and Sherlock Holmes-style hats.

Despite my being fairly confident that little if any animosity would be directed at Frankie and his people, there were one or two cutting remarks flying around. Richard stressed that it was inevitable, reason doesn't always prevail, he said, when faced with a bad memory from the past. I had to have a word with a woman, related, I was told, to the wedding party who, inches away from Frankie's face, promised the big man that if it was the last thing she ever did, she would see him dressed up like the clown he was. People have long memories.

Frankie must have sensed it. He shoved The Twins quite forcefully. In response, they held their hands out, pleading, and vigorously shook their heads. The threatening look in Big Frankie's eyes was not one I would have ignored, but still, The Twins stood their ground, shaking their heads and grabbing on tighter to the buckled belts on their coats. Attention from all quarters was inexplicably drawn to them.

People, who moments earlier had been struggling with the cold and a degree of apprehension about the day ahead, were now pushing against each other trying to catch a glimpse. Of what, I didn't know, but there was a feeling in the air that something was afoot.

Frankie pulled at the belts of their coats. Like ships in a wild sea, The Twins rocked back and forth in physical protest against Frankie's attack. To no avail. Frankie's swiftness was too much for them.

Gasps punctuated the air as the heavy overcoats fell away. Frankie looked round him, almost, it seemed, in an effort to catch everyone's eye.

'Will this do, eh, will this pay for the hurt, humiliation and distress caused by my, I admit it, less-than-professional tailoring that day, eh?' he asked, a pleading tone adding a painful edge to each and every word.

Personally, I wouldn't have been overly willing to accept this show as an apology, seeing as how it wasn't actually Frankie being humiliated, but the odd nod or two and sideways glance among some in the crowd seemed to be at odds with my thinking.

There before us were The Twins, dressed, it seemed, for their appearance in a forthcoming edition of one of TV's afternoon shows. The fat one with the barrel chest and the straggly hair wore a green apron festooned with a big red tomato over his regular clothes; his co-contestant, the tall, thin Twin with the closely cropped black hair, was all done up in his brand-spanking-new red apron. Aye, with a big green pepper to the fore.

Frankie looked expectantly at them. They had the look of defeated men as they each reluctantly drew from their coat pockets a white peaked cap, blue lettering splattered across each one, and put it on. Frankie told me later, when the whooping and hollering from my lot had died down, that he had arranged for them to be in the audience only; they weren't actually going to be contestants on *Ready, Steady, Cook*.

Humiliation enough, I would have thought.

Do you think…

I was going to ask Frankie for his opinion, but the notion was, I suppose, too far-fetched to actually be asked. I just tossed the idea over in my head as we began to slowly disengage ourselves from this farce and take hold of the day in hand.

What if, in the past, we could have arranged for some – no, sod it – all of our local politicians to appear on shows like *Supermarket Sweep*, *Name That Tune*, *Catchphrase*, *Family Fortunes*, or if they had really pissed us off, put them in close quarters to Jimmy Tarbuck in *Winner Takes All*? We could have buried them in humiliation, never to see them again. And, if we did see them again, there was always *The Golden Shot*, *Countdown*, *Fifteen to One*…

Only a rambling thought; best kept to myself, eh?

I told Frankie, as we walked along together, that this day would see changes; it was going to be worth it. It was no time for doubts. I tried to sound positive, but my major concern was the lack of media coverage. John Aldridge being unveiled as the new manager of the Northern Ireland football team was worth a few more columns than us, I would have thought.

It seemed nearly everyone had heeded our warning and toned down the banners, excluding anything overtly traditional that could be misconstrued as sectarian. We had to be united on this. I looked round me and, at that moment, felt very proud. Proud that I was part of this, part of a new dawn for these people.

Perhaps.

It was up to them. And us.

I looked round me; there was no way I would ever betray this lot, no way. Not now. Whatever chance I had with my estranged wife, I would leave in the lap of the gods. I would not sell anyone down the river, not for my own selfish purposes.

Well, mum, do you think I got it right, eh? You'd have approved, wouldn't you? I mean, who'd have thought, me coming back to Belfast and it being the making of me, eh, who'd have thought?

But worryingly, there was nothing, nothing at all I could do to stop the mass arrests of all of us. We had to go to Stormont. Miss Webster said we should, and we had to trust her, even though I knew the Englishman was waiting for us. That fear provided a tough, but ultimately unsuccessful, opponent to the wonderful feeling of being part of this terrific day. I looked around and saw rows of smiling, determined faces, all apparently ready for whatever the day threw up.

We had, there was no denying it, managed to unite some of our people; this was a cross-community effort. They might not actually make a film about me, but sure that fame thing, I don't think it's all it's cracked up to be.

'We should have had some music or singing,' I said to Cathal and regretted the suggestion almost immediately as Richard caught my eye.

'No, Richard, no. I need you close by me. You and Pat. Don't want you off elsewhere.'

Not somewhere up there where the fields are alive with the sound of music…

It seemed to pacify him, although I found it hard not to return Pat's knowing smile.

ONE LIMP, ONE ALLOWANCE
BEND THE RULES, NOT MY BACK
INCAPACITY IS NOT A CHOSEN CAREER PATH

The placards and banners were there in abundance, most with either red or blue writing on white backgrounds. I spotted Father Rice in his holy garb; he appeared to be handing out cards. Who knows, maybe he was offering discounts on penances for sins committed, or maybe a deal on repointing walls? You could never tell with that man. Still, it was good to see him.

Frankie blew a whistle and I took a deep breath. I smiled and winked at Bertie and Alice who had come up from Dublin for the day. I noticed the good priest kept a distance from them. They moved forward in what was a fairly neat little sequence, possibly gleaned, but in need of practice, from a recent line-dancing championship. I was constantly looking through the crowd, amazed at the sea of faces all out for the "cause".

Suddenly, I noticed a banner that I felt, while undoubtedly apt, was not really appropriate for the type of atmosphere we were trying to create. I pointed it out to Frankie.

DSS BASTARDS

'Oh aye, take your meaning, Tom. But that one's personal. I think we can keep that one,' he said.

And then, like the parting of the Red Sea, people seemed to move to allow me a fleeting glance of the banner carrier.

The big boots, the duffel coat.

'Is that frigging Cecil?' I turned to Frankie and threw my gaze back again towards the figure who more than resembled the giant Civil Servant. Only this time, my view was blocked as the crowd diligently moved forward. Frankie merely laughed. No amount of pleading would make him confirm or deny the presence of his nephew.

We soon arrived at City Hall, encountering shoppers who appeared not to have any idea what we were on about. Frankie blew his whistle and we stopped. Jimmy, our local postman, was still out of breath and red faced as he struggled with a full sack of yet-to-be delivered mail. He and Alice exchanged shy, furtive smiles in the pouring rain. Bertie was more preoccupied with getting his knees to follow the rest of him to notice anything untoward taking place.

'Here, take this,' said Frankie, handing me an envelope. 'Cecil told me to give it to you.'

I opened it. Three words: GO TO STORMONT. I caught Assumpta's eye at that moment. She winked and gave me the thumbs up.

Miss Webster had asked this of us. And now Cecil was doing the same. I had to trust him. *We* had to trust *them*.

I led the people. To what, I didn't know, but there was no way I was going to be responsible for stopping that tide. I don't think I could have, even if I had wanted to. Cathal grinned over at me. Maureen gave me a dirty look. Must remember to tone down my vocal opposition to vegans, if only for Cathal's sake.

We marched onwards and it was Pat who was first to spot our numbers were swelling. It appeared that we were being joined by a combination of people who will traditionally join any movement of people, regardless of its purpose, and others who believed in us, for new banners waved in defiance of the rain.

A red banner with white lettering:

THE RIGHTS OF THE PEOPLE TO SELF-DETERMINATION IS PARAMOUNT. WE WILL DECIDE WHAT WE ARE ENTITLED TO.

A white banner with red lettering:

NOT AN INCH, UNLESS IT ADDS A FEW NOUGHTS TO THE IEA CHEQUE.

A few protest and support banners, seemingly from other eras, and totally unrelated, were being unfolded and offered to the gaze. Some people will support anything. I agreed with the claim that Brian Clough should have been England manager: had my doubts about the benefits of seeing Gay Byrne imprisoned; saw the potential health benefits of allowing queuing OAPs to swig from gin bottles on pension day in local post offices. For the life of me, I couldn't see why anyone local was concerned about the union rights of circus clowns, until I saw the banner:

CIRCUS CLOWNS MAY BE FIGURES OF FUN, PUT OUR BIG FEET IN THINGS, FREQUENTLY FALL OVER, SO WE DEMAND FINANCIAL PARITY WITH NORTHERN IRELAND POLITICIANS.

We ploughed on through the streets, ignoring the aggressive tooting of bus horns and crude gesticulations from other motorists, until we reached the outer area of the city and were pleased to be met with hand waving and clapping, timid though some of it was. One woman struggled to slide down a ladder, dropped her bucket and chamois, and fell awkwardly. She smiled warmly at us. I threw her over a claim form with my phone number on it.

Weariness then began to creep up on me, presenting reality in all its colours as the long road up to the imposing Government building that was Stormont suddenly came into view. Images of my country's recent past flashed into my mind. God! Anything can happen to you in this country! Some of it State sanctioned. I felt the sickness of fear embedded in my stomach. I sure as hell didn't trust Fortesque-Smith. He must have known Roger the Codger had gone. The bastard tried to con me.

Frankie blew his whistle. The crowd stopped. A silence descended. We could see about half a dozen of the rusty blue and white Ulsterbuses lining the route, and a number of Burger men standing beside them.

By the look of them, we were not to be offered Happy Meals.

Into the lion's den, then.

Frankie blew his whistle and with an impromptu chant, led, of course, by Richard, suddenly erupting, we walked forward at a steady pace. The people of the North were united.

I didn't join in the chant. Thankfully, I didn't know the words to it, although I seem to recall the giant out of Jack and the Beanstalk always appealed to me; he had a directness I admired:

Fe-Fi-Fo-Fum
I smell the blood of an Englishman
Be he alive or be he dead
I'll grind his bones to make my bread.

Racist? Probably. But the pantomime giant might just have been offering an alternative to the sodium-laden, high-fat bread of the day. Only a thought.

Cathal suddenly started shouting, 'Look! Look! There he is! There's Aldo.'

The chanting ended.

Indeed, there *was* John Aldridge. And strangely, beside him, the Bishop of Down and Dromore. Was he there to give John his blessing or was he going to be his assistant? I would have thought Jimmy Nichol would have proved a better man for the job. They were both surrounded by TV cameras and photographers.

Presumably, Aldridge had signed on the dotted line and was now being introduced to the media and the rest of us as the new manager of Northern Ireland.

I decided I really should be at the front of the crowd when we came to an enforced halt as we surely would. I couldn't imagine the West Midlanders had instructions to let us through and up and into Stormont. I shouted across at Cathal and my two uncles, telling them to follow me. I nodded to Frankie. We all moved through the crowd to the front. I couldn't help but notice Pat counting as we moved and Richard singing something softly. Or maybe praying. I felt at that moment that we needed prayers slightly more than a soft rendition of something from *Oklahoma*.

I spotted the Englishman coming out of the building, dressed in his official issue black suit. He stopped and stared at us. Even from a distance, it was possible to notice a big smirk on his face. He took out a hankie and blew his nose before pushing his glasses back up into place. He walked slowly towards us.

Where was Miss Webster?

Frankie was a few yards ahead of me when he stopped and held his hands up. The black guy from Birmingham was inches from our faces.

'Hello, Mr Dooley,' he said warmly, and after taking a couple of furtive looks around him, he handed me a piece of paper. 'Maybe you would like to have a look at our new takeaway menu, Mr Dooley.'

I took the paper from him. 'Kind of you,' I said, trying hard to mask my annoyance. 'We're really not in the mood for some smart-arse games.'

'Have a look, Mr Dooley. Remember it's our *takeaway* menu, if you get my drift. It's a bit limited, but I think you will like it.'

There was one word on the paper. On the takeaway menu. One word.

The Englishman.

Suddenly, our attention was dragged to a commotion behind us, the sound of an engine and the loud tooting of a horn. A large lorry came ploughing through us as we quickly made space for it. I was frightened. Jesus! What was going on? John Aldridge looked confused, and so he should.

The lorry screeched to a halt as the TV cameras left the new Northern Ireland manager and focused on the vehicular interruption. The back doors of the lorry opened up and four women of varying ages got out, the fitter ones helping the less able ones to the ground. A ramp appeared from the back and a wheelchair came flying down, followed by a fragile woman, her hair tied up in a red polka dot scarf, taking slow steps until she rested herself in the chair. I turned round quickly to see the Englishman running towards us.

'We're ready, Miss Webster,' the woman said.

A small woman with a pointy nose and razor-sharp blue eyes descended from

161

the lorry. She was wearing a tweed suit, and on her head was a green beret with a pin in it. She looked over at me. 'Mr Dooley, I presume?'

'Miss Webster, I presume?' I said, walking over to her and offering her my hand. She shook it gently.

'Miss Webster!' The booming voice of Fortesque-Smith. 'What is going on?'

'Keep calm,' I called out to everyone. 'This is a peaceful demonstration, do not on any account be provoked.'

We grouped in the middle, flanked on the right by the West Midlanders, on the left the lorry ladies, now lined up in a row with Miss Webster in front of them. She turned and walked over to her boss.

'Miss Webster, what is the meaning of this? I thought you said the media was at the football ground, at Windsor Park?' said the Englishman.

'Oh, did I? Sorry,' she said and then took out a booklet from her inside pocket. 'This, Mr Fortesque-Smith, is a copy of the Civil Service Terms and Conditions. No doubt you are familiar with it?'

I eagerly scanned the crowd. I couldn't see it. Anywhere. The DSS BASTARDS banner. I hadn't a clue what the hell was going on, but I had a good feeling about it and I felt Cecil should be here. In at the end, big man.

'Mr Fortesque-Smith, it is my duty to request your resignation.'

The Englishman looked dumbstruck. Cameras surrounded him like vultures and his eyes blinked violently in response to the accusing media voices. John Aldridge was now seemingly old and boring news. The Englishman swallowed deeply. The boys from the Black Country approached him, the black guy with a pair of cuffs in his hand. I wondered what bus Mr Fortesque-Smith would be travelling on today.

Chapter Fourteen

Later that evening in the club, we watched the News. And we taped it. To watch time and time again. Our record of a memorable day, 1 April 2004. The unthinkable happened. And we were part of it. A big part. Cecil's mobile was on Voicemail. 'Nice knowing you, Tom,' was all it said. I really wanted to speak to him. God! Cecil, ye bastard! Jesus! We had some times. Frankie declined my offer to come and join in. He felt he should wait awhile before coming into our district again. Like confetti, he said, people with grievances are scattered everywhere.

For most of us it was our first time on TV and Alice was smiling widely and commenting how well she looked while berating Bertie for his stooped appearance. I so wished Siobhan and Mairead could be with us but Siobhan had a bit of a cough, best for her not to come out. My day would have been perfect. I called both of them earlier and told them to watch the News.

We watched as Miss Webster, in full view of the TV cameras and the media photographers, presented the five women to the Englishman. He looked confused. One after the other threw the accusation of sexual harassment at Fortesque-Smith. The woman in the wheelchair looked straight into the camera as she related her tale of sexual woe.

'On my Zimmer, I was, I swear to God. I was defenceless. I'm only a humble cleaner, like. I had just finished dusting his desk and I was feeling a wee bit tired. I was trying to get into a chair for a wee rest, like, but he pushed it away so I couldn't get near it and he, well, you know, sort of, well, it's embarrassing to talk about it in front of all you telly people…'

'He dillied with her dally,' another woman shouted into the camera.

'Dillied with her dally? Wouldn't exactly squeeze him onto the front pages of the *News of the World*,' said Cathal from behind my left shoulder.

'No, but most likely a misdemeanour down the Embroidery Guild,' I said.

'Oh, right. Sure. I'll check with my uncle some time,' offered the Scouser.

We all watched keenly as the black Brummie calmly but forcefully took the Englishman by the arm and led him towards the door of the building. It seemed he didn't want to humiliate him by putting on the cuffs in full view of the media. Decent bloke. We heard Fortesque-Smith shouting he had never seen any of the women in his life. The five women, meanwhile, continued to tell their stories, some of them becoming more fanciful by the moment. Miss Webster looked on unabashed.

'Miss Webster, could we please have a word?' It was a BBC Northern Ireland reporter. 'Miss Webster, these are very serious allegations. How are you going to prove them? It is, after all, the word of these women against a respected Civil Servant.'

Miss Webster never spoke, merely walked over to the lorry, waving the camera crews towards her. They scurried over, cameras and sound equipment poking their way through the crowd. Inside the lorry, we were treated to half a dozen NO SMOKING signs stuck at the back.

'It is with great reluctance that I have to inform you that, in addition to the very serious offences described here today, Mr Fortesque-Smith, my colleague, has been involved in the rather serious crime of receiving these signs, which have been illegally removed from a warehouse in the Republic of Ireland. Now, at this particular time when we are all bending over backwards to be civil and agreeable, not to mention accommodating and helpful, to the government of the Republic, it is a particular act of betrayal to find one of Her Majesty's Civil Servants involved in such things.'

'Indeed, Miss Webster. Puts the odd four or five cases of sexual harassment into the shade, eh?' announced a reporter.

'Indeed. Could well jeopardise cross-border trade – tourism, even. By Christ! Smuggling! Our traditional cross-border activity! And, hey, we don't want their draconian laws making their way up here, now, do we? In my opinion you can't beat a good pint of Guinness accompanied by a spliff.'

What a woman! We all cheered. All those years of Civil Service training and not a bit of it truly touched her. My type of woman.

At that moment I thought of big Cecil and his and our struggle with an Englishman; big Frankie and his opposition to the South of Ireland because of the Virgin Mary's favouritism; my own doubts about their new oppressive smoking and drinking laws; and what about this seemingly quiet wee Civil Servant rising up against the Establishment? I realised there and then that we Northerners could unite as we all shared, in one form or another, a degree of opposition to the old traditional enemies.

The trick, however, was timing. Getting us all united against the one thing at the right time.

We repeatedly freeze-framed that moment and, just as we were about to watch it for the umpteenth time, in walked the vegan, dressed as a nun. I nudged Cathal.

'So, it's too late. Maureen went ahead and joined up?' I said to him, slapping him considerably on the back. Still, he had his hero, Aldo, close by now. Not for long, if tradition was any indication. Still, if we beat England…

'Aye, she has. Well, it was either that or Cher,' said Cathal.

'Cher?'

'Aye, the two of us are off to a fancy dress party.'

'Ye big bastard ye. You had me all worried about you.'

'Well, I wouldn't have gone had things not worked out today, so there was no point in telling you.'

I wanted to ask Cathal what he intended going as, but before I could, he offered an explanation.

'Who do you usually see a nun with? Another nun, perhaps? Well, I'm not dressing up as a nun. I could go as a priest, but think of the potential scandal. Father Cathal seen with Sister Maureen in an intimate clinch. No, the Catholic Church is in enough trouble without my adding to it. It's a quandary, no mistake. Anyhow, there was only one costume left in the shop.'

'So?' I asked.

'So, Sister Olive now has her Popeye.'

So, this was it. As I watched the drinks flow, and sucked in the air of joyous celebration, I could think of one person only. My mother. Just like she had said, I had indeed returned to Belfast and, yes, quite possibly, it might well be the making of me.

I caught a glimpse of my uncle Richard on the dance floor as he attempted to do the Waltz with Miriam, the behavioural therapist. They didn't seem to notice the band were playing *The Birdie Song*. I recalled his words from earlier.

'Jesus, son, your mother is so proud of you, so very, very proud.'

'*Is* proud? *Is?* Do you mean… has she been in touch with you?' I felt a bit daft asking this.

'Tom, your mother is always with you. Oh, and she says that no matter what Cathal says, you're not to drink Guinness. It makes you sick.'

I couldn't help but laugh as I watched Father Rice, all dressed up in his clerical garb, in heated debate with Alice and Bertie; might they have been querying their placing in that Line Dancing Competition? After a couple of minutes, the priest walked away, his face flushed with a grin, and with two fingers of his right hand in the air. Perhaps he had relented and suggested he should have placed them second.

Assumpta was, quite uncharacteristically, standing at the bar with Emmett, Sammy Devine and my uncle Pat. They looked over and all three gave me the thumbs up. I winked at them. Cathal was a few feet away from them, rocking on his heels, as he dissolved into a fit of laughter with some of the locals. Colum McGeough was frantically pulling at his jacket and, when he got his attention, pointed to the stage. The band began what turned out to be a more than passable version of Willie Nelson's *You Were Always On My Mind*.

I could feel the warmth of the people, people who had been so much part of my recent life. Many had always been a part of me. I remembered thinking and feeling one thing as I looked around.

I was home. I was so home.

It was about four o'clock in the morning when I got back to the house. I fell into a chair. Popeye was already lying on the sofa, snoring loudly. I could feel my eyelids getting heavy, but I was determined to stay awake and relive the past months.

I thought of the dreadful moment when I heard my mother had died as Cathal and I planned our career as male escorts, how I felt as Mairead and I returned to Belfast...

My thoughts, however, were interrupted by my mobile phone ringing. At this hour, who the hell...

'Is that Mr Thomas Dooley?' It was an American accent, a Southern drawl.

'Yes, yes it is,' I replied, trying hard not to slur my words too much.

'Mr Dooley, this is William Jefferson Clinton.'

'Who?' I still had alcohol inhabiting my brain cells.

'Bill Clinton, Mr Dooley.'

'Oh, the President?'

He laughed. 'No longer, I'm afraid, Mr Dooley. To get to the point, Mr Dooley, I have been informed about the wonderful work you have been doing there in Ireland and tonight we saw the pictures of what happened at Stormont. It's a grand thing you have done there, Mr Dooley.'

'Thank you, Mr President... eh... I mean... Mr Clinton. That's mighty kind of you.'

Cathal's love of Country and Western rubbing off on me and coming in handy there.

He then asked me what my future plans were. I told him I felt I had done everything I could with regard to helping the people with the IEA. I said I felt it was time I concentrated on getting my family back. He said he was sure that Mairead and I would get back together and added that he thought I would be knighted very soon and that Siobhan would, in the future, be offered the crown of Miss World. I said I hoped there would be no repeat of the suspicion surrounding the crowning of Chris de Burgh's daughter. He told me not to worry, that Siobhan would tell the organisers to stick the crown where the sun don't shine...

'Just a word before I go, Mr Dooley. Think about something for me, will you? Think about joining the DSS and changing things from within. I found out during my time in Ireland, and my interest in your future there, that it is always better to bugger up a system from within than to merely dent it from the outside. Must go now, Mr Dooley. Hillary is late home again. I have my suspicions about her, you know. If she's up to something, I'll catch her out. Only fair I return the compliment, eh?'

I had just spoken to the one-time President of the United States of America. God! Things were on the up and up, no mistake. Maybe they will make a film of the life and times of Tom Dooley yet, working-class hero. And, sod it, I'll play myself.

The next day I awoke with a start. I shook my head and tried to recall the previous night's conversation. Jesus! *I had been speaking to Bill Clinton.*

Cathal was still snoring away. I got up and shook him awake. He wasn't best pleased. I told him about the call.

'A call last night from Bill Clinton?' he asked, rubbing his eyes.

'Yeah, I can't believe it. Bill Clinton called me.'

'On your mobile?'

'Yeah, on my mobile,' I answered, a little irritated at his interest in trivia and not what Bill and I had discussed.

'Tom, you gave your mobile phone to Samuel Devine last night, remember? To let him call his cousin in Boston to tell him about him getting the IEA.'

'So?'

'You never got it back. Sammy said he wanted to ring his sister in Australia later on and you, Mr Generous, you said, "Keep it, Sammy. Keep the phone."'

'But, so what happened last night was a… was a dream?'

I felt demoralised.

Later that day I called round to see Mairead. She was very open with me, didn't mince her words. She told me straight. Yes, for Siobhan's sake, she might, just might, think about us getting back together again.

'Jesus, do you really think that after all you put me through I will roll over like some puppy dog? Do you think I will just float back into your life like nothing has happened? Yes, Mairead, no, Mairead, three bags bloody full, Mrs Dooley, eh, do you?'

Jesus, who was making me say these words?

'Yes, I do, Tom Dooley, yes I do.' Mairead's green eyes just stared at me, a mischievous smile completing the picture I had been longing for.

'Aye, well, you make sure you don't step out of line again…'

Oh, please…

'Me… me step out of line?' She paused and her face broke into a heart-jolting smile reflecting what I had always known. And had joyously accepted, all those years ago when we were teenagers, as her flushed face denied that Mairead Canavan loved Thomas Dooley. I have, if I am truthful with myself, revelled in it ever since.

Mairead and Tom Dooley were meant for each other.

'Are you staying for dinner?' she asked before teasingly adding that Siobhan was staying over in her friend's house that night.

'Dinner tonight?' I asked

'Yes, tonight, Thomas Dooley.'

'Can't, Mrs Dooley.'

'What do you mean, you can't?'

I looked her straight in the eye as I held both her hands in mine.

'Today, Mrs Dooley, I have things to sort out. I need to consider the future. You see, things are looking great at the moment, that's for sure, but there is so much more to do. So much more. You see, I have a dream…